STILL MISSING

Still County Thrillers
Book 5

LAUREN STREET

STERLING &STONE

STILL MISSING

Chapter One

"GET READY FOR IT," Rita said, sliding out the safe deposit box.

She placed the metal drawer on the table inside the vault at Elk Mountain Equity and flipped back the lid.

Cash's mouth fell open as stacks of crisp bills came into view, over half a million dollars' worth.

"What the fuck?"

"That's what I said." Rita pulled out several bundles and stacked them neatly on the table. "I've counted over six hundred and twenty grand."

Cash picked up a bundle. "This one's from 1986." He flipped it over. "Bills look like they've never been used."

"I didn't find anything dated later than that."

He thumbed the edge of the wad, fanning it. "And Otto never mentioned this?"

Rita shook her head. "Nope. Only cash he ever talked about was you."

Cash let out a forced chuckle. "No wonder my ears burned so much growing up."

Rita suspected Cash missed her father more than she

did, now that Otto was gone. Not that she didn't think about him. But their relationship had never been easy.

She gave Cash a glib smile. "Don't worry, the things Otto and I said about you are nothing compared to what me and Thomas say."

Cash furrowed his brow. "Double funny." He fanned the stack of bills with his thumb. "You check if it's counterfeit?"

Rita plucked up a bill. "Of course. I'm a cop, remember? Though you'd probably spot a fake faster than me."

"Is this how the jokes are gonna go all night?"

"You're the one with the felon for a father."

Cash tossed the bundle onto the pile. "I wouldn't be so sure about that anymore. For all we know, this could be ransom money. Maybe a bribe."

Rita glared at him. "I sure as hell hope not."

"Stolen?"

"Not flagged. I looked up old bank robberies in Wyoming. But nothing with a loss this big."

"Bills are too clean, and the denominations too large, for drug money," Cash said.

"Exactly," Rita said. "Most are fifties, which would've been worth a lot more in 1986. I even checked with the FBI. But no leads."

Cash poked around the bottom of the box. "And this is the jewelry?"

Rita nodded. "Probably Otto's mother's."

"What are you gonna do with it?"

She shrugged. "Might ask Ruby Joe if she wants it."

Cash gave her a look. "But you're not talking to her yet."

Rita's gaze slid away. "That's right."

Silence settled between them as Cash rummaged through the rest of the box. He pulled out an envelope of snapshots, flipping through them before holding one up. It showed Otto with an unfamiliar woman, his arm draped across her shoulders.

"Who's this?"

"No idea," Rita said. "Another mystery Otto left behind. Though maybe not as pressing as the six hundred twenty grand. I should ask around."

Cash handed her the photo, then grabbed another envelope from the bottom of the drawer. He peered inside. "Empty."

"Yeah, it was when I found it." Rita leaned against the wall, shifting her weight to ease her aching feet. "There are some ink smudges inside—maybe it held a newspaper clipping at some point."

Cash returned the envelope to the drawer, then stared silently at the money.

Rita pushed off the wall, though her knees protested. "What are you thinking?"

Cash met her eye. "Don't really want to say it."

"Say it," Rita said. "That's why I brought you here. I value your opinion."

A muscle in Cash's jaw tightened. He nodded. "Okay. Is there any chance…Otto took a bribe?" He rubbed his neck, shrugging. "Thomas was still working the streets when these bills were printed."

Rita rolled her shoulders. "I wish I had an inkling. But I just don't know. It doesn't sound like Otto. Then again, I would've sworn he'd never hide a half-sister from me right under my nose. Or that his own sister practically runs this whole place." She blew out a breath. "I used to think *you* weren't being straight with me, Cash." A bitter laugh escaped her. "How wrong I was."

Cash grinned and leaned in for a kiss. "That's why you're marrying me. Finally."

Rita kissed him back, then laughed.

Then they stacked the money, and returned it to the drawer, which Rita slid back into the wall.

"Got any plans for it?" Cash asked.

"Nope," Rita said. "Holding onto it for now, I guess."

"You don't like guessing," Cash pointed out.

"Right," she admitted. "Are you willing talk to Thomas? See if he knows anything?"

Cash frowned. "What makes you think he'll talk to me? I haven't spoken to him in years."

"Well, the last time I talked to him, I hung up. Might've blown his eardrum slamming the receiver. And he's not my biggest fan at the best of times. If he'll talk to either of us, it's you."

Cash shifted. "He's not gonna talk to either of us. He only talks to Alan."

"Easy peasy, then," Rita said. "You don't even need to talk to your dad—we can get the dirt from his lawyer."

Cash rolled his shoulders. "No guarantees he'll spill to Alan, either."

Rita touched his arm. "Of course not. And there's no guarantee Tom was even involved, let alone heard any rumors. But I appreciate it."

Cash gave a slow nod. "Have you told anyone else about the money?"

Rita shook her head. "No. Besides Thomas, let's keep it between us."

"Natch," Cash said.

Rita kissed him again. "Thank you for doing this for me."

Cash smiled, rubbing the small swell of her belly. "I'm doin' it for *us*. Everything's for us now."

Rita took a steadying breath and smiled. "For us."

Chapter Two

Cash pulled his black pickup into the gravel driveway and parked next to the BMW crossover.

"Home sweet home," he said with a boyish grin.

Rita smiled back, then popped the door open and heaved herself out of the passenger seat. She still wasn't used to living this far out of town. Overhead, the Wyoming sky deepened to sapphire, the evening's first stars flickering above the skeletal silhouettes of apple and plum trees lining the southwestern edge of the property.

Then she stopped, listening.

Cash did too. "What's up?"

Rita hesitated before answering. "The silence."

Cash cocked his head. "What about it?"

"It's different from Otto's."

She turned away from the fruit trees and toward the house. In the twilight, the stucco walls took on a blue hue, while the wooden window trim appeared blood-red. The last rays of light gleamed off the metal roof. She rolled her shoulders. "I'm still adjusting to life outside of town."

Cash laced his fingers through hers. "Any regrets?"

Rita met his gaze. "Since I can't regret expecting a baby with you, I assume you mean putting my name on the mortgage."

He shrugged. "Maybe. Seeing as it's mostly your credit score that got us this place, what with Tom Gabriel's long shadow still following me around. But I was actually asking about selling your dad's place. That was all you had left of him."

Rita chewed her lip. "Not really. I've got a safety deposit box full of his puzzles." She kissed him. "Besides, I'm happy Jason's in the place, giving it new life."

Cash's shoulders relaxed. "Well, it's a new life out here too." He craned his neck to take in the stars.

Rita followed his gaze. "Sure ain't the Big Apple."

"You don't really miss it," Cash said. "I know you better than that."

"Of course not," Rita said. "Can't see the stars like this there."

"For a while, it seemed like you were missing Dale. But now you're here, with me." His hand moved over her belly. "Making a new life."

She lifted his hand from her bladder. "Speaking of new life, the new life is nudging me to go pee."

Cash followed her up the walkway and unlocked the front door, stepping aside to allow her entry.

Rita hurried inside, shivering. The house felt cold. "I hope the furnace isn't broken."

"Stay positive," Cash said, shrugging off his coat.

She opened the closet, the door squealing across the floor as it sagged off the broken top hinge. "It's hard *not* to be a determinist when everything in this place breaks." Reluctantly, she removed her puffer jacket and hung it on the rod.

Cash hung his coat besides hers. "Considering we

solved the situation of the backed-up septic system, we can handle anything." He closed the closet door. "It's just cold in here because I opened the windows to air out the fumes." He waved a finger through the doorway, to the rear of the house. "I'll be finished painting tomorrow—putting the final touches on the living room."

Rita softened. "Nice." She stepped in to him, finally accepting a hug. And felt a little warmer. She tilted her chin to look up at him. "Your sudden burst of domestic enthusiasm is both baffling and impressive."

Cash laid his cheek against her temple. "Guess I'm finally moving on from my old place. Dust to dust, ashes to —" His arms tightened as he caught himself. "Sorry, Rita, didn't mean to be insensitive." He looked up, too, but at the ceiling. "And Otto, sorry, old man."

"It's okay," Rita said. "Dad would've appreciated your humor. Maybe your domestic urges have nothing to do with your old place burning down." She moved her hand to pat his belly, the way people had started patting hers. "Maybe you're nesting, too."

Cash slid a hand over her backside. "I like that theory." Then he gave it a light slap. "And by the way, the baby's room is ready. I installed the closet shelves this morning and replaced the baseboards."

She snuggled closer. "You're downright heroic."

He chuckled, then pulled away. "And your duty belt's digging into me."

"Sorry," Rita said, releasing him and kicking off her boots. "I'll go strip off this uniform."

Upstairs, Rita stowed her service weapon in her gun locker, then changed into heather-gray sweats pants and a T-shirt.

Downstairs, Cash was moving around the living room, closing the wide-open windows. Their queen-sized mattress and box spring sat in the center of the room, flanked by two moving boxes serving as makeshift nightstands. On the wall above the head of the bed hung a framed needlepoint of a bison, Wyoming's flag waving behind it.

"Hi, Dad," Rita murmured.

Cash glanced at her. "Talking to ghosts?"

Rita pointed. "You put up Irene's needlepoint. I named him Otto."

Cash grinned. "He look okay there?"

"Yeah. Though I'm not sure how I feel about sleeping under his watchful eye."

"I'll move the bed upstairs soon," Cash said, closing another window. "Then we'll have privacy again." He moved to the last window. "Come tell me about your day while I make some burgers."

"Sounds good," Rita said, pulling on her boots again. Soles squeaking, she followed him into the kitchen. "I can't tell if I'm hungrier or thirstier these days."

Cash crossed to the sink and washed his hands. "Do you have to wear those?"

Rita looked down at her baggy sweats. "I know they're not the most attractive pants I own. But given the rate my mid-section's expanding, expect things to get even baggier."

"I was referring to the shoes," Cash said, drying his hands on a kitchen towel.

Rita looked behind her. "Am I tracking slush in the house?"

"No, but they're fucking annoying to listen to."

"I know," Rita said. "I'm the one who has to listen to them all day. But my back hurts. If I take them off, I won't have any arch support on the tile. And my feet are too swollen for my runners."

Cash pulled out a chair at the table for her. "Then have a seat."

"Thanks," she said sinking into the vinyl cushion.

He tied an apron around his waist. "What are you drinking these days? Water, juice, or ginger ale?"

"Have we got any coconut water?"

Cash rummaged through the fridge and pulled out a ribbed can. "Last one."

Rita cracked it open and raised it. "A toast. I'm officially in my second trimester—and I haven't puked in two weeks."

Cash tapped his beer can against hers. "I'll cheers to that."

As she sipped, she took out the photo of Otto and the unknown woman. Whether Otto's embrace was friendly or romantic, she couldn't tell.

"Hell, I've seen Otto hug fellow cops closer than this. Did these two work together?"

Cash flashed a crooked smile. "Maybe he was taking her into custody."

"Funny," Rita said. She looked closer at the snapshot. "I don't think this was taken in Wyoming."

Cash halved an onion on the cutting board, then set aside the knife. "Oh yeah?"

"I thought these blurry white rectangles in the background were stucco buildings." She tapped the photo. "But now I think it's the Hollywood sign, out-of-focus."

Cash approached and leaned over her shoulder.

"And this jagged shadow?" Rita pointed. "Could be made by palm fronds."

"That's fair," Cash said, nodding.

She quickly Googled 'palm trees and the Hollywood sign.' A flood of images popped up, many taken from South Windsor Boulevard.

"But Otto never went to LA," Rita said, more to herself than Cash.

Cash returned to the cutting board on the counter. "Maybe he had a twin brother."

"Good grief, let's hope not," Rita said with a laugh. "I can't handle any more skeletons in Dad's closet."

Cash chopped the onion. "Once the door's open, it's open."

Rita sighed. "That's for damn sure. And it's always the younger generation who opens it, without a clue what's inside. But by then, it's too late."

Cash set down the knife. "Have you thought about seeing that therapist I recommended?"

Rita crinkled her nose. "I made an appointment."

Cash resumed chopping. "That's good."

"It's a six-week wait."

He placed the chopped onion in a bowl. "It'll be worth it."

Sighing, Rita rested her elbows on the table. "I still don't see how you're the authority on therapists."

He looked up from salting the onion. "I have a felon for a father, remember?"

Rita dropped her chin in her hands. "Maybe the therapist can give me some answers about *my* dad."

Cash tore open the pack of ground beef. "Why not ask Carol about the photo?"

Rita scoffed. "Absolutely not."

"She's your mother."

"And you don't speak to your father."

"Not the same," Cash said. "Mine's in prison."

"And my mother drives a shit-brown van that's seen better days. I'd be fine if she drove it right out of state."

Cash chuckled. "Won't make a difference if you keep stalking her on YouTube."

Rita glared at him. "Fine, I'll message Carol."

She took out her phone and tapped: *We need to talk.* A second later she added a smiley face. Then hit 'send.'

"There," she said, setting aside her phone. "And for the record, I'm not stalking her. I only want to see if she's taken down that video of our fight."

Cash added pepper to the meat. "Has she?"

Rita snorted. "No. And you wanna know what she said when I reminded her?"

"I have a feeling you're about to tell me," Cash said, kneading the ground beef.

"She asked me to film a grandbaby drop with her."

Cash's eyebrows shot up. "Drop a baby? Whose baby? Your baby? Not my baby."

"It's a social media thing," Rita said. "She's calling it a First-Time Nana 'Nouncement."

Cash blinked. "Say what?"

"Don't worry about it," Rita said. "You should be more worried about the things her fans say about me."

Cash winked. "That you've got a hell of a left hook?"

Ignoring him, Rita navigated to Carol's YouTube channel, SilverNomad. "You should read some of the shit that's on her page." She found the popular video in question and scrolled through the comments.

"Most of these are wondering if Carol has"—Rita made air quotes—"'reconciled with her daughter.'"

"And has she?" Cash asked with a winsome smile.

Rita cut him a look. "Listen to this comment: *Why is her daughter so angry?* Or how about this one: *Who would treat a mother like that?*"

Cash shaped a burger in his hands. "You probably shouldn't read these."

"I know I shouldn't," Rita said, scowling. "Here's a hot

one: 'What kind of person walks out of their mother's life?'"

Cash scoffed. "The kind who knows a bad deal when she sees one."

Rita scowl deepened. "Yeah, well, I didn't walk out on her. She ran away from us." Rita's shoulders dropped. "Except Otto isn't here anymore to remember that part of my history." Tears burned at the back off her eyes. "It's only me and Carol now."

Cash grinned. "You got me."

Ria nodded, feeling better. "Yeah."

"And the baby."

She smiled. "Yeah."

"And the grandbaby dropping thing to look forward to."

She laughed. "Promise me something, Cash?"

"Sure. What?"

"That you won't pass any skeletons onto our kid."

Cash smiled, hamburger meat clinging to his knuckles. "I swear on my life."

Rita touched her belly. "Me too."

Chapter Three

RITA ROLLED OVER, reaching for her phone. She unplugged it from the charging cable and checked the time. "Morning already?"

Beside her, Cash stirred. "You didn't sleep?"

"Not really," Rita said. "But I peed five times."

Cash patted the small curve forming just below her belly button. "Six times," he corrected, pressing a kiss to her cheek. "But who's counting?"

Rita dragged herself out of bed, upstairs, and into the bathroom. After a quick shower, too tired to bother with the blow dryer, she wrung the water from her hair and pulled it into a tight ponytail. She dressed in her uniform, listening to the sounds of Cash moving around in the kitchen downstairs. Before heading down, she took a photo of the snapshot—Otto and the mystery woman, frozen in time.

Downstairs, Cash had a hot mug of black tea awaiting her, along with a packed lunch.

She kissed him. "Once again, you're my PFH."

He cocked an eyebrow. "PFH?"

"Personal fucking hero."

"My pleasure," he said. "In fact, I can do this for you every day for the rest of your life." He passed her the paper lunch bag. "Or, at least for the rest of my life. That's the limit of my guarantee."

Rita laughed. "Thanks. I'll see you at dinner."

"You're leaving now?"

She took a sip of tea. "I want to run an errand before work."

"What about breakfast?"

Rita shrugged, then reached for the fruit bowl. "I'll take a banana and a cereal bar."

Cash frowned. "You're growing a baby."

"Yes," Rita said, rummaging in the pantry for a breakfast bar. "Apparently out of protein bars and cups of tea."

Cash's frown deepened. "There's still a lot of caffeine in tea, you know. Give me five minutes—I'll whisk up some eggs and squeeze a grapefruit."

"Squeeze a—?" Rita shook her head. "Since when have I ever been someone who drinks grapefruit juice? When I moved back from New York, I wasn't even eating salad, and look how long it's taken you to change my mind about that."

"About what? New York, or salad?"

Rita matched his frown. "Both, obviously. But in this case, salad."

"You still don't like salad."

"Exactly. People don't change overnight."

Cash's gaze softened. "I know that."

"Which is why I'm not drinking the grapefruit juice."

"Got it," Cash said, stiff. He studied her. "Your hormones normal?"

Rita growled. "What do you think?" Her fingers closed

around something at the back of the cabinet. "Aha!" She held up a raspberry oatmeal bar.

"Those things are mostly sugar." Cash opened the fridge. "I've got a hard-boiled egg you can take." He tossed it to her.

Rita caught it and dropped it into her lunch bag. "Fine. I'll see you tonight."

She kissed him one last time, then headed to the foyer, where she bundled herself in layers of outerwear: neck gaiter, thermal vest, and puffer jacket.

Outside, the cold wind raked through her damp hair, sending a sharp chill straight to her scalp, as though an ice pack pressed against her skin. She shut the door behind her and walked to the driveway, unlocking the black BMW X6 with a press of the key fob.

Settling into the driver's seat, the heated leather seats molded around Rita and filled the cabin with their distinct scent. She started the ignition and drove to the Still County Sheriff's Office.

Parked at the curb, she took a breath, then peeled the banana. Once she'd eaten, she stepped out into the cold, bracing against the wind as she climbed the front steps.

Inside, the familiar scent of old linoleum hit her. She cracked a smile. She'd gone nose-blind to it long ago, but today, it was like stepping into the station for the first time all over again.

She walked up to reception, where Mary Lou sat typing, her silver beehive wobbling in sync with her rapid keystrokes. She wore a fluffy angora sweater pinned with a plastic badge featuring Elvis Presley's portrait and the words *The King Lives On.*

Mary Lou glanced up, then did a double take. Her gaze narrowed. "What are you doing here?"

Rita pulled out her phone. "I need to ask you about

this photo of Otto." She swiped to the image of the snapshot, then turned her the screen to face Mary Lou. "Do you know who this woman is?"

Mary Lou plucked the phone from Rita's hand and studied the screen in silence. Then she thrust it back. "Nope. Never seen her before."

"Did Otto ever mention Los Angeles?"

Mary Lou raised an eyebrow. "That where this is taken?"

Rita nodded. "Yes."

"Dunno," Mary Lou said, turning back to her keyboard.

A beat of silence stretched between them. "Well," Rita said, pocketing the phone, "that's all I needed. Thanks for your help."

Mary Lou shrugged. "No problem."

Rita craned to look in the bullpen, but the room appeared vacant. "Give my regards to Jason when you see him."

Mary Lou grunted.

Rita set her jaw. "I'll take that as a 'yes.'"

Folding her arms, Mary Lou sat back in her chair. "You two had some real choice words when you announced decamping to the enemy." She held Rita's gaze. "Hard to forget something like that."

Rita shifted, boots squeaking on the soft linoleum. "Sure, things got a little heated, but I don't remember saying anything—"

"Hi, Rita," Jason said, walking through the SCSO entrance. "Thought I saw your car out there."

"Not really mine," she said, with a weak smile. "Company car. Comes with the job."

Mary Lou snorted. "You mean the job comes with a bribe?"

Jason smirked. "The car's just a perk, isn't it? The real bribe was the helicopter ride to dinner at the Faculty Club in Casper."

Heat crept up Rita's neck. She pressed her teeth together, forcing a neutral expression. "Well, I'll see you around."

Then she headed for the door, feeling hotter by the second.

"Wait up," Jason called after her.

Rita hesitated, her shoulders tensing before she stopped.

"What'd you come by for?" he asked, standing close.

Rita kept her voice low. "Some personal information."

"Which you now have," Mary Lou said loudly. "So you can be on your way."

Rita shot her a look, then left, her shoes squeaking down the front steps. She took the cereal bar from her pocket and tore open the package. She ate it in four bites as she crossed the street to Bighorn Bean Coffee Shop.

"Morning," Skylar greeted her from behind the counter. "You're late today."

"Cash made me tea," Rita said, pulling out her wallet. "But I'll take another. A London Fog, please."

"Coming up." Skylar frothed the milk, then slid Rita a to-go cup along with a sleeve of saltines. "On the house."

Rita smiled. "Thanks, you're my personal fucking hero. Even though I'm officially over morning sickness now, I think I've developed a cracker habit."

Skyler laughed. "Muffin?"

Rita nodded. "Please. Surprise me." As Skyler packaged up a muffin and Rita swiped her debit card, she gave Skylar's hair a second glance. "I like the green."

"Thanks," Skylar said, passing Rita the muffin in a bag.

"Wasn't intentional, but I consider it a happy accident. I was going for neon yellow."

Rita cocked her head. "Neon green suits you."

Back in the BMW, she sipped her London Fog and ate the muffin. Still not feeling full, she followed it up with the hard-boiled egg Cash had given her.

Then she checked her phone. No response from Carol to the text message. Rita navigated to YouTube. No new uploads on SilverNomad, either. And the video of their fight was still up.

With a sigh, Rita put down her phone and started the engine. She headed for APEX. At the front gate, the young security guard peered into her window.

"Morning, Brett," she said.

Brett raised the gate with a smile. "Morning, Boss."

Rita drove in, parked in the stall labeled R. Jonas, Head of L.E.O. (Law Enforcement Operations) and stepped out.

Passing through the double-glass doors, Ginny the receptionist greeted her. "Good morning, Ms. Jonas."

Giving a wave, Rita replied in kind, headed for the elevator. She swiped her badge across the security panel, then rode to the top floor. The doors opened onto a glass promenade with a stunning view of the mountains. She paused to admire them, sipping the last of her London Fog.

Then she stepped into her office, a space that had once belonged to Ken Saunders, and before him, Boyd Farmer. Determined to leave their shadows behind, she'd had the walls repainted a warm butter yellow and hung one of Otto's favorite paintings: a storm gathering over Devil's Tower, or "Home of Bears," as it had more commonly come to be known in recent years. Dark clouds billowed over the iconic butte, and a distant fork of lightning reflected nature's power.

Rita had also tried to replace the seating in the office with more comfortable options, like the ergonomically designed desk-chair she'd had at the SCSO. But APEX policy dictated every office to contain the same standard furnishings, which meant tolerating the modern vinyl sofa which was about as comfortable as sitting on a piece of dry toast.

She hung up her puffer jacket on a steel coat-stand and peeled off her utility vest. Then she stood at the window, looking over her new domain.

Chapter Four

Rita's phone rang with a FaceTime call. She picked up and said hi to Angela, APEX Executive Director.

"How's the baby?" Angela asked.

"Still on the inside," Rita said.

Angela laughed. "What have you got for leads?"

Rita rolled her shoulders. "We're still looking for evidence. Have there been any further thefts?"

"Have there been more chemicals compounds showing up at competitors? Not recently," Angela said with a patronizing edge. "But it's hard to tell with corporate espionage."

"You're not kidding," Rita said, sighing. "We'll keep scrolling through footage."

"I'm the first to know if you find anything," Angela reminded her.

"Of course," Rita said, hoping her own response didn't sound terse.

Angela laced her words with a smile Rita could hear through the cell phone. "I knew I could trust you to go after the truth, Rita."

Rita cleared her throat. "That's because trustworthiness is a rare quality of character around APEX. At least considering some law enforcement alum I know."

Angela's voice hardened again. "If we don't get to the bottom of this, my job's on the line. And if my job's on the line, Jonas, your job's on the line. If we can't stop the leak, the board will axe the both of us."

"Yikes," Rita said. "Sounds serious."

"It is serious," Angela said. "And you should be thankful for your job, considering you could be riding that desk back at the SCSO, sitting on your bladder and doing paperwork while some rookie does all the fun stuff. You should be respectful of the opportunity to be a team member at APEX, making a difference."

"I'm a contractor, not technically an APEX team member, if that's what you call employees," Rita said. "And I'm not sure tracking down stolen staplers is saving me from boredom or making much of a difference. Especially since the stapler wasn't even stolen in the first place. It happened to fall into a trash can, until the custodian collected it."

Angela took a beat before responding. "That's why you're such a good candidate for the job, Rita. We really need someone who can track things department to department, and keep things tight within the operation."

"Yeah, well, you can remove babysitting from the job description, because I've had enough of that rookie you sent me. Guess what he's doing today? Playing hooky."

Angela chuckled. "That's rhymes. Rookie, hooky."

Rita suppressed an impatient sigh. "That's because he's a child. Probably needs nursery rhymes to go to sleep at night.'"

Angela cleared her throat. "Yeah, sorry about that... What's his name, Greg?"

"Craig," Rita said. "Craig Dillard." Then she let out the sigh. "As green as he is, I'm working on whittling him."

"That's all I can ask," Angela said.

Rita grunted as she ended the call, then grabbed the receiver from her sleek glass desk and dialed reception.

"Hi, Ginny," Rita said when the receptionist picked up, "has Craig signed in yet?"

"Not yet, Ms. Jonas," Ginny said.

Rita thanked her and hung up before heading down to her Beemer. Her boots were starting to rub sore spots on both of her big toes. Doing her best to ignore them, she sank into the driver's seat and fastened the belt.

Rolling over speedbumps as she left the parking lot, her stomach growled. Not again. She'd left her bag lunch in the office.

Waving at Brett, she passed through the gate and turned left, making her way toward APEX Hills.

She pulled up at Craig's duplex, parking in the right-hand driveway next to his pickup. Rita slid out from behind the wheel and walked to the door. She rang the bell, depressing the button for an extra few seconds.

Eventually a shadow moved on the other side of the glass panel beside the door. It opened, and Craig stood standing with a towel wrapped around his waist, his hair dripping on his base shoulders. "Jonas?"

"Do you know the time?" Rita asked.

"No, I was in the shower."

"It's eight-thirty."

Craig's eyes widened. "Oh, shit."

"Yeah," Rita said. "Oh, shit."

Craig ran his hands over his damp hair. "I'm sorry I'm late, I had a late night."

"I noticed," Rita said, nodding her head towards a bra

lying on the foyer floor. "You've got two minutes to get in the car or I'm firing you."

Craig went pale. "You wouldn't do that."

Rita shrugged. "Gotta do what I gotta do. I answer to Angela."

Craig bristled. "You're crankier than usual today."

"Didn't have much breakfast," Rita said. She held up her phone and showed him her clock app. "I'm using the timer," she said. "You've got four minutes."

Craig nodded, then ran up the carpeted stairwell behind him.

Leaving the front door open, Rita walked back to the crossover, shoes squeaking. She got into the driver's seat and watched the timer countdown for three minutes.

As she waited, Rita tried not to think about how much she missed working with Jason.

The timer buzzed and Rita turned the ignition. As she started to reverse, Craig ran out of the house, barefoot and bare-chested, carrying his boots and coat and almost tripping on his shirt sleeves.

Rita put on the brakes.

Craig ran around to the passenger's side and tried the door. It was locked. Rita hit the button to unlock the door and he climbed in.

"You're getting dressed in my car?" she asked.

"Thought you said it was a company car," Craig said, buttoning his shirt.

Rita gave him a look, then resumed backing up.

"What do you expect?" Craig said. "Last week you weren't very happy about me brushing my teeth in here." He flashy her a toothy smile. "So I prioritized."

"Gee, thanks," she said, rolling out of the driveway. "Please don't bleed on the upholstery."

"Huh?" Craig lowered the visor and looked in the

mirror. Then he used a fingertip to blot at a shaving wound on his chin. "It was a rush job."

"I can see that," Rita said, shifting gears into drive. "And this is your last warning."

Grumbling, Craig bent over to pull on a pair of socks and his boots. For some reason, his never squeaked.

"Do you understand?" Rita asked.

Craig sat upright again, gave a silent nod, and stared ahead through the windshield.

The dashboard lit up and chimed, signaling that the passenger hadn't fastened the seatbelt.

"Buckle up," Rita said.

Craig grunted. "Don't need to tell me, Jonas."

Rita shot him a glance. "Oh, really? You seem to need an alarm for everything." She cranked the wheel and merged into traffic, heading back to APEX. "At least I'm getting plenty of parenting practice."

Chapter Five

Seated at the conference desk behind her computer console, Rita's phone pinged with a text notification. Glancing at the screen, she checked the caller ID. It was Carol:

I'm in Casper shooting footage, will stop by later. What time do you want to meet at the house?

The house.

As in Otto's. Rita's childhood home. And Carol's former place. Tempted to send a message explaining she didn't want to meet, Rita paused to compose her response:

We'll meet at the picnic tables by the children's play area at Chester's Gas-N-Go. You know the one, south of town.

She sent the message, then sighed and rubbed her eyes. Across the table, Craig was slumped at his computer, looking like he might fall asleep. She tossed a saltine at him.

He jolted, then sat upright. "I know what time it is," he said, blinking and looking around. Then he shook his head clear. "Sorry, Jonas, I spaced out for a moment."

"We only just got started," Rita said. "We've got hours of this ahead of us."

"There's nothing here," Craig said. He rolled his shoulders. "We could be…doing other stuff."

Rita smirked. "Like finding staplers? Look, we've been over this before."

Craig sighed. "Everyone thinks this is a waste of time."

"Not Angela," Rita said. "She called this morning to check if we'd found anything."

"And we haven't," Craig said. "So what'd you tell her?"

"That we'll keep trying. We've still got hours of security footage to go through."

Craig stared at her. "We do? We can't just watch tape all day."

Rita raised an eyebrow. "Why not?"

Craig floundered. "Because I've got tactical training, for one. And seriously, have we even got proof this 'leak' exists?" He made quotation marks with his fingers. "We don't even know what these 'proprietary compounds' are used for."

"It doesn't matter," Rita replied. She cracked her knuckles. "Whatever your opinion, it's up to you and me to do the job, partner."

"Well, if everyone thinks Jim took something," Craig argued, "why not just fire him? A hell of a lot easier than watching endless security footage."

"Because what if he's innocent?" Rita said. "We fire the wrong guy, and the leak keeps happening."

"Well, if he's innocent, he might not like knowing I've practically got his whole damn day memorized," Craig said. "Every morning, between ten and ten-ten a.m., he heads to the bathroom on the next level for, on average, twelve minutes. And I don't even need to refer to my notes to tell you that."

Craig paused to take a sip of water, then continued. "At eleven, he takes his break, grabs a cup of coffee and treat from Ginny's snack cart, and spends exactly fifteen minutes playing solitaire on his laptop. On the dot. He swaps between purchasing a blueberry muffin for a bagel with cream cheese."

"Except Wednesdays," Rita said. "When he gets a coffee and a cinnamon roll from the snack cart."

"Right," Craig said. "Then at noon he texts his wife, no idea what they talk about, but it's always at the same time."

"At twelve-thirty he eats in the lunchroom, usually a rice bowl." Rita said. "He's lowering his glycemic index these days."

Craig set his elbows on the conference table, pretending to be casual while flexing his biceps. "Rice? Sure, that'll fix his blood sugar." He smirked. "And the cinnamon rolls, and bagels, and muffins—"

"Speaking of food," Rita said, "I'm starving." She unwrapped the sandwich Cash had made for her.

"At one, Jim returns to his desk, where he takes off his suit jacket and folds it over the back of his chair. Then he loosens his tie and unbuttons his collar like a goddamned ritual." Craig ran his hands over his head. "He takes another break at three, playing more electronic solitaire for fifteen minutes. From three-fifteen to five, he focuses on backing up his files and processing his email inbox." Craig moved his hands to rest them behind his head. "After that, he heads home." Craig yawned. "God, we know everything about this guy. He's like clockwork."

"Which should make our job easier," Rita said, biting into the sandwich, lettuce crunching. "If we know his routine cold, we'll spot something unusual eventually."

Craig blew out a breath. "I just want some action around here."

"The argument that broke out at the Collins and Anderson presentation was thrilling."

"That ended up being an HR issue," Craig said. "We didn't do anything."

"Yeah, I don't know much about that kind of conflict resolution, either," Rita said.

"What kind of conflict?" Craig asked.

"The kind where I don't arrest people." Rita took the last bite of her sandwich. "But that situation was tense, and you have to admit, when the Post-Its were thrown—and I'm talking, pads of 'em, not singular sticky notes—we were both wondering if things were going to turn physical."

Movement flickered on the other side of the sand-blasted glass conference room door.

"Here comes Ginny with the snack cart," Rita said. "Maybe a little caffeine will help you."

The receptionist pushed open the door and nudged the cart inside.

Craig jumped up to hold open the door. "Let me get that."

Ginny blushed. "Thanks. It's a little awkward pushing this thing around." She bumped the corner of the table as she rolled up. "Sorry 'bout that."

"Better the table than my knee," Rita said.

Ginny blushed again. "What will you have, Sheriff Jonas? I mean, Ms. Jonas?"

Rita picked a ham and cheese sandwich, a bag of grapes, and some salted peanuts.

"Eating lunch again?" Craig asked, selecting a variety of power bars, chocolate-covered almonds, and a chocolate milk.

"Come to think of it, I'll have some chocolate-covered almonds too," Rita said, as Ginny noted the items for their tabs. Then she threw a look at Craig. "And I have a lot of lunches to make up for. I didn't eat for two months."

Then Ginny waved goodbye as she rolled out the cart, Craig holding the door for her again.

Once she'd left, he tore open a protein bar and bit into it. "Think I'll take my morning break now. Got a call to make."

"I need a bathroom break," Rita said, gathering her items. "I'll see you back here shortly, for more fun."

"Looking forward to it already," Craig said, chewing his protein bar as he gathered his things.

Rita headed for the door. "Don't be late."

Chapter Six

Rita awoke to Cash shaking her shoulder.

"Your phone's ringing," he grumbled, half asleep. "And it's definitely not morning."

Rita rolled over and picked up her phone, answering it in the dark.

"Ms. Jonas, it's Gord," one of the security guards at APEX said. "We've got trespassers. I was doing my rounds and come across an opening in the fence. Some of the chain links have been cut."

"Ten-four," Rita said, clearing her throat. "Could you call out Dillard and Middleton, please? I'm on my way."

Rita rang off and pushed herself out of bed, groaning.

"You're going out at this hour?" Cash said.

"Trespassers out at APEX," Rita said.

Cash grumbled. "Doesn't mean you need to deal with it, do you? What about the security guards?"

"I won't be alone. Craig and Martin will be there."

Cash frowned. "Not exactly encouraging."

Rita snapped on her maternity bra, making a mental note that she was going to need a new one soon. "Martin's all right." Then she dressed, snapped on her duty belt, and fetched her firearm from the locker in the closet.

"Well, I'm wide awake now," Cash said as she emerged from the closet. "You know I'm going to lay here awake until you're home safe and sound again."

Rita leaned over the bed and kissed him on the cheek. "I'll keep your baby and me nice and safe." Her stomach growled. "Shit. I'm hungry again."

"Maybe we should make you a snack cart, like Angela's so-called morale-boosting snack cart initiative."

"It's been boosting *my* morale," Rita said.

"I thought you were annoyed that you had to pay your own tab instead of APEX picking it up?"

"I got over that when I tasted the cinnamon buns. And Ginny always has perfect bananas. How does she do that? She drives that cart into everything from elevator doors to glass pillars in the lobby, and still, those things are never bruised."

"Enough said. If we get a cart in here, will you let me sleep?"

"How about a bar fridge? I could use some ice cream."

"Are you bonkers?" he said, rolling over. "It's freezing out."

"Not bonkers," she said, "only pregnant. See you tomorrow."

"Already is tomorrow," Cash mumbled, his face buried into the pillow.

Rita went downstairs, locked the door behind her, and pulled out of the driveway. As she drove, she nibbled on the crackers. They were dry and pasty, but at least they kept her stomach quiet.

The roads were empty, the traffic lights all turning green as if clearing a path for her. At APEX, the parking lot was nearly deserted, only a handful of cars clustered near the security post.

She parked her Beemer, stepped out, and walked up to the guards' hut, where Martin stood outside, talking through the window to the security guard on duty. Both of them were focused on something on their phone screens.

"Hi, guys," Rita said.

Martin looked up. "Evening, Ms. Jonas."

The security guard, Gord, held up his phone. "I was showing Martin where the fence was cut. That's how the trespassers got in."

Martin turned his screen toward her. "I've marked it on the security map."

"What's our timing?" Rita asked.

"I do my rounds every three hours," Gord said with a shrug. "Fence was fine earlier."

"And Craig's not here yet?"

Martin shook his head.

Rita sighed. "Jesus Christ. All right, let's go, Middleton."

"You should take the golf cart," Gord said.

"Good idea. I'll drive," Martin said to Rita. "Gord already showed me the way."

"Need anything before heading out?" Gord asked.

"Better flashlights," Rita said. "And you got any headlamps?"

"Yeah, hang on." Gord ducked back inside the hut. A moment later, he returned with a handful of headlamps and flashlights.

Rita and Martin each took a headlamp, adjusting the straps, then Rita took an extra for Craig, in case he showed up.

Then she gestured towards the back of the security hut. "Let's go."

They walked around the building to where a jet-black golf cart, emblazoned with a reflective APEX logo, was parked.

Rita slid into the padded leather seat as the cart hummed to life. Martin tapped the digital display on the dash, switching on the LED headlights. The beams of light cut through the low-hanging frozen fog. Martin pressed the pedal and they were off.

They'd rolled only a few yards when vehicle headlights cut across their path. As Gord raised the gate, a pick-up pulled into the parking lot.

Craig jumped out, hit the fob to lock the truck, and ran across the lot to the golf cart.

"My commute here is twice as long as yours," Rita said as Craig approached.

He blinked at her. "It is? Well, where the hell do you live?"

"Not in APEX Hills, that's for sure," Rita slid across the bench, brushing up against Martin. "Get in and let's go."

Craig climbed into the cart and sat where Rita had. "Bench is nice and warm," he said.

"No doubt," Rita said. "I felt my entire body's warmth leaching into the upholstery. Enjoy. Let's go."

But Martin idled the cart. "Your safety is compromised, Ms. Jonas."

Rita blinked at him. "It is?"

"This cart isn't made for three riders. You haven't got a handhold."

"True," Rita said. "But it's fucking cold tonight so we're all gonna ride. You'll just have to take it easy, 'cause if you hit the brakes hard, it's me who gets launched."

Martin nodded and pressed the pedal with care. "Got it."

The golf cart rolled forward with a quiet *whirr*, leaving behind the brightly lit guards' hut as they headed for the bluff. The crisp night air nipped at their faces, but a small built-in heater under the dashboard pushed out just enough warmth to take the edge off the chill.

Martin steered along the fence line toward the back of APEX property. They passed a patch of grass where Lisa's body had been burned, now fully restored, the vegetation returning as if nothing had ever happened. No one spoke her name anymore. It was as if the condo development that had taken her place now owned it more than she ever had.

Another five minutes later, Martin eased the golf cart to a stop at the edge of the bluff, its headlights carving twin beams through the frozen night. Something reflective glimmered ahead, then vanished just as quickly.

"That's the fence up there," Martin said, stepping out and leaving the cart's lights on to pierce the darkness. He flicked on his headlamp.

Craig followed, switching his on as well. Rita climbed out last, her boots half-crunching, half-squeaking against the frozen ground. She switched on her own headlamp and surveyed the bluff. It was a jagged expanse of uneven rock, its crevices filled with tufts of frost-coated grass. The wind swept across the exposed terrain, rattling the bare trees that stood like silent sentinels.

Pulling her puffer tighter, she buried her chin in the collar against the cold and followed Martin toward the fence. A thin layer of snow clung to the ground, slick underfoot.

"Watch your step," she said, her voice nearly lost to the wind. "It's icy out here."

Martin swept his flashlight over the ground before

raising it to locate the fence. "There," he said, training the beam on the chain link.

The metal had been slashed vertically about four feet, then shoved inward. The jagged edges of the links glinted under the light, some reflecting clean silver where they had been sliced, others blackened as if scorched.

"That's big enough for someone to fit through," Craig said.

Rita studied the cut, then turned and swept her light across the ground. A glint of metal caught her eye. Something lay partially hidden in the grass, reflecting the harsh beams of her flashlight and headlamp. She knelt beside it. The blade of a power tool gleamed in the dark.

"It's an angle grinder," she said, rising and turning to face the others.

She took a step toward them, then stopped. The grass in front of her was flattened, a clear track leading all the way to the fence. Something heavy had been dragged through here. In some places, the compressed grass shimmered with moisture. She crouched, touched it. Sticky and warm.

She called out, "We've got blood."

Straightening, she pulled her weapon, then turned toward the tree line, the most likely place for trespassers to take cover. Craig and Martin followed her lead, sweeping their flashlight beams in the same direction.

The light flashed across a pale mass.

Rita's breath caught. "There's someone there."

Craig steadied his flashlight beam. Martin angled his to match. The three intersecting lights illuminated a bare-chested figure with the head of a deer standing in the woods.

No, not standing. Hanging.

The body dangled limp from a thick branch, teal-green

ropes looped under its armpits, and arms hanging lifeless. A four-point shoulder-mounted deer's head replaced the man's own. Glassy eyes stared forward in an empty, eternal gaze. And an encircled star had been carved deep into his torso.

Dropping their flashlights, Craig and Martin turned away and vomited into the grass.

Stepping back, Rita lowered her beam and dug into her puffer pocket, pulling out the packet of saltines. She extended it toward them.

"Cracker?" she asked.

For the first time in days, her stomach felt fine.

Chapter Seven

"WELL, he definitely didn't die here," Rita said, studying the macabre tableau set against the silent backdrop of the woods. "Not enough blood."

Craig pulled himself to his feet. "Should we call the cops?"

Rita gave him a flat look. "We *are* the cops." She swept her light over the area, searching for any sign of the perpetrator, or the missing head. "The body's on APEX land. Our jurisdiction, our problem."

Craig wiped his chin with the back of his hand. "Well, hell. This is some crazy-ass kink."

Rita rolled her eyes and turned to Martin. "Middleton, call Casper Forensics. Ask for the medical examiner, Dylan Bruce."

"Ten-four," Martin said, stepping away to make the call. In the distance, an owl hooted.

Rita moved closer, her headlamp and flashlight combining with Craig's, their beams slicing through the dark like strobes at some theatrical death rite, the shadows shifting like mourners in a funeral procession.

The body dangled from a branch, suspended on a simple pulley. It swayed slightly in the breeze, the branch above creaking under the weight. Chunks of bark and broken twigs had snagged in the deer's antlers.

"No shoes," Craig muttered, pointing at the man's bare feet. The toes had turned a lifeless gray.

"I wonder if this is all he was wearing when he was murdered," Rita said. "Or if his clothes were taken by the killer."

"Like his head?" Craig said, his voice tight.

Rita glanced at him. "Think we'll find his shoes with it?"

Craig squared his shoulders. "Wouldn't rule it out."

Rita took a slow step around the body. "I was curious about your training," she said.

Craig shot her a wary look, but she was already moving, boots crunching against the frost-hardened ground as she circled the body. Her light flickered over the man's chest, illuminating the deep, crude pentagram carved into his skin. Around the incisions the flesh had puckered.

She exhaled sharply. "Hell of a job."

Her beam traveled upward to the severed neck. Raw strands of sinew and tissue clung to the smooth underside of the deer mount, while the ragged edges of the cut were charred.

"You think an angle grinder did this?" she asked. "Took off the head *and* cut through the fence?"

Craig burped, covering his mouth. "You mean the one that cut the fence?" He shook his head. "Dunno."

Rita took another step, angling her flashlight toward the left side of the man's neck. "Looks like he's got a tattoo."

The black blade of an ornate dagger extended up the

severed neck, standing alone, as the hilt had been lost with the head. The edges of the tattoo were distorted by the roughly severed tissue, giving the impression of a knife broken in half.

But Craig's gaze was averted. "Here's another wound," he said, pointing to the man's wrist.

"Sliced and burned like the neck," Rita said. "But no bleeding."

"If you say so," Craig said, looking green again.

"Maybe the killer tried to remove his hands as well," Rita said. "Then changed their mind."

He stifled an acidic burp. "Or got interrupted."

"You okay?" Rita asked.

Craig nodded, but Rita was unconvinced. She gestured over his shoulder. "Here's Deputy Middleton."

"I've alerted the gate staff that the medical examiner will be arriving shortly," Martin said, approaching.

"Thanks," Rita said. "Did they—"

A crack sounded in the woods and Rita spun, pulling her weapon. Craig and Martin pulled theirs as well, a heartbeat slower than Rita.

"Stop!" Rita called out. "Police! Reveal yourself!"

No response came.

Rita repeated the command.

Silence.

She met Craig's eye, then Martin's, and gestured for the three of them to fan out and head towards the woods. The beams from their headlights and flashlights bounced over the uneven ground. Underfoot, twigs snapped and the wind whispered through the spindly trees.

As they crossed the bluff, something rustled. Rita turned the beam of her flashlight towards the sound. A buck bolted across the shafts of light, crashing into the woods.

Craig fired a shot, the sound ripping through the silent woods and echoing across the bluff.

Rita dropped to the ground, heart pounding in her ears. "Stop!"

Craig froze.

"Jesus," Rita said, the cold temperature of the ground seeping into her chest. She rolled onto her side, senses reeling. "What the hell are you doing?"

Craig lowered his weapon. "I thought it was the perp."

Panting, Martin crossed to Rita's side and stooped down. Despite the frigid air, sweat beaded his forehead. "You okay?"

Martin offered a hand and she grasped it, her muscles still coiled to fight or flee. She pulled herself up to standing and the world spun. She planted her feet shoulder width apart, anchoring her shaky legs to the ground.

"Thanks," she said, releasing his hand. "You okay?"

Martin nodded, his mouth set in a grim line. He rubbed his left ear. "Still can't hear shit." Then he turned and walked two paces over to Craig and punched him in the jaw.

Craig dropped with a bellow. "What the fuck?"

Martin shook out his hand/ "You almost shot me and Rita."

Craig worked his jaw. "It was a simple mistake."

Martin tapped his temple. "Fucking simple is right."

"Easy, guys," Rita said, dusting off her uniform, "everyone's okay."

But she was still trembling.

Chapter Eight

"Evening, Dylan, Tilda," Rita said, walking to meet the Casper Forensics Team coming over the bluff. They were already suited up in Tyvek, hair tucked inside the drawstring hoods.

"Technically, it's morning," Dylan Bruce said, looking over his horn-rimmed glasses at her. Even at this hour, the medical examiner didn't look any less sharp-witted as any workday in the morgue.

"Hi, Rita," Tilda said. "I heard you changed sides, but I didn't quite believe it."

Rita shrugged. "I'm still adjusting. I meant to call you to let you know, but every night, I fall asleep right after dinner."

"You got a lot on your mind these days," Tilda said. "Or in this case, in your belly. How's the baby?"

"So far so good," Rita said. "And to be honest, my entire decision was made with the baby in mind."

"Did you get a pay increase?" Tilda asked.

Rita gave her a look. "Only reason I'm here." She cocked her head towards Craig. "Of course, Deputy

Dillard might think I'm here for the joyous experience of training him up to follow in my footsteps, but he'd be mistaken."

Tilda laughed.

"I appreciate your understanding," Rita said, "because the team didn't take it so good."

"Stands to figure," Tilda said, ever pragmatic. "Deputy Perry upset?"

Rita blew out a sigh. "Hell, yes. Even though he made Sheriff."

"Well, it's nice to work with a familiar face, even if it is the unfortunate circumstances of murder."

"And what a murder it is," Rita said, gesturing towards the body.

"That's a new one, for sure," Tilda said.

Rita led the team towards the body. "New one for me, too."

Craig burped as they ground drew up to the body, hanging limp from the ropes.

Rita pumped a thumb towards him. "New one for him, too."

"You'll get used to it," Tilda said, cheery. "I once worked a crime scene in Casper that had a hollowed-out sheep's carcass."

Dylan Bruce made an interested sound.

"I saw my share of weird shit in New York," Rita said. "Like this alligator in a guy's bathtub who'd eaten half his roommate. The guy's roommate, that is, not the alligator's."

Tilda made a face. "Which half?"

"Well, that's what made the whole thing so disturbing," Rita said. "It wasn't a clean half; more like collection of various body parts that together made up half the guy."

"So who got arrested?" Tilda asked.

Rita obliged the forensics examiner with an eye roll, and everyone but Craig laughed.

Bruce set down his kit and a stepladder. "Where's the head?"

"Beats me," Rita said. "Though I can't say we did a very thorough search, out here with our flashlights."

Tilda crunched through the frozen underbrush, stopping in front of the hanging body. "Goddamn," she muttered, tilting her head to take it all in. She pointed at the shoulder mount. "A lot of work went into both of these cadavers."

"You think the killer and the taxidermist are one and the same?" Martin asked.

"There's no shortage of shoulder mounts around here," Rita said. "Seems like everyone in Still has an uncle who's made them one."

Craig curled his lip. "I think the killer's more likely to be a Satanist than a taxidermist."

Bruce scoffed. "A pentagram isn't inherently evil."

"True," Tilda said with a shrug. "But most people share the same cultural biases as Deputy—"

"Dillard," Craig supplied.

"I think there's something inherently evil about decapitation," Martin said.

Bruce snorted, then stooped to open his kit. "We'll set up a search for the head and you two officers can pitch in."

Craig swallowed, swapping a look with Martin. Behind them, a tech switched on a row of standing perimeter lights. The harsh white light chased away the shadows, flattening the trees as though they were cardboard cutouts, lending the body a waxen appearance.

"You got an ID for this fellow?" Bruce asked.

"Haven't found any," Rita said. "He's got a distinctive

tattoo, though only partially visible—er, obviously. But none of us here recognize it."

"'Cause it's common," Craig said. He wagged a finger at his own neck. "Lot of guys got daggers here."

"Then let's get down to it, shall we?" Tilda said, squinting up at the body.

Bruce unfolded the stepladder. "Or in this case, up to it."

"That's rock climber's rope," Tilda said. "My ex was into that. Used to keep some coils of the stuff in the garage. It's not cheap."

"It did the job right," Bruce said. "Other varieties might have cut into the cadaver's underarms."

Tilda gestured to the pulley system. "The killer's essentially built a belay system here." Her gaze traveled to the tree trunk, where the rope was wrapped tightly around the base. She pointed. "Tying off the rope here prevented the body from slipping back down due to gravity."

Bruce joined her at the tree trunk, and they proceeded to discuss the feat required to raise the body into the trees.

Walking out of earshot of the two examiners, Rita pulled out her phone and scrolled through the contacts. Her finger drifted between Jason and Mary Lou.

She dialed Jason. It rang five times, then flicked over to voicemail. Rita disconnected, then moved her thumb to dial again when a call came in from Jason.

"Jason," Rita said.

"Rita. Is the baby okay?"

"The kid's fine," Rita said. "Though it'd probably like to be in bed sleeping as much as me at this moment. But I've got a body out here at APEX."

"Oh, shit," Jason said, still sounding sleepy.

"You got any missing persons reports come in?" she asked.

"No," Jason said. "Let me look at my phone closer." Silence settled on the call while he checked for messages, then said: "Nothing's come in to us. What do you know about the victim?"

"We didn't find any ID. Guy doesn't even have shoes or socks."

"It's freezing out," Jason said.

"One hundred percent," Rita said, switching the phone between her hands while she blew on them to warm them up. "Vic is a white male, maybe five nine or five ten. It's hard to tell because he's missing his head. He has a tattoo of what looks like a knife on his neck. Which is ironic because it's exactly at the place where his neck was severed."

"Got it," Jason said. "Sounds bloody."

"Looks like he wasn't killed here. Crime scene could be on your patch."

"Got it," Jason said. "We'll keep an eye out."

"There's some other weird shit about the body, too," Rita said. "But I'll tell you later. Nothing that can't wait, I don't think."

"Er—okay," he said, sounding unsure.

Craig walked over, waving for Rita's attention.

"I gotta go, Jason," she said. "Thanks for your help."

"You're welcome," he said, hanging up.

Rita disconnected and walked over to Craig. "Got something to show you," he said. "This way."

He strode toward the fence, ducked, and slipped through the hole. Rita followed.

On the other side, they scrambled through the ditch and climbed onto a dirt road, its surface a patchwork of frozen ruts and churned-up mud. Older tire tracks stood rigid, preserved in ice, while others had fractured into jagged ridges and shallow, half-frozen puddles. Where a vehicle had passed more recently, the frost-crusted earth had buckled under its weight, smearing once-distinct treads into a slushy, chaotic mess.

"Over here," Craig said, waving Rita a few feet along the shoulder. "Blood."

Wine-colored patches glowed in their flashlights, frozen into brittle layers like sheets of shattered stained-glass. Along the embankment, which dropped away into the ditch, frozen drops beaded the dead grass, like garnets.

"Well, at least we know how the body got here," Rita said.

Craig pointed with the beam of his flashlight. "I think the vehicle pulled over here and dumped him."

Rita nodded, looking back at the rift in the fence. "And dragged him to the bluff. Would have taken some strength, seeing as the victim is probably heavier with the deer's head than his own."

"Although less the weight of his shoes," Craig said with a shrug.

Rita motioned left, then right. "We'll each take a direction. Walk about a hundred yards along the shoulder."

Craig adjusted his headlamp. "Got it."

"You go left," Rita said. "That loops back toward Still. I'll head right, toward APEX."

"Ten-four." Craig turned and disappeared into the darkness.

Rita went the opposite way, sweeping her flashlight over the ground. For several paces, all she saw was slush. She pulled out her radio and called Martin.

"Middleton speaking," Martin said.

"I'm thinking through the reason the body might be brought out here," Rita said. "Maybe the vic's an APEX employee. Can you find out if anyone was unaccounted for at work today?"

"Sure, I'll check it out," Martin said.

Two minutes later, he messaged: *Only one employee didn't show today. Macy Baker in finance. Kid was sick. Everyone else accounted for.*"

Thanks, Rita messaged, continuing along the dirt track. She pocketed her phone. The body dump location wasn't the only puzzle. What was the meaning of the deer's head and carving the guy up like a jack-o-lantern?

She rounded a bend and saw the lights in the distance. The forensic technicians had set up the perimeter lights, illuminating the place like an evening softball game. Yellow tape was strung like patio lanterns, and the parking lot was full of cars. A regular party scene if one didn't know better.

She paused, catching a glimpse of the body still hanging in the trees. Bruce stood on a footstool taking photographs as though he were examining a marble bust in a museum of antiquities.

In her pocket, Rita's phone vibrated with a text notification. She stopped and looked the screen. It was Cash.

Everything OK?

Rita gave his message a thumbs-up, then typed: *Dunno when I'll be home.* Her fingers were frigid from the cold, her toes just as numb. She stiffly tapped out another message: *Dead body.*

Chapter Nine

RITA WALKED UP TO THE GUARDS' hut and rapped on the glass.

Gord stuck his head out. "Hi, Ms. Jonas. How's it going up there?"

"Still plenty of work to do," Rita said. "Your shift must be over by now."

Gord rolled his shoulders. "Martin just finished taking my witness statement. I was packing up to head home."

"Before you go," Rita said, taking out her notebook, "do you mind updating me about last night?"

"Okay."

"Did you hear anything unusual?"

"Like I told Martin, nothing in particular."

Rita had a feeling he was holding something back. "Any power tools?"

His brows lifted. "Power tools?"

"Like an angle grinder."

Gord blinked. "An angle grinder? What for?"

"We found one by the vandalized fence panel. Presumably it was used to cut the chain-link fence."

A faint flush rose to his cheeks. "I wear headphones to stay awake, Ms. Jonas."

"You were listening to music?" Rita asked.

He nodded. "I tried audiobooks like my uncle who drives a truck, but they only put me to sleep faster." He shrugged, the color fading from his face. "Gotta have something with a beat to keep me going." He averted her gaze. "But I'll stop if it's a problem."

Rita waved a hand. "No need. Whatever gets you through the shift. But adjust your headphone settings so you can still hear outside noise."

Gord looked relieved. "Sure thing, Ms. Jonas."

"Did you have your eyes on the lot," Rita asked lightly, "or were you reading a book?"

Gord gave a small laugh. "If you're asking about suspicious vehicles, didn't see nothing other than a few folks heading home late. Sometimes the research lab will stay open overnight, depending on the experiment, but right now, no one's on the premises at night except security."

"How many on shift?" Rita asked.

"Aside from our supervisor, there's four of us, taking rounds in the guard's hut here, and patrolling the fence line."

"Who was supervising last night?" Rita asked.

"Len," Gord answered. "Martin went to talk to him and the other guys, Danny, Dave, and Manuel were on with me last night."

"And no surveillance cameras up there?" Rita asked.

"None," Gord confirmed. "No lights neither. There's no wiring that far back."

"Got it," Rita said, closing her notebook. "Thanks."

With that, she turned and headed back toward the crime scene, wishing for another ride in the golf cart. The sun was coming up, but her toes didn't feel any warmer.

At the highest point of the bluff, yellow crime tape cordoned off the scene. Inside the perimeter, the half-naked, deer-headed body lay rigid on the frozen ground. Around it, figures in Tyvek suits moved with slow deliberation, their protective gear stretched tight over thick puffer jackets.

Bruce turned as Rita approached.

"We got him down," Bruce said, the wind rumpling his drawstring hood. "We're taking him in." He turned away from the gusting air currents. "Not the easiest working conditions this morning."

"I'll say," Rita said, shivering. She gestured to the corpse. "Still has the shoulder mount on."

"It's fastened in place somehow," Bruce said, adjusting his glasses. A gleam of curiosity lit his eyes. "I'm looking forward to having a better look."

Rita grimaced. "Have fun with that."

Tilda joined them, exhaling a breath.

"No ID, no personal belongings," she said. "Other than the mass of frozen blood on the road and a very obviously damaged chain-link fence, there's not a lot to work with. As elaborate as this body dump is, it's also a very stripped-down crime scene."

"You've got some rope and an angle grinder to work with," Bruce said, offering a grin.

Tilda matched his expression. "True enough. I lifted a nice set of prints from that angle grinder." She turned to Rita. "I'll be in touch as soon as we get an ID."

"Appreciate it," Rita said. "I'm still puzzling why anyone would bring the body here in the first place. It seems like an awful lot of work to get it through the fence, let alone string it up in the trees."

"Agreed," Tilda said. "Can't have been any easier to hang that thing up than it was for us to take it down."

"The deer's antlers wouldn't have been easy to fit inside the cabin of a vehicle," Rita said, "so I think the killer used a pick-up truck. Plus the killer would have packed coils of rope."

"And an angle grinder," Tilda said.

"Right," Rita said. "With the sound of the angle grinder, the chance of discovery was huge, not to mention round-the-clock security at APEX. Why risk it?"

"Sounds like we all have some questions to answer," Bruce said. "Talk to you soon, Jonas."

"Thanks," Rita said. "It's good working with you guys. Obviously, the circumstances aren't great, but you know what I mean."

Tilda smiled. "Get some rest. You must be exhausted."

Rita nodded. "And starving. Though I'm also nauseated, so sleep might win." She glanced toward the rest of the team, where Craig assisted in combing the area. "I'm leaving Craig with continuity. He'll see you guys out."

The inspectors bade Rita goodbye as she crossed to Craig. The wind had picked up, tugging at the yellow crime tape and carrying the sharp scent of frozen earth.

"Search team's wrapping things up," he said, breaking away from the search party. He exhaled. "No head, no shoes, no socks."

"Tilda told me," Rita said. "That head is going to turn up somewhere and surprise us all." She echoed his exhalation, then, "I'm leaving you in charge. Middleton's talking to the security guards. I need you to stick around while Forensics packs up."

"Ten-four," Craig said.

"And I'm taking the golf cart," she added. "These boots are killing me. You can radio Middleton to drive it back up here."

Then she turned and made her way down the path, riding the golf cart back to the guard's hut.

The soft seat was a welcome relief from the aches in her feet and the cold air biting at her skin. She keyed the engine, feeling the gentle acceleration as the cart smoothly rolled down the slope. Within minutes, she reached the guards' post, the sound of the cart's tires crunching against the gravel.

In the parking lot, the day was stirring to life. Gord had gone home, replaced by another guard, but the gate remained raised as employees trickled in for another shift. Casper's forensic team managed the flow of traffic, directing vehicles into vacant stalls, away from the official vehicles.

Among them, she spotted the SCSO truck. Jason sat behind the wheel. In the passenger seat sat his new deputy, Candace Watkins.

Rita walked over. Jason lowered the window.

"Didn't expect to see you here," Rita said. "This is APEX's jurisdiction."

"I know," Jason said. "Just wanted to check in. See how you're holding up."

Rita nodded. "I appreciate that."

Jason gestured to his passenger. "This is Deputy Watkins."

"I remember." Rita gave Candace a tight smile. "Hunter recommended you. Fresh out of the Academy, right?"

"Top of her class," Jason said before Candace could answer.

Rita glanced at him. "Education's not the same as experience."

Jason stiffened. "Then it's good she's getting some."

Rita looked at Candace again, who had gone pale, her lips pressed into a thin line.

"You're gonna cut your teeth on this one, that's for sure," Rita said.

"Foul play?" Candace asked.

Rita grimaced. "Very foul. But there's nothing to see. This isn't your jurisdiction."

Jason blew out a breath. "Jesus, Rita, we came by to help."

Rita stilled. "Oh, yeah?"

"Wanted to confirm we haven't got any missing person reports." He set his jaw. "But if one comes in, I'll let you know."

Rita narrowed her eyes. "That's really why you came?"

Jason frowned. "What do you mean?"

Rita shrugged. "Just wondering if you're here for the case or your career." She flicked her gaze toward Candace. "Same goes for Deputy Watkins."

Jason let out a growl. "You want the truth? Still's a small town, Rita. I grew up here. When someone dies, I want to know who they are." He voice cracked. "I might know them."

Rita's shoulders eased. "Fair enough. I'm sorry, Jason. I'm exhausted."

"I get it," Jason said. "We gotta go anyway. Call-out to the Gas-N-Go."

"What's happening at Chester's?"

"Stolen property," Jason said. "Though not sure what yet. Call just came in." He glanced at his watch. "And it's still damn early."

"Well, while you're looking for stolen property," Rita said, "I'm looking for a head. If you see one around town, let me know."

Candace gasped and blinked. "A head?"

But Jason chuckled. "That's what you wanted, Rita."

Rita frowned. "Huh?"

"To get ahead?" Jason smirked. "That's why you left for Genius HQ, right?"

"So you're funny now, too?" Rita rolled her eyes, though she was relieved Jason was teasing her like old times. Even if he did punch where it hurt.

She flashed him a smile. "I thought I was the punny one."

Jason rolled his shoulders. "Must be a lingering legacy from Blaze. For all the crap you gave me about leaking information to him, he was the one dripping nonsense into my head. Like wordplay."

Rita wanted to laugh, but instead, she said, "The way you talk about him, it sounds like you two aren't playing anymore."

Jason gave her a look. "Of course not. It wasn't gonna work out in the long run. Like you said, he was always tryin' to glean intel."

Rita gave a nod. "In the end, that was the mature thing to do."

Jason flared. "What the hell does that mean, 'the mature thing to do'? I just figured this would be the easiest way to enforce my boundaries, that's all. Didn't have to 'grow up' or nothin'. I only made the right choice, like I always try to do."

"Of course," Rita said, stumbling over her words. "That's what I meant."

Without a word, Jason turned the ignition. Then he started to roll up the window.

"Thanks for keeping an eye out for our head," Rita said, raising her voice to be heard over the engine. "We still don't have an ID."

Then the window closed and the SCSO truck pulled out of the parking lot, wheels crunching over the rock-salt.

"Fuck," Rita said, her breath hanging in curtains. For a moment, she stood in the parking lot contemplating her BMW. But she was too tired to drive.

She turned and trudged inside the front doors of APEX. Ginny, bright-eyed in the morning, gave her a cheery salutation.

Rita grumbled a good morning, swiped her access card, and rode the elevator upstairs to her office. Before making herself some oatmeal in the microwave, she dropped onto the couch for a moment. She just needed a few minutes to rest before getting behind the wheel. She yawned, then closed her eyes…

Chapter Ten

RITA'S FOOT caught on a root, twisting her ankle. She stumbled, dirt flying into her face as she hit the ground. Pushing herself up to hands and knees, she paused to take a breath, trying to steady her racing heart. Where the hell was she? To her right, something bolted through the brush. Was that a mule deer?

No, not a deer. A man with the head of a buck.

Rita jerked upright, her breath catching in her chest. She blinked, the vision vanishing. She was in her office at APEX, the faux-leather sofa sticking to her skin. She rubbed her face and swung her legs to the floor. Her back protested the shift in position. The modern sleek sofa felt more like an upholstered ironing board than anything comfortable.

With a sigh, Rita fished her phone from her pocket. Her thumbs quickly flicked across the screen, finding a series of texts from Craig. He was tired. And asking when he could go home.

Rita tapped out a quick response telling him to hang on, that she'd be right there. Then she stood. The shift in weight pinched her bladder and she hurried out of her office to the bathroom at the end of the corridor.

A few minutes later, she stepped out and took the elevator downstairs. The cavernous foyer buzzed with chatter. Two dozen or so employees had gathered, leaning against walls or standing in small groups. Some wore lab coats, others dressed in casual business attire, but all wore expressions of astonishment. Instead of working, they were caught up in a flurry of rumors.

She marched straight up to Ginny at the reception desk, receiving several glances as she passed the gossiping staff.

"Everyone's talking about it, Sheriff Jonas, I mean, Ms. Jonas," Ginny said, catching herself.

Rita smiled lightly. "Why don't you just call me Rita?"

Ginny nodded, solemn.

"What's the word on the street?" Rita asked, inviting the gossipers.

Ginny's eyes widened. "Satanists."

Rita rolled her eyes. "There's no evidence of that, so everyone can relax. I'm heading back up to the scene if anyone needs me."

The building's glass doors slid open with a soft hiss as she stepped out into the fresh air.

To the right, the chemical storehouse loomed, and to the left was a gravel track that wound its way back down to the guards' hut and the parking lots.

She crossed the path and cut through the grass, heading back up the bluff to the crime scene. As she approached the crime tape, she found Craig asleep in one of the white plastic patio chairs the employees used in the unofficial smoking section behind the guards' hut. Martin must have brought it up in the golf cart.

Rita touched his shoulder. "Deputy Dillard."

Craig jolted awake, yanking his gun. But before he could aim it, Rita snatched it from his hand and unloaded the clip.

"Ms. Jonas," Craig said, blinking in the frigid sunlight.

Rita handed back his gun. "Go home."

Craig pried himself out of the chair, re-holstered his gun, and trudged away.

Rita considered calling after him to tell him to put the chair back where he found it. Or at least drink a Coke before getting behind the wheel. She sighed. When it came to Craig, why did she always feel like she was talking to a teenager?

She refocused, sweeping the area with fresh eyes. Using landmarks, she mapped out a mental grid, then moved in steady, deliberate passes. The frosted grass crunched underfoot as she scanned for anything overlooked by the forensics team.

But there was nothing to find. With a growing urgency in her bladder, she headed back to the golf cart and drove down the bluff toward the office.

Inside, Rita strode past reception, swiped her badge to open the elevator, and made a beeline for the bathroom. The moment she sat down on the toilet seat, she let out a long sigh of relief.

After washing her hands, she splashed warm water on her face and retied her bun, trying to smooth away the evidence of four hours spent sleeping in her office.

Back at her desk, she fired off a quick message to Cash, letting him know she was still at APEX, and not to worry, she had napped.

On her desktop computer, she pulled up the staff profiles, filtering for white men. A quick scroll revealed five employees who hadn't clocked in. One was on sick leave, two were on vacation, one was attending a conference in Paris, and another was on parental leave.

One by one, she called each of them, confirming they were alive, and every single one took the opportunity to ask about the body. The office gossip had clearly blown all the way over to Europe.

Setting the receiver down, she turned back to her keyboard and pulled up the NCIC database. The search bar blinked at her, the computer humming softly. She typed in a detailed description of the tattoo, the style of the illustrated blade, its distinct placement, the ink's color, and hit enter.

The results were slow to load. Hundreds of entries filled the screen, most without photographs. Rita leaned forward, scrolling through the list. Without visuals, the search was practically useless.

She tried another approach, calling law enforcement in Cheyenne, Casper, and Beaumont to check for missing persons not yet entered into NCIC. But each department came up empty.

Sighing, she shifted to missing persons reports that might match her John Doe. But none had a tattoo that matched. And without an ID—least of all, a head—she had no idea who she was looking for. She didn't even have a solid guess at his age.

Leaning back, she let her head rest against the chair and gazed out the window. The afternoon sky stretched out in a deep royal blue, fading at the horizon. In the parking lot, a string of taillights flickered like gemstones stitched to the hem of a sapphire cloak as employees headed home.

Rita logged off, tidied her desk, and gathered her things. One last stop at the bathroom, then she made her way down to her car, slipping into the driver's seat and joining the slow-moving line of vehicles pulling out of the lot.

Tonight, the drive along the rutted rural road felt longer than usual. Her eyelids were heavy, but so was the renewed pressure in her bladder, an inevitable consequence of sitting in a bucket seat and rumbling over potholes. Because she was too fucking tired to avoid all of them.

When she finally pulled into the driveway, the porch light was already on. She smiled, unbuckling her seatbelt and pushing open the door, almost too tired to move.

Her boots hit the pavement with a squeak. Everything felt heavy, her eyelids, her bladder, the exhaustion settled deep in her bones.

But then Cash was there, lightening every aspect of her being as he gathered her into his arms…

Chapter Eleven

RITA STIRRED, blinking awake to find Cash's face close enough to count his eyelashes.

"You should probably wake up now," he said.

She groaned, stretching out on Irene's overstuffed floral sofa. It was not her taste, but her spine approved. "What time is it?"

"Seven."

Rita sighed. "You're right. Otherwise, I won't sleep tonight. Thanks for waiting. I needed that nap."

"No problem," Cash said. "Can't promise the meatloaf ain't dried out, though."

Rita blinked at him. "You make meatloaf?"

"Don't everybody?"

"I don't."

"Dad always made it when he was on kitchen patrol. We'd even eat it for breakfast. Chuck meat, breadcrumbs, Worcestershire, a couple eggs and slam it in a pan."

Rita's stomach growled. "Help me up," she said, wiggling off the couch.

Cash gave her hand up and she shuffled to the small bathroom off the kitchen. When she returned, Cash had plated the meatloaf.

She sat down to a mouth-watering plate of roast potatoes and meatloaf. Cash offered her Heinz ketchup and BBQ sauce, and she accepted the latter.

"It's amazing," she said through a mouthful.

"You're welcome," Cash said. Then: "So the town's talkin'…"

"Oh, yeah?" she said, clearing her tongue with a sip of water. "So what's the talk?"

Cash grinned. "Satanists."

"You don't sound convinced."

"I'm not."

"Me neither," Rita said. "Yeah, there's a pentagram carved into the victim's torso, but that kind of thing doesn't usually mean much. Even if some wannabe cult is involved, they probably don't even know real satanic practices. If I start chasing that angle, I'll just end up following theories the killer doesn't even understand."

"Smoke and mirrors, huh?" Cash said.

"Uh-huh," Rita mumbled through a mouthful of meatloaf. "This is fucking good, by the way." Then she sighed. "Without a head, IDing the body's a pain in the neck."

Cash chuckled. "You're funny."

She stuck out her tongue at him. "Not as punny as Jason." Her phone rang, making her jump. She swiped to answer. "Hi, Tilda."

"I've got good news," Tilda said.

"Hang on." Rita stood, gesturing to Cash that she was stepping outside.

The cold air hit her as she shut the door behind her, hugging her arms. "Brr. Should've brought a jacket."

"You always 'should have' brought a jacket," Tilda said. "It didn't ever get cold in New York?"

"Of course it did," Rita said. "But this kind of cold? It's criminal."

Tilda snorted. "It's Wyoming."

Rita shivered. "I know, I grew up here."

"Yes, you did," Tilda said with a laugh. "You ready now?"

Hugging herself tighter for warmth, Rita smiled. "Ready."

"I've ID'd the victim," Tilda said. "Theodore 'Teddy' Brandon Lake. DOB: January 6, 1982. Home address in Tampa, lapsed Florida driver's license, and a four-year-old mugshot."

"Mugshot?"

"A bit of a terror on the road, I'd say," Tilda said. "I've already emailed everything."

"Well, now I'll know what kind of head I'm looking for," Rita said.

"There's more," Tilda said. "That print off the grinder, running it now. Next, I'll check the rope, see if I can get a brand name."

Rita thanked her, then hung up.

Still shivering, she opened her email and pulled up Teddy Lake's mugshot. The tattoo matched.

"Bingo," she said.

She also accepted the Google Calendar invite from Dylan Bruce to attend tomorrow's autopsy at 10 a.m. Rita accepted, then stepped back inside, rubbing her arms to warm up. "I gotta go into the office."

Cash blinked at her. "Now?"

Rita nodded, coming into the kitchen. She laid her phone on beside her plate of meatloaf, her hand trembling.

Cash caught it up and put it to his lips. "You're as cold as an ice cube."

He released her hand and she rubbed them together for warmth. "After I'm done at the office, I'm gonna head straight to Casper, since I'm already out that way. I'm going to catch the autopsy in the morning."

"You're exhausted," Cash said. "You think it's a good idea to drive into Casper tonight?"

Rita shoveled some more meatloaf in her mouth. "I know my capabilities, Cash. I'm a better driver than you. I'll be fine."

He pushed aside his plate, resting his elbows on the table. "Maybe this has nothing to do about your driving capabilities, but the fact that I'd rather my future child ain't on the road at this time of night." He shivered as if he'd been standing out on the porch, too. "I reckon it's real frosty out already."

Rita leaned in to kiss him on the cheek. "I'll call you when I get to the Best Western."

"Your lips are cold too," he said.

"Then why don't you do something about it?"

He laughed, then kissed her on the mouth, tugging her lower lip into his mouth.

When he let her go, her lips were definitely warmer. "I'm gonna go pack my bag."

He nodded. "Can I do anything for you?"

Rita gave him a small smile. "Pack me some snacks, please?"

Cash smiled back at her. "You got it."

Five minutes later, she returned downstairs with her overnight bag. Cash met her at the front door with a packed Rancher's Pantry reusable shopping bag and another kiss.

Rita thanked him for the snacks and drove to APEX

HQ. At eight o'clock, the place was nearly empty. Gord was back on night shift, wearing headphones and looking like he hadn't slept much.

She gave him a nod as she passed. "Evening."

He waved back and greeted her, his voice louder than necessary. "Hello, Ms. Jonas." The words echoed across the cold blacktop.

Upstairs in her office, Rita ran Teddy Lake's name through the database. One DUI and two road rage convictions—once using a tire-iron on the other vehicle, the other time pulling a driver from a car and assaulting him. She printed out his record, mugshot, and driver's license photo.

A quick Google search filled in more gaps. Teddy had been a high school football star in a small Florida town, with teachers and state-wide sources predicting great things for him. His father, a retired cop, had passed six weeks ago from a stroke in the early stages of Alzheimer's. The obituary listed his surviving family: wife Loreen and sons Theodore Jr. and Lucas. A daughter, Brandi, had died at age four from a brain tumor.

Rita picked up her landline and called Tampa PD. After introducing herself, she explained they had a dead body by the name of Theodore 'Teddy' Lake.

"Can you locate next of kin and make the notification?" she asked.

The officer checked their system. "We've got a possible contact for his mother. We'll notify her and let you know when it's done."

"Thanks," Rita said, leaving her details.

She pulled out her phone and forwarded Teddy's mugshot to Jason, marking him as the victim. Then she switched off the office lights and headed to her car.

Passing the guards' hut, she gave Gord a wave, then drove to the Gas-N-Go to fill up. The BMW burned through gas twice as fast as her Honda had, or any of the clunkers at the SCSO, but at least APEX covered the bill. Sliding the nozzle into the tank, she hit the premium button.

With a yawn, she got back in the car and drove to the Best Western in Casper.

Chapter Twelve

RITA WOKE UP EARLY, stomach growling.

She rolled over and reached for her shoulder bag lying on the floor. Snagging the strap, she dragged the bag closer to the bed, to rummage inside.

But no power bars.

Not even saltines.

She sighed and lay back, then picked up her phone from the side table.

Not surprisingly, Craig didn't pick up. She left a voicemail stating she was in Casper for the autopsy and if there were any calls from the press, he was to direct them to her.

She padded to the bathroom to finish her morning routine, then changed into khakis and a sweater. It was a relief to be out of the APEX uniform. It was too tight, with narrower legs than the SCSO's. And head-to-toe black made her feel like the Grim Reaper.

She slipped on her well-worn all-weather shoes, grateful to be rid of the squeaky boots. Leaving her room, she followed the aroma of coffee and hash-browns downstairs to the dining room.

Inside, a half-dozen business professionals sat at black-veneer tables, eating with plastic forks. Others moved through the buffet line. Rita fell into step, piling her paper plate with sausages, scrambled eggs, and hash browns before grabbing a yogurt, two muffins, and a pair of bananas.

As she sat and ate, a call came in from the D.A. She licked sausage grease from her fingertip and swiped right to answer.

"Hi, Hunter."

He skipped the salutations. "I hear you've got a dead body."

Rita chewed some potato. "Part of one."

He chuckled. "Heard a rumor about a chimera."

"It's no joke," Rita said, swallowing. She cleared her mouth with some orange juice. "There's a shoulder mount in place of the victim's head." The suited trio at the neighboring table laughed loudly and Rita tucked the phone closer to her ear. "I think it's a mule deer, but it could be a white tail. Hasn't got a tail to know for sure."

"Christ," Hunter said, sobering. "You got any leads?"

"So far, we're still piecing it all together," Rita said. She bit into a muffin. "Hope you don't mind the pun."

"Are you somewhere private to talk?" Hunter asked.

"Not really," Rita said, over the chatter of the dining room.

"I'll get the details later, then," he said. "I'm eager to hear about this one."

Rita rang off and finished her breakfast, eating the second banana on the way.

Outside, her breath unfurled in thin white ribbons in the crisp morning air. Frost laced the windshield, melting swiftly as she flipped on the defroster. The engine purred to life and the vents blew out warm air, filling the cabin with heat as she adjusted her mirrors and backed out of the stall. The heated leather driver's seat warmed her back.

Leaving the hotel parking lot, she drove to Casper Hospital. The roads were quiet, the last streaks of ice evaporating on the asphalt. When she pulled into the hospital's sprawling lot, she parked away from the entrance.

A bit more space, a clearer view.

And she'd been here too often lately.

As she stepped out, the cold nipped at her face. But inside, the hot air was sharp with antiseptic. Sterile, yet laced with uneasy memories—long nights at Otto's bedside, the hum of machines, the weight of waiting. She exhaled, steadying herself, then rode the elevator downstairs to the morgue.

She signed in at the reception desk, exchanging a brief nod with the clerk before stepping into the adjoining room to don her PPE. Pulling on the gloves, gown, and mask, she adjusted the fit carefully, ensuring nothing was out of place before stepping into the autopsy room.

Here, the air was cool and moving in gentle currents due to robust air filtration systems, the metronomic hum blending with those of the refrigeration units and overhead fluorescent lights. The sterile brightness bleached away all warmth, sending hard reflections off the stainless-steel tables and counters.

On the central table lay the body, its waxy skin almost translucent beneath the lights. With the shoulder mount now removed, the neck was a gaping wound, ragged and dark, with tattered edges where the flesh was torn. Blood had long since drained from the body, leaving a sickly yellowish tint to the skin, while lividity mottled the lower limbs purple and pink.

Dylan Bruce stood to one side, wearing full PPE. Inspecting the remains, he dictated notes into a recorder clipped to the collar. He paused speaking, looking over his horn-framed glasses sitting low on his nose as she entered.

He paused the recorder. "Jonas."

"Bruce," she said.

The medical examiner gestured toward the remains. "Preliminary report: no gunshot wounds, no sharp-force trauma prior to death. Toxicology's pending, but the liver shows signs of chronic alcohol use. Plus his stomach contents confirm it."

"Cause of death?" Rita asked.

"My best guess? A blunt force impact to the head." His brow crinkled. "Shame we don't have it to confirm."

"Shame we have to guess," Rita said.

"At least we don't have to guess about the decapitation," Bruce said. "It happened post-mortem."

Rita's shoulders relaxed. "Thank goodness for small mercies. Did the angle grinder do the job?"

Bruce shook his head. "No, the skin isn't singed. This is the work of a handsaw. Maybe a hacksaw or a bone saw."

"The tools of a taxidermist?"

Bruce nodded. "A fair assumption."

"Not that it narrows the field of suspects," Rita said. "Hunting's a popular pastime in these parts."

"As is taxidermy." Bruce adjusted the recorder clipped to his collar. "The shoulder mount was originally attached to a wooden plaque, as is standard. The base was removed in order to shove the mount onto a piece of bent rebar. The rebar was then driven into the torso, following the spinal column. It's crude but effective; it kept the head stable enough for transport and display."

"Rebar would have added a reasonable amount of weight to the body," Rita said.

"Whoever did this was determined and strong," Bruce said.

"And had the help of the rope pulley."

Bruce nodded. "Even so, moving and hanging this body would likely have required the strength of a someone as large or larger than the victim. And our victim is a healthy weight. Even without a head."

"And what about this?" Rita asked, indicating the arm lying closest to her. A large incision spanned the wrist, reducing the joint to a series of sinewy strips, exposing the bone. "Is this an attempt to sever the hand?"

"Possibly," Bruce said. "The cuts are rough and shallow, almost hesitant."

Rita frowned. "Seems out of character, considering the effort put into the pentagram."

"True," Bruce said. "Although it could also indicate interruption."

Rita leaned over Teddy Lake's torso. "And yet there was all the time in the world for this handiwork."

Bruce met her eye. "Thankfully, like the head, done so after death." He traced the lines by hovering a gloved finger, pointing out the edges of the wounds. "The flesh around each incision is dry, with no signs of bleeding or fluid loss."

Rita shuddered. "At least he didn't feel it."

The medical examiner gave a slight nod. "Though it doesn't rule out ritual sacrifice. Each spoke has been carved with confidence and intention, without a pause. Almost like taking pride in it."

He pointed to the center of the star. "There's an initial in the middle."

Rita leaned closer. "Looks like an 'M.'"

"I agree," Bruce said.

"Could be significant."

"Likely."

"Although turn him upside down," Rita said, "and

you've got a 'W.' Which might tie in with the pentagram. *Wicca*, maybe?"

"I don't think the plan was to hang him any other way that right-side up," Bruce said. "While the head was securely fixed with the rebar, the effect wouldn't have been the same if the antlers were dragging on the ground. Plus, an 'M' could spark just as much speculation."

"Murder?" Rita said.

Bruce winked. "Or mayhem."

"Mule deer?" Rita said.

Bruce's eyes twinkled. "Actually, Tilda confirmed the mount *is* a mule deer." He turned off his recorder and stepped back. "That's all I've got for now. I'll send you the full report once toxicology comes in."

Rita smiled behind her mask. "Thanks, Bruce."

Then she exited the autopsy room and stripped off her PPE. She took out her phone and texted Tilda: *Leaving the morgue, how about lunch at the Olive and Grape?*

A second later, Tilda thumbs-upped the message and replied, *See you in 15.*

Rita put away her phone and gave the morgue clerk a wave before heading outside. In the parking lot, a frigid breeze cleared away the residue of chemicals in her nose.

Rita rubbed her belly. "That's enough death for now, baby."

Chapter Thirteen

WHILE WAITING for Tilda at the Olive and Grape, Rita flipped through the notifications on her phone.

Jason had texted. He and Deputy Watkins had done a thorough sweep of Still but found no sign of a crime scene or a head. Jason assured her they'd keep looking.

She sent back a quick thank you and promised to check in soon. Then she opened an email from the Tampa Police Department, confirming they'd located Loreen Lake and made the next-of-kin notification. The email included her contact information.

A shadow fell over the table. Rita closed her phone and looked up as Tilda slid into the booth.

"Nice place," Tilda said. "I've heard about it but never made the trip."

"It's worth the drive across town," Rita said. "I recommend the lasagna."

The server arrived, took their orders, and disappeared again.

Tilda leaned in with a knowing smile. "So, how's the pregnancy roller coaster?"

Rita snorted. "The hormones are kicking my ass." She rubbed her temples. "Even my brain feels exhausted."

The server passed by, dropping off a basket of warm focaccia.

Tilda shook her head. "Pregnancy's rough, but I think you're talking about overwhelm."

Rita arched a brow. "Overwhelm? Like the way my knees feel? Because they're killing me. Is this going to last all nine months?"

Tilda grimaced. "Oh, it'll get worse. But don't worry, you'll stop complaining about your knees by the time acid reflux sets in. And by overwhelm, I mean burn-out. You got a lot on your plate, and I'm not talking about focaccia bread."

Rita shrugged. "To be honest, the gig at APEX is easy. A stapler went missing last week."

"Was it used for vandalism? Or assault?"

"It fell into a trash can and got rescued by the custodian."

Tilda laughed. "Okay, but that's just work. What about everything else? Your dad died. You moved. You got engaged to a guy whose business literally burned down. Your father-in-law is a convicted felon. And on top of all that, you're still finding your footing at a new job while pregnant." She folded her arms. "You don't need a forensic investigator to see the evidence."

Rita laughed, then felt her phone vibrate in her pocket. She pulled it out. It was Jason. She sent the call to voicemail and slipped the phone away as the server arrived, balancing two steaming baked lasagnas with side salads.

They thanked the server, and Tilda took a sip of her ice water before leaning in. "I've got some information for you."

"You ID'd the print on the angle grinder?" Rita asked.

Tilda nodded. "Donald Horgan."

"The mechanic?" Rita said. "He's got a criminal record?"

"No," Tilda said, "he submitted his prints for employment. He used to work for Casper PD as a mechanic."

"That's interesting," Rita said. "So what happened?"

"Guys down in the shop said they moved to Still to take care of his mom-in-law, been there ever since."

"So where does he work now?"

"At the Gas-N-Go."

Rita chewed thoughtfully, then swallowed. "The other day Jason mentioned there was a theft at the Gas-N-Go. Maybe it was the angle grinder."

"Speaking of grinding," Tilda said, "this is lasagna is delicious. The meat's perfectly seasoned. I'm going to have to bring Bennett sometime, after practice, when her appetite doubles mine."

"How's the hockey season going?" Rita asked.

"Excellent," Tilda said. "Though I'll admit, the early morning driving isn't my favorite part of the experience."

As they ate, they chatted about Tilda's daughter and the updates Cash had made to the home he and Rita had recently bought. Like Rita, Tilda expressed her admiration for Cash's domestic skills.

"You should try his lasagna," Rita said. She tapped her fork on her plate. "As much as I love the lasagna here, Cash's easily outshines it.

"Then you owe me a dinner invite next time he's cooking," Tilda said with conviction.

After the server cleared their plates, they settled the bill and stepped out into the parking lot. The midday sun did little to cut the chill. They hugged, puffer jackets slipping and swishing against the other like Rita's new camping slippers.

"Good idea to meet up," Tilda said with a hug. "Have a good drive back to Still."

Rita smiled and bade her good-bye before walking toward her car. After getting inside the warm interior, she took a moment to listen to the voicemail from Jason.

"Rumor mill says the body was chopped up with an angle grinder. One was reported stolen from Chester's gas station. And I doubt that's a coincidence."

"I doubt it too," Rita said to herself, buckling into the seatbelt.

She sent Jason a thumbs-up, then texted Cash to let him know she was heading home after making one stop. Pulling out of the lot, she merged onto the freeway.

As Rita neared Still, she came up behind a silver van traveling below the speed limit. She pulled into the inside lane to get a better look. The vehicle had a distinctive teardrop rear window and a side-panel decal that read *SilverNomad.com*, accented by a sleek arrow pointing forward.

Rita did a double-take. "What the hell?"

She inched forward for a better look at the driver. Carol sat behind the wheel, her freshly colored hair sleek from a flat iron. Her cheeks, too, appeared smoother. And a pale gloss shimmered on her noticeably plumper lips. It wasn't just the van that had gotten a makeover in Cheyenne.

Rita faced forward, punched the gas, and surged ahead.

She didn't ease off the pedal until the van's headlights disappeared from her rearview mirror. Only then did she let out a breath.

Chapter Fourteen

RITA PARKED at the Gas-N-Go and breathed. Carol had never seen Rita's BMW, and she hoped her mother hadn't recognized her.

In the afternoon gloom, the fluorescent lights above the pumps cast a cool glow on the cracked asphalt. Beyond the pumps, sun-faded posters papered the windows, coaxing customers with deals for propane, firewood, and energy drinks. To the left, the mechanic's shop stood open for business, its garage doors rolled up and the sound of tools filling the air.

She stepped out of the BMW and crunched across the gravel lot, her boots squeaking as she pushed open the glass door to the store and stepped inside.

An acrid aroma of old coffee and motor oil hung in the air. A wire rack by the entrance displayed local postcards and maps and air fresheners shaped like pine trees. Along the back wall, a cooler hummed, filled with sodas and energy drinks.

Chester, restocking the cigarettes and razor blades beneath the glass countertop, looked up when he saw her.

He straightened, adjusting the oversized belt buckle on his jeans. "Well, how do you do, Sheriff?" Cowboy hat askew, he flashed her a grin that didn't quite reach his eyes. "Though I don't suppose I can call you that no more, huh?"

Rita returned a tight smile. Passing a rack of chip bags and packaged snack cakes (which she'd never paid much attention to in the past), her mouth watered. But she kept her gaze fixed on Chester as she walked up to the counter.

"Still fill up my car here, same as I always did, Chester."

"Except you got a new ride," he said. "How is it, working for the other side?" Chester folded his arms and leaned against the metal shelves behind him, stocked with everything from high-powered flashlights and bug zappers to inflatable boats with plastic oars, all coated in decades of old dust. "Must be real nice, sittin' pretty playin' cops and robbers in the private sector, while the rest of us deal with that dinky-ass deputy you left behind."

"I presume you're trying to insult Sheriff Perry," Rita said, her tone as biting as the wind. "Did Sheriff Perry show you his new dinky-ass badge?"

Chester tongued his cheek. "At least he brought that pretty young thing with him. Deputy Wet-Kiss, isn't it?" He chuckled. "Gotta say, that uniform didn't do her no favors. I'd rather have met her swinging on a pole. You know, ever since The Revue closed—"

"Her name is Watkins," Rita cut in, her tone sharp. "And she's got a dinky-ass badge, too. She could write you up for harassment before you finish your next sentence. "

Chester raised his hands in mock surrender. "All right, all right, Jonas, don't get your feathers ruffled."

Rita narrowed her eyes. "My feathers are fine, Chester. It's your tail I'm about to ruffle if you don't cooperate."

"Me?" Chester said, his eyebrows jumping. "How'm I uncooperative?"

Rita paused, taking a patient breath. She moistened her lips. "I'm here to talk about the angle grinder stolen from the mechanics' shop the other day."

Chester grunted. "I doubt it's stolen, probably just misplaced around here. But Donald is damn anal when it comes to his tools. He's only sayin' it's taken just 'cause it ain't in its usual spot."

"When did it go missing?" Rita asked.

"I don't know," Chester said, "and why the hell should I tell you anyway? This ain't your jurisdiction, you're on the other side, remember?" Then he looked around her shoulder as a customer came through the doorway. Dismissing Rita, he asked the young man, "How can I help you?"

The newcomer grabbed a six-pack of Pepsi and stepped up to the counter. "Pepsi," he said.

Blocking the man, Rita put her elbow on the counter and fixed her eye on Chester. "If you don't want to answer the questions here, Chester, I'll take you to *my* jurisdiction and we can talk it over at APEX."

The customer reached around Rita, holding out a twenty-dollar bill. "I got cash."

Chester snatched the bill, counted out change, then met Rita's glare again. "Go ahead then, get it over with, so you can stop interfering with my business."

"Have you noticed any rope missing as well?" Rita asked, as the young man exited with his six-pack.

Chester blinked. "Rope?" He shook his head. "Nope."

"Can I see your stock?" Rita asked.

Sighing, Chester came out from behind the counter. Rita followed him down an aisle, passing bottles of motor oil and windshield washer fluid, to where several varieties of tow ropes, nylon rope, and bungee cords hung on a pegboard. But nothing looked like the teal climber's rope she was looking for.

"Thanks, Chester," Rita said, forcing a smile. "And how about the security footage?"

"The SCSO already took it," Chester said, pushing past her.

Rita followed him to the counter. "Is Donald Horgan around?"

Chester busied himself, arranging keychains on a spinning rack, all of them sporting slogans like, "Get Lost in Wyoming," "Still Searching…but at least I'm in Wyoming," and, "Still haven't left Wyoming—It's that good!"

"Check the garage," he said without looking at Rita.

Without a word, Rita strode to the steel side-door of the convenience store. Low voices echoed and tools clanged. She pulled it open and poked her head through to the mechanics' shop. Two men stood conversing beside a Ford F-150 on a lift.

"Donald Horgan?"

Both men looked over, then the one closest approached, carrying a wrench in his thick-set hands. His dark blue coveralls were faded at the knees and elbows and bore faint stains of engine grime despite repeated washings.

"Can I help you?" he asked.

"I'm Rita Jonas, Head of APEX Security. You're Donald Horgan?"

The mechanic bobbed his head. "I go by Don. Are you here about my angle grinder?"

"Yes," Rita said. "It was found on APEX property."

Don crumpled his brow, grease trapped in the creases in his forehead. "Out at APEX? Well, I'll be damned." His face relaxed. "I knew I hadn't misplaced it, like Chester insisted."

"Any chance you were out there last night?"

"At APEX?" Don chuckled. "Not a chance. Spent the night at home with my wife. She made a real nice casserole."

"The angle grinder has been entered into evidence," Rita said.

Don's expression returned to its former state of consternation. "Evidence? Like in a crime?"

Rita nodded. "Yes."

The mechanic made a sound in his throat. "What kind of crime?"

"I can't answer that at the moment," Rita said. "But I'd appreciate seeing where it's stored."

"Of course."

Horgan waved her to the back of the shop, to his work-bench, a sturdy setup that held every tool in its place. A pegboard above displayed wrenches and screwdrivers hung in orderly rows, while below a row of cubby holes held various power tools.

He pointed to an empty space among the cubbies. "This is where I keep it. Sheriff Perry asked me to track down the serial number and I jotted it down on a card, but I haven't gotten around to calling it in yet." He gestured at the lift behind him. "Heavy snow's forecast and the Gusikowskis got to haul some feed up pasture." Don opened a small drawer to extract a business card. "Cattle are already struggling with frostbite conditions."

"I can send the number into the SCSO," Rita said as he passed her the card. She photographed the serial number, then passed him back the card. "Anything else suspicious?"

"Nope," Don said. "Nothing else missing. Nothing damaged."

"What do you think happened to the angle grinder?"

Don shrugged. "If someone came in here to steal it, surely one of us would have seen it on the security footage."

"Where are the security cameras in here?" Rita asked.

Don pointed to one that aimed towards the back garage. "Only the one. But it has a clear view of the shop, including my bench."

"And do you know if anyone watched the footage before the SCSO took it?"

Don nodded. "Sure, Chester had a look first, then called me in to have a look." He nodded towards the other mechanic. "Jerry works in Beaumont most days, but if we're running tight, he'll lend a hand. He was here yesterday when Chester was reviewing the tapes. We all had a look but didn't see no one in the shop."

"Thank you," Rita said.

Don wished her a good day, and Rita departed the mechanics' shop and returned to the Beemer.

Before she drove, she called Craig. When he didn't answer, she called APEX reception.

"Hi, Ginny, it's Rita. Is Deputy Dillard in today?"

"Yes, he is, Ms. Jonas." Ginny said.

"Can you tell me if he's up in the conference room?" Rita asked.

The receiver was muffled, then Ginny's voice returned. "He's outside."

"Oh," Rita said. "In the parking lot?"

"No," Ginny said, "outside reception."

"Outside the front doors?"

"Yes."

"It's cold," Rita said.

"Yes."

"Well, what's he doing there?" she asked.

"He's talking to someone."

"Who?"

"Umm…" Ginny's voice was thin, stretched taut as she craned her neck to peer through the glass doors. "I don't know her…but she's cute."

"I don't doubt it," Rita said.

"Do you want me to go get him for you?" Ginny asked.

"Don't worry about it," she said, "I'll catch him when I come in."

Ginny giggled. "That's funny, Ms. Jonas. You sound like a copper."

"I *am* a copper," Rita said.

Ginny coughed. "Right, Ms. Jonas."

Rita sighed. "If only it were so easy as arresting Craig's ass…"

Chapter Fifteen

RITA WALKED through the APEX parking lot, scanning for Craig. Seeing no sign of him, she headed inside.

She walked through the foyer to the conference room and peeked inside. Craig sat at the computer, watching footage. He looked up at her and waved.

Rita grunted and refrained asking him if Ginny had given him the heads up.

Then she went upstairs to her office and sat at her desktop computer. She pulled up a photo of the angle grinder found at the crime scene and compared the serial number to the one Donald had given her. It matched.

The Gas-N-Go wasn't exactly convenient to APEX, being at the other end of town. So was the body dismembered back in town? And if so, why transport the body (retrofit with the deer mount) across Still?

Rita picked up the telephone receiver and called the SCSO. Mary Lou answered.

"Hi Mary Lou, it's Rita."

"What can I do for you, Ms. Jonas?" Mary Lou asked.

Rita ignored her formal tone. "The angle grinder stolen from the Gas-N-Go is the same one we found at the APEX crime scene. I'm calling to request access to the security footage."

"I'll send it over with Deputy Watkins," Mary Lou said with curt professionalism before disconnecting.

Rita hung up and glanced at the time. Almost five. Cash would be preparing dinner. Rita's stomach growled at the thought. Instead, she'd have to wait for Candace.

She sighed again and pulled out her notebook. Reviewing, she found the contact details for Theodore's mom, Loreen, and dialed the number.

It rang through and an automated voice announced that the voicemail was full. Rita hung up, then waited a few minutes. Then she tried again. Still no answer, the voicemail still full.

She moved her hands to the keyboard and looked up Loreen Lake on Google. But aside from a mention in Teddy's obituary, Rita found nothing.

Next, she typed Lucas Lake into the search bar and discovered he was a teacher with the Tampa School Board. She noticed the pattern of email addresses for the district and composed one to Lucas introducing herself. After giving condolences, she asked to arrange a time to talk to him about his brother Theodore.

Then Rita hit send. A few seconds later, the email bounced back. Rita checked her spelling and formatting in the address. Then reversed Lucas's name and tried again. Again, the email bounced.

Rita then ran a search on the APEX database. But there was no Theodore Lake. The closest was Theron Lakehead, but he was stationed in the Arctic and looked nothing like Teddy.

Rita checked the time, almost 5:30. Where the hell was

Watkins? She stood and glanced out the window. The deputy stood at the entrance of the parking lot, chatting with Craig. Candace threw back her head, laughter spilling into the cold air like white clouds.

Rita pulled out her phone and dialed Craig. Watching from the window, she saw him glance at the screen and ignore the call. She hung up and called Mary Lou at the SCSO instead.

"What is it?" Mary Lou answered. "I'm just about to leave."

"Could you radio Watkins and tell her to quit flirting with Prince Charming in the parking lot and get her ass upstairs?"

A beat of silence followed. Then Mary Lou said, "I don't work for you anymore."

"Do it," Rita snapped, then hung up and shoved her phone back into her pocket. Arms crossed, she watched as Craig said something else, making Candace laugh again. This time, she placed a hand on his shoulder.

A moment later, Candace straightened, touching the radio on her shoulder strap. Her posture stiffened, then she spoke briefly to Craig before heading inside the building. He lingered, watching her go before finally getting into his car and driving away.

Rita debated going down to the foyer to meet Candace, but her bladder had other priorities. When she emerged from the bathroom, Candace stood waiting by the door, at the door waiting for her.

"Good evening," Rita said, slipping past her and crossing to her desk. "I was getting ready to leave for the day."

Cheeks flushed, Candace extended a brown cardboard pack. "Mary Lou sent this over."

Rita took the packet and tore it open. A USB stick fell out onto the desk.

"Thanks," she said, even though the last thing she wanted to do was to spend another minute watching footage.

Chapter Sixteen

"ANGLE GRINDER PICKED UP," Cash said beside her in bed, his voice flat and gaze locked on his laptop screen. He paused the footage to jot down a time stamp on his notepad, evening stubble roughening his jaw.

Propped up beside him, Rita kept eating, scooping up the last bite of pasta.

"Angle grinder returned," Cash said, recording another time stamp.

"Just like every other instance," Rita said, setting her empty bowl on the moving box beside the bed. She eyed the needlepoint bison on the wall. It stared back at her, its eye highlighted with gold threads.

"One of these times," Cash said, "someone ain't gonna put it back."

"That's right, Deputy," Rita said, burrowing into the pillows. "Tell me when it gets interesting." She yawned. "I think I'm too tired to brush my teeth."

Cash grunted, his attention fixed on the laptop. "At least we know it was in use on Thursday."

The soft glow of the floor lamp coaxed Rita's eyelids to close. "You definitely sound like a deputy now."

"Holy fuck."

Rita opened her eyes. "You spot the thief?"

Cash tapped the computer screen. "I found a problem with the footage."

Rita pushed up on her elbows. "What is it?"

Cash pointed to the date and time on the lower right of the viewfinder. "Watch."

He hit play, and Rita kept her eyes on the numbers. In a split second, the time jumped forward by an hour.

She blinked. "What the fuck?"

Cash rewound it, and they watched it again. "Sometimes the cameras at my shop would glitch," he said. "But I had an old system, and this one is digital."

Rita nodded. "Yeah. I've looked at a lot of footage in my day, and this stuff is clean."

"Maybe it's a software error."

"If that's the case, it's an awfully convenient one," Rita said. Then she kissed him. "Thanks. You're almost as good as Jason."

Cash laughed and kissed her back. "I hope you mean that about my detecting abilities and not kissing."

Rita laughed with him. "Might get you a bonus."

He grinned. "I like the sound of that."

"Don't get too excited," Rita said, "I'm exhausted." She heaved herself off the bed and collected their empty pasta bowls. "It'll get you a night off the dishes."

Cash was thanking her when his phone rang. He set aside the laptop and checked it. He cringed. "It's Alan Crawford."

"Our favorite family lawyer," Rita said drily.

Cash put the phone to his ear. "I'm gonna take it."

Rita gave him a nod and carried the dishes into the

kitchen. She set them on the counter and started filling the sink with water. She squeezed in a dollop of dish soap. How had Irene managed all these years without a dishwasher? As the sink filled, she glanced out the back window, but the night was too dark to see anything beyond the dim, yellowish reflection of her own face.

Behind her, heavy footsteps sounded on the kitchen floor. Cash walked in, bristling.

"What happened?" Rita asked without turning around.

"Alan said that if I have questions, I'm welcome to ask Thomas myself. Thomas won't answer through Alan or over the phone."

"Sounds like extortion," Rita said, setting the clean bowls in the drying rack. "Clearly, he wants leverage to get you to visit."

Cash grunted.

"You don't have to break your streak of no contact just for this investigation," she continued. "That money might not have anything to do with Thomas in the first place. And even if it does, there's no guarantee he actually knows anything useful."

Cash nodded, but the doubt in his eyes lingered.

"Unless," Rita said, pulling the drain in the sink, "you actually *want* to see your dad. In which case, this might be as good an opportunity as any."

Cash exhaled sharply, rubbing the back of his neck. "I don't know. Standing up at the podium at your dad's funeral...it got me thinking. I might be doing that for Thomas any day now."

"It's a fair point," Rita said, drying her hands on a dish towel.

Cash tensed his jaw. "The man was an asshole."

Rita gave him a crooked smile. "So was Otto."

"At least you knew your dad loved you," Cash said.

"He wanted to protect you. I was written off the second I didn't join the goddamn family business."

Rita sighed. "Look at our relationships with our parents, Cash. What if we screw up this kid? Are they gonna grow up to hate us, too?"

Cash frowned. "Probably."

They both laughed, the tension lifting for a brief moment. Then Cash said, "You didn't hate Otto."

Rita softened. "True."

His gaze locked onto hers. "There's nothing this kid could ever do that would make me turn away. I've known too many people in hard places to ever stand in judgment."

Rita nodded. "Same."

Her phone rang, interrupting the moment. She glanced at the screen: Jason.

"Hey, Jason," she said, answering the call. "What's up?"

"Sorry to bother you so late," he said, "but did you stop by the house today?"

"No," Rita said, "why?"

"When I got here, the back door was unlocked. And the laundry room window was open a few inches more than I'd left it. You know I always lock up."

Rita's stomach tensed. "Thanks for letting me know. Keep me posted if it happens again."

Jason hesitated before answering. "Sure. Sleep well, Rita."

She wished him a goodnight and hung up, then leaned into Cash's embrace.

Chapter Seventeen

RITA STEPPED INTO THE GAS-N-GO, the door jingling behind her. Behind the counter, Chester stood hunched over his phone, his usual cowboy hat sitting askew. He glanced up as she entered, his expression as unwelcoming as it had been the day before.

"You here on personal business?"

Rita frowned at him. "Hardly. I always pay at the pump."

"Well, y'ain't in uniform."

"I'm on my way to meet my mother," Rita said with an edge. She met his eyes. "And on my way, I'm conducting some official business."

Chester folded his arms. "You find the bastard who took Don's angle grinder?"

"No," Rita said, "there's a problem with your security footage."

Chester's eyebrows shot up. "File's corrupt?"

"It's possible," Rita said, "which is why I'd like to see the original, please."

Nostrils flaring, Chester shoved his phone into the back pocket of his jeans and trudged across the shop.

Rita followed him into the back office, where the air was thick with the malodors of stale coffee, old paper, and motor oil. Overstuffed shelves sagged under piles of paperwork and dusty car parts wedged between outdated printers and fax machines.

She sat at the worn desk, its surface marred with scratches and rings. Chester leaned against the wall next to her.

She reached for the computer mouse, once white, now stained brown from years of grime. The mouse pad wasn't much better, greasy and faded, the Gas-N-Go logo barely visible.

She clicked to open the security footage folder. Finding the file in question, she double-clicked and fast-forwarded to the time-stamp Cash had noted.

Once again, the footage jumped.

"Check it out," she said to Chester, pointing to the number in the lower right of the computer monitor.

Chester leaned closer. "Huh?"

"The time skips," she said. "The two frames knit together where no one is in view." She replayed the segment.

"What the fuck?" he said.

Rita turned to look at him over her shoulder. "What do you think caused that?"

He scratched his neck. "I didn't even know it *could* do that."

Rita watched him for another second. "Was the power interrupted at any time last night?"

Chester shrugged. "Don't remember any outage."

"Can I see the electrical panel, please?"

"It's 'round back." Chester pushed off from the wall and waved for Rita to follow.

She rose from the desk and followed him out of the cramped office, down a narrow corridor. They passed a staff bathroom and a storage closet before reaching the back door.

"For fuck's sake," he said, jabbing a finger at a few words scrawled in black marker on the wall: *Electrical Panel.* A few inches above the writing, an empty nail jutted out. "The key's missing."

Rita blinked. "Is this where the key is normally kept?"

Chester tapped the black letters. "Can you read?"

Ignoring the question, Rita asked: "Right *here*, just inside the back door?"

Chester rubbed at his neck again. "I know it ain't as convenient as before, having to come through the door for it. But at least it gets lost a whole lot less than when I kept it outside."

"Right," Rita said. "So who would have had access to the mechanics' shop overnight?"

Chester shrugged. "Anyone with a key, since you can go in through the side door."

"Is there a nail around here with a key?" Rita asked.

"No," Chester said, "that would be stupid."

"Now there's a thought," Rita said.

"I cut some extras and gave them to my key-holders."

Rita took out her notebook. "Who are the key-holders?"

Chester cleared his throat, thinking for a moment before counting on his fingers. "There's me, Don, Jerry, the two janitors, my assistant manager, Myrtle, though she only works tourist season and spends winters in Arizona, and all the gas jockeys."

Rita's hand moved fast to keep up. "How many gas jockeys are there?"

Chester thought some more. "Right now, I got five. But I had to let some lads go not too long ago, so there might be some spare keys floating around town. Oh, I gave one to Edith-Mae, too, 'cause I was tired of her picking the locks. Damn kid broke a window, too, once." He adjusted his hat. "I'm sure of it."

Rita closed her notebook. "At least a dozen keys out there."

Chester chewed on a thought for a moment. "Good thing I got the alarm system."

Rita nodded. "Who knows the code to disarm it?"

Chester blinked at her. "Well, all the same key-holders, of course."

Rita let out a breath. "Of course they do. Can you send me the contact details for all of these people?"

Chester leaned forward to scan Rita's notebook. "Sure, if you could send me that list you got there?"

"Probably not," Rita said. "Take a photo."

Chester pulled his phone from his back pocket and fumbled to snap a picture. Then Rita pushed ahead of him to open the back door and step outside.

"Let's go have a look at that electrical panel."

Outside, the fresh air was a welcome relief after the stale confines of Chester's office. He led Rita around the side of the building to the back, where a metal cage meant to protect the electrical panel hung crookedly, barely clinging to its last two hinges. The plaster wall around it was cracked and scuffed.

"Damn lock's gone," Chester muttered.

Rita scanned the area. "Padlock?"

"Yep," Chester said, kicking at a pile of debris near the back door. "Painted it orange so I'd stop losing it." He sifted through discarded gas cans and crumpled soda flats. "Should be easy to spot."

Rita studied the exposed panel. "No security camera back here?"

Chester shook his head. "Nope."

"So someone could've come through the back door, shut off the alarm, grabbed the key from the nail, unlocked the cage, cut the power, stolen the angle grinder, tampered with the footage, turned the power back on, locked up again, and walked out without ever being seen?"

Chester exhaled through his nose. "Guess so."

Rita gave him a tight smile. "I happen to hate guessing. Which is why I love recommending better security." She nodded her head towards the front of the station. "I'm gonna go talk to the jockeys."

Chester grunted. "Don't scare away any customers."

Rita walked around the side of the building and over to the two young men lounging against the pumps, caught up in conversation. One, wearing sunglasses despite the cloud cover, stood with his arms crossed over his chest. The other, with long hair tied back in a ponytail, stood with hands in his pockets. Both wore oversized puffer jackets embroidered with the Gas-N-Go logo, clearly designed for men twice their size.

As Rita neared, they looked over.

"Hey, Jesse," said the one in sunglasses, "I think it's time for breakfast."

"Oh, yeah?" Jesse, the one with long hair, replied. "Why's that?"

The guy in sunglasses chuckled. "'Cause I smell bacon."

Jesse grinned. "That ain't bacon, Rod, that's a—"

"Ain't the Sheriff anymore," Rita said, strolling up.

Rod spat on the asphalt. "No shit?"

"I work at APEX now."

"What, you a scientist now?"

"Head of L.E.O.," she said.

"*Meow,*" Jesse meowed.

Rita cut him a half-serious look. "Stands for Law Enforcement Operations."

Rod snorted. "Same difference. Once a cop, always a cop."

"I'm here about a missing angle grinder," Rita said. "Chester says the two of you hold a master key to the station. Is that correct?"

Their heads bobbed in unison. "Yeah."

"Can you show them to me, please?" Rita asked.

Jesse stalled. "Not unless you show us your badge first."

Rita sighed, then smiled with her teeth. "Of course." She pulled out her APEX badge. "Happy?"

The gas jockeys looked at each other.

"Um, I lost my key," Jesse said, lowering his voice. "Rod's been covering for me while I've been trying to find it."

"So you haven't told Chester?" Rita asked.

"No," Jesse said. "Don't want to get fired."

Rita looked at the one in sunglasses. "Rodney, is it?"

He nodded.

"You got your key?"

He nodded again, reached into his pocket, and pulled out a key attached to an orange boating float.

"You worried about dropping your key in the Platte?" Rita asked.

Rodney shifted his feet. "Maybe the reservoir."

Rita raised a brow. "The reservoir?"

Blushing, Rodney shrugged. "I like to hang out up there."

"Of course," Rita said. "It's a real scene Saturday night."

"Chester gives them to us like that," Jesse said, indicating the keychain.

Rodney nodded. "Says it makes 'em harder to lose."

Rita looked back at Jesse. "Except you lost yours?"

He nodded. "Yep."

"And yours is on a flotation keyring, too?" Rita asked.

"Yep."

"And you both have the security code for the alarm system, yes?"

Laughing, they both nodded.

Rita glanced between them. "What's so funny?"

"Guess what the code is."

Rita smiled. "I don't guess."

"Come on, Sheriff," Jesse said, "take a stab."

Rita cringed at the metaphor. "Not the sheriff anymore."

"What, they don't got no sense of humor over at APEX?" Rodney asked. "Come on, take a guess."

Rita gave them a genuine smile. "Okay," she said. "One, two, three, four."

"Close," Jesse said. "One, one, one, one."

"Actually," Rodney said, "it's one, one, one, one, one."

"When Don noticed the angle grinder was missing," Jesse said, "he told Chester to set a new code. But damn fool didn't do it."

"Why not?" Rita asked.

"Didn't wanna memorize it, is all," Jesse said.

Rodney chuckled again. "He's a lazy fucker."

"Well, I'm encouraged that you two aren't lazy," Rita said. "So I'll let you get back to your duties while I go do mine." She scraped her boot along the pavement. "Looks like there're some cigarette butts to sweep up to do around here." she said. "Wouldn't want to set a bad example for the customers."

Then she thanked them for their assistance and walked away. As Rita crossed the lot toward her car, her phone buzzed with a new message. She checked her notifications and saw a text from Jason asking to meet her at APEX.

Rita texted back, *Ten-four.*

Chapter Eighteen

As Rita drove past the guards' hut and into the APEX parking lot, her eyes landed on the SCSO vehicle parked near the entrance. She pulled into a spot and got out of her car, making her way over to Jason, who was sitting in the driver's seat, dressed in civilian clothes.

He rolled down the window while the passenger-side door swung open. A young man stepped out, puffy sacks under his eyes and a two-day beard. He walked around the side of the truck, a backpack slung over his shoulder and his footsteps echoing in the lot.

The man's face looked familiar. She took a step towards Jason, meeting his eye. "What's up, Sheriff Perry?"

Jason glanced at the young man and pointed. "This is Lucas Lake."

Rita blinked. "Teddy Lake's brother?"

The man ducked his head. "After the cops came and told me what happened to him, I flew to Casper. Then caught the bus to Still."

Jason hooked his arm on the ledge of the open window.

"He showed up at the SCSO this morning. Candace gave me a call."

Lucas's shoulders shook with a self-conscious laugh. "Fell asleep in the cells. That Elvis fangirl gave me a mug of warm milk and it knocked me out."

"You wouldn't be the first hitchhiker to catch a nap," Rita said. "And Mary Lou's gonna love being called a fangirl."

"I offered Lucas a room at my place while he's here in town," Jason said. "If you don't mind dropping him off after you talk?"

Rita nodded, biting her lip while she adjusted to Jason calling Otto's place his.

Lucas ducked his head. "Nice to meet you, Sir— Ma'am—"

"Rita Jonas, Head of Law Enforcement Operations at APEX," Rita said. "It's a mouthful. You can call me Jonas. The department goes by L.E.O."

Lucas nodded. "Uh, okay. That's kind of cute, Leo."

"Maybe," Rita said. "It's a rebranding thing by the new boss. And she's anything but cute."

"Oh," Lucas said, "okay."

"Come on," she said, nodding towards the glass exterior of APEX. "We'll go up to my office and chat."

She took a step, then stopped, glancing back at Jason. She drew up to his open window.

"Hey, I got a question about the Gas-N-Go."

Jason leaned forward, resting his right forearm on the steering wheel. "Yeah?"

"When you were taking Chester's theft complaint, what did you make of the electrical panel being vandalized?"

"Didn't know it was," Jason said. "Deputy Watkins did the site check, and she didn't mention it. I'll get Mary Lou to send you the time Watkins was out there."

"Thanks," Rita said. "The key and the padlock to the cage on the electrical box are missing, too."

"I'll ask her about it," Jason said. "It's possible she missed something."

"The padlock is orange," Rita said. "Makes it harder to miss, Chester said." She dropped her voice. "Got something else to tell you."

Jason leaned closer. "Yeah?"

"Chester's security footage has missing tape. Time-stamp skips ahead more than an hour."

"I'll look into it." Jason said, straightening in his seat.

Rita saluted him and stepped back as he started the ignition. "Thanks for dropping off Lucas."

While Jason pulled away, Rita walked back to Lucas, waiting on the pathway.

"Let's go," she said.

She led Lucas through the glass front doors of APEX and across the cavernous space. Their footsteps echoed against the polished floors.

"Your brother shortened his birth name to Teddy," Rita said as swiped her access card to call the elevator. "Do you go by Luke?"

Lucas snorted. "Never." He gave her a lopsided grin. "Luke Lake?"

Rita laughed as the elevator chimed. The doors slid open and they stepped inside. "Oh, geez, you're right."

"Well, I do appreciate you didn't think of it right away," Lucas said. "'Cause every kid at school did."

"I don't doubt you got teased. Kids called me Jone-Ass."

Lucas gave an empathic wince as the doors slid open to the upper floor. "Kids at my school used to say, 'Lucky Luke Lake licks lost locks.'"

Rita frowned. "What does that even mean?"

Lucas shrugged. "No clue. But they thought it was hilarious."

"Do all kids do stupid shit?" Rita said as she strode into her office. She brushed a hand over her belly before gesturing for Lucas to take a seat. "Have a seat."

Lucas set his overnight bag on the floor and took a seat on the faux-leather sofa. "Thanks."

Rita crossed to the mini fridge and opened the door. "Can I offer you bottled water, orange juice, or…" She paused to pick up a small pink carton and read its label. "Some kind of yogurt drink with probiotics, prebiotics, and açai berries." Rita looked in the fridge again. "Oh, and one can of Coke rolling around in the back."

"I'll take a water, thanks, and that Coke, too, if you don't mind?"

"No problem," Rita said, grabbing two bottles of water and the Coke.

She passed him the can and a bottled water, then cracked her own bottle of water. "Have you been to Still before?"

"Haven't left Florida since we moved there," Lucas said, cracking the can of soda.

Rita sat at her desk. "When was that?"

"I think I was five," he said, taking a sip. "So that would have made Teddy somewhere around seven, and our sister about three."

"Did your family stay in touch with anyone here?"

He shook his head. "Which is why I'm eager to find out what he was doing here."

"I was hoping you could tell me." She opened the desk drawer and took out her voice recorder. "I'm going to record out conversation."

"Uh—why?" Lucas asked.

"It's standard procedure to ensure we have an accurate

record of what's discussed. You're a valuable witness in the investigation."

"There's an investigation?" Lucas asked. "About his death?"

"Yes," Rita said. "Tampa PD didn't tell you?"

Lucas shook his head. "They said he died suddenly. Unexpectedly." His voice wobbled. "Well, no shit, he was fine when he left."

"Please confirm your name and consent to being recorded?" Rita said, extending the device.

Lucas obliged, then lifted his gaze to meet Rita's. "The cops never told me how he died." His fingers tightening around the Coke can. "Could you?"

Chapter Nineteen

Staring at Rita, Lucas put down his empty Coke can. "His head is missing?" he said at last. "Why?"

"I don't know," Rita said. "One guess would be to have delayed identification. But I've never been one to make guesses."

Lucas moistened his lips. "Is that how he died, beheading?"

Rita's shoulders relaxed. "No. The medical examiner confirms that Teddy was deceased prior to decapitation."

Lucas chugged some Coke. "That's a good thing, right?"

Rita chewed on her lip. "I'd say."

Lucas' hand shook as he took another swallow. "How...*did* he die?"

"We can't know that exactly until we locate the head," Rita said.

Lucas gave a bewildered nod. "Is it possible he died of natural causes?"

Rita hesitated. The last thing she wanted was to crush whatever hope he was clinging to, but wishful thinking wasn't evidence. "There's no indication of heart failure," she said, keeping her tone even. "We're still waiting on the toxicology report."

Lucas was silent for a moment. Then: "Alcohol."

"Yes?" Rita prompted.

"Teddy drank a lot," Lucas said. "Too much. I always worried he'd get into an accident or land himself in trouble." He let out a slow breath. "And now my worst nightmare's come true."

"That was a heavy concern to carry," Rita said.

Teddy nodded. "I'm sure you'll find alcohol in his bloodstream."

"Yes," Rita said. "Plus the coroner found signs of cirrhosis."

"Shit, that's how our dad was gonna go. Cirrhosis and early-stage dementia. It was bleak for him." He drank some cola. "But in the end, it was a heart attack that took him." Lucas' voice stretched thin. "It was a blessing, really. Saved him a lot of suffering."

"I'm sorry you've recently lost your father, too," Rita said.

Lucas dropped his head, studying the industrial carpet. "A cop's life was hard on him. Plus, Dad never got over losing Brandi—that's our little sister." His hands screwed around the Coke can. "When she died, they both started drinking heavily. Dad was always worse than Mom because he never seemed to be able to bring himself to cry. Mom's just going the scenic route, falling asleep by seven every night, slowly pickling herself, year in and year out."

"That's a lot of loss for one family," Rita said.

Lucas' thumbs dented the can. "It was hard to live up to a ghost. Everything out of their mouths was 'Brandi would have liked this' and 'Brandi would have liked that.' 'Brandi would be getting married,' 'Brandi would have named her kids after them.' Jesus Christ, she died at four years old. Who the hell knows what she would have liked or didn't like?"

"How did she die?" Rita asked.

"Brain tumor," Lucas said, his voice hollow. "All these years later, I still know her fucking diagnosis, prognosis, treatment, and palliation better than I know my own damn dental schedule."

"Do you drink, Lucas?"

Lucas shook his head, setting aside the crumpled can. "Maybe I should take it up."

"Did your brother know anyone here?" Rita asked.

"I don't think so," Lucas said. "At least not that I know of. Never heard him say so."

"Did Teddy think about moving away from Florida? Considering your family spent time living in Casper, did he want to come back to see this part of this country?"

"Doubt it," Lucas said, his voice becoming steadier. "My brother and me didn't remember much except the snow. And Dad always said Still was in the sticks and he'd never been so happy as when he'd left. So no, I wouldn't have thought Teddy had plans to come back."

"Why did your family move away from Casper?" Rita asked.

"Because Dad was a cop," Lucas said. "Moved around a bit in his training."

Rita studied him for a moment. "Are you happy in Florida?"

Lucas laughed, uneasy. "It shows, doesn't it, ma'am?"

Rita sat forward. "I beg your pardon?"

"It shows that me and Teddy are about as different as they come, even though we're brothers."

"How so?" Rita asked.

Lucas grinned. "He was a true Floridian, just like Dad."

Rita raised a brow. "And what exactly is a true Floridian?"

He flushed slightly. "Beaches, boobs, and beer."

"Hm," Rita said, considering. "Guess that makes me a true Wyomingite. I like big sky, boots, and beef dip." She shifted her position, soles squeaking against the floor. "Though maybe not these boots."

Rita's phone vibrated in her pocket. "One moment." She paused the recorder and checked her phone.

It was Carol: *Are we still meeting?*

Rita bit back a curse, remembering she'd missed their meetup. "Pardon me, Lucas," she said, getting up from her desk, "I need to attend to a family matter. I won't be five minutes."

Lucas bobbed his head. While he ripped open the package of a protein bar, Rita stepped out of the office.

Standing on the other side of the glass door, she typed a response to Carol: *Busy at work.*

Her phone pinged in response: *I didn't think APEX was open on Saturdays.*

Rita sighed. *OT. Need to reschedule.*

Then she gazed across the concourse to the view of mountains beyond, awaiting Carol's response.

Her phone pinged. *I don't see how that can work, I'm leaving town tomorrow morning.*

Rita messaged back: *Meet me at Bighorn Bakery at 17:00.*

Really? Shop talk with your mother?

Rita clenched her teeth. *It's a habit.*

Carol replied: *I guess 5pm will work.*

The thread went silent. Rita stared at the darkened screen for a moment, then turned back to the office. Lucas was polishing off the last bite of his protein bar.

"Thanks for your patience," Rita said, sitting at her desk. She started the recorder again. "How do you think Teddy got here?" she asked. "He doesn't have a driver's license."

Lucas snorted. "Just 'cuz he ain't licensed doesn't mean he can't drive. Not that I'm saying he drives well, mind you. But if he couldn't get a buddy to lend him a car, he'd probably hitchhike."

"And considering you don't think he had any contacts here, can you think of any reason why he would want to come here?"

Lucas shook his head while he chewed. "Nope."

"Did he say or do anything unusual in the past few weeks?"

Lucas licked his fingers clean, thinking. "Not the past few weeks, but…"

"Anything is helpful," Rita said.

He took a swallow of water, clearing his mouth. "It's stupid, but he was spending more time with Dad."

"Which is odd why?" Rita asked.

"'Cuz Teddy hated Dad."

"Why was that?"

Lucas wiped his mouth with the back of his hand. "He got in trouble with the police once. Assault."

Rita nodded.

"And Dad refused to bail him out. He told him he had to learn the lesson, that he deserved the penalty. If we fucked up, it was our problem."

"Was Teddy often violent?"

Lucas was quick to shake his head. "No, he just gets rowdy when he drinks. But as many swings as he takes, he also hands out hugs."

"Did Teddy have any interest in the occult?"

Lucas coughed, thrown off by the question. "Not that I know of. Like I said, he liked bikinis and Budweiser."

"And how about the initial 'M'?" Rita asked. "Does the letter have any special meaning to him?"

"M?" Lucas frowned, taking a moment to think. "Not really. He's a die-hard Bulls fan, never gonna support Miami. He worked at Maloney's Irrigation, but that was only one summer. And he hasn't talked to his ex, Melissa, in ages."

"Do you know how things ended between them?" Rita asked.

"I don't think there were ever any fireworks," Lucas said. "They didn't date long and the relationship sort of fizzled out. She's married now, with some kids, I think. Far as I know, I don't think they've ever been in touch again."

"What do you do, Lucas?" Rita asked.

Lucas sat straighter. "I'm a teacher, junior high science."

"At which school?"

His smile faded. "I left my last job to help Mom take care of Dad. Real grunt work, you know, cleaning his pissed bedsheets and helping him scrub up in the shower." His voice turned brittle. "Not sitting there with a beer in hand and my feet up, listening to Dad's cop stories, for the hundredth time, the way Teddy got to."

Rita felt a pang. Otto hadn't been coherent enough to tell stories in the end. And what she'd give now to ask him about his past.

"Your father spent more time talking to Teddy?" she asked.

Lucas nodded, his sadness returning. "I try to tell myself Dad was confused. That he thought I was Teddy sometimes, the way he sometimes thought I was the postman or neighbor." He shrugged. "But I'm not stupid."

"Were you close to Teddy?" Rita asked.

Lucas met her eye. "What's close?" He rolled his shoulders. "We weren't much alike. Lived different lives. And let's be real, our circumstances were never fair. But when you go through the same shit, it makes you family, whether you like it or not."

Thinking about the years she and Otto had spent adjusting to Carol's departure, Rita nodded. "I know," she said.

And she did.

Chapter Twenty

"THANKS FOR THE LIFT," Lucas said as Rita pulled into the packed gravel driveway at Otto's house.

"Glad to do it," Rita said. "How long do you plan to stay in town?"

Lucas tugged on his chin. "Don't know. How long do these things usually take?"

Rita dropped her hands from the steering wheel. "Unfortunately, there's no playbook. But if you do choose to leave, let me know so I can contact you with any future updates."

Lucas nodded. "Sure."

"Did Teddy have a cell phone?" Rita asked.

Lucas nodded again. "Of course," and he gave her a number with a Florida area code. Rita jotted it down in her notebook, then read it back to him before Lucas got out of the vehicle. He climbed the three treads to the door and rang the bell. Hands clasped behind his back, his backpack pulling at his shoulders, he looked like a Boy Scout waiting for inspection.

A moment later, Jason opened the door, waved him in, and shut it behind them.

Rita put the crossover into reverse but stopped when her phone rang. It was Tilda.

"I got the brand name of the rope," the forensics examiner said. "It's Craggy Peak. I talked to the manufacturer, only local distributor is Casper Mountain Sport."

Rita thanked her and hung up, then reversed out of the driveway. She headed for the freeway, passing the Gas-N-Go en route to Casper.

Arriving at The Casper Chronicle, Rita pulled into a narrow parking lot beside the newspaper's squat brick building. The building was topped with a faded blue awning, the newspaper's name stenciled in gold letters across the front window.

Inside, the air was thick with the scent of newsprint and coffee. A receptionist with a clipped hairstyle and chunky sweater glanced up as Rita walked in. Her fingers ceased tapping, the low hum of a copier filling the silence.

Rita smiled. "I'd like to—"

A side door banged open and Blaze Wright strode up to her. He grinned, his eyes as bright as his pastel polo shirt tucked into his waistband, snug around a middle that had started to soften with age. "How can I help you, Ms. Jonas?"

"Blaze," Rita said. He was one of the few locals who remembered she no longer used the title "sheriff." "So I'm not the only one working on a Saturday?"

"News never sleeps." Blaze flashed another grin, his veneers catching the light. "You looking to place an information request?"

Rita pulled out two pieces of paper with photos of Theodore Lucas. "I got a mugshot and a driver's license."

Blaze put on a pair of reading glasses and looked closer at the printouts.

"Two different haircuts," she said. "Can you make sure they're both in the system?"

Blaze nodded, his own hair combed with a little too much gel. "Come on back."

She followed him through the side door through which he'd appeared. Entering a large newsroom, they passed several cubicles quietly buzzing with conversations.

Blaze led her into a corner office. The space could use a fresh coat of paint, but the walls were mostly overshadowed by framed front-page stories showcasing Blaze's past work. Several local and state-level awards were neatly arranged on a shelf, accompanied by a few quirky items, an antique camera, an old typewriter, and fan memorabilia for bands like Wham! and Duran Duran.

Blaze sat at his desk while Rita took the chair opposite. He popped open his laptop and positioned his fingers on the keys. "Give me the descriptions."

Rita supplied the vitals from the documents, then added case-specific information: "His body was located in Still last Thursday."

Blaze glanced at her as he typed. "Whereabouts in Still?"

"That's not relevant to the ad," Rita said.

"Residents will want to know," Blaze said.

Rita ignored him. "We're looking for witnesses who may have seen him. Or offered him a ride. They can contact APEX for more information."

"Got it," Blaze said, typing quickly and nodding. "Am I putting down your direct line at APEX?"

"Yeah," she said, then supplied her number. "And I got a hot line." She read out Craig's number from her phone contacts, then told Blaze to add Mary Lou's line at the SCSO.

"Almost done," Blaze said, his fingers moving swiftly. Then he spun around his laptop to face her. "What do you think?"

Rita leaned forward to read. She checked it over. The description was clear, and the contact information correct. She sat back. "Yep, that's it."

Blaze took off his eyeglasses and closed his laptop with a click. "It'll go in the next edition."

"Thanks," she said, getting up and heading toward the door. "I appreciate it."

Before driving out of the lot, she called Craig. No answer.

She blew out a breath and texted him: *If you don't answer my next call, consider yourself fired.*

Rita's phone lit up as Craig called her.

Skipping the salutations, Rita said, "I'm running an ad with your number as the witness line for Teddy Lucas's death."

"You're using my cell as a hotline?"

"Yeah. Anyone who calls, get their name and contact info. Record whatever details they have and tell them I'll follow up."

"So I'm basically an answering service?" Craig asked. "Why don't I get to interrogate them?"

Rita leaned against the headrest. "Can you handle it, or should I put Middleton on it?"

"I can do it," Craig said quickly. Then, after a beat, "Does this mean I don't have to watch any more footage?"

"For now, yes," Rita replied. "But I've got something else for you. I need you to ping Teddy's cell."

She didn't wait for a response before hanging up. Checking the time, she turned the ignition and headed toward Casper Sport, a massive box of a building on the town's rugged outskirts.

The beige and forest-green façade might have blended into the surrounding hills if not for the snow-plowed piles at the ends of each row of the lot. The cruel wind cut across the asphalt, and Rita hurried inside through the sliding glass doors.

The air smelled of rubber boot soles and metallic camping gear, laced with the earthy scent of leather hunting vests. Faint country music drifted over the speakers.

She scanned the overhead placards, spotting *Mountaineering* between *Waterproof Outerwear* and *Camping Equipment*. Her boots squeaked on the polished concrete as she walked down the aisle, passing an assortment of carabiners and quickdraws, their gleaming finishes flashing under the fluorescents like trout in a stream.

At the end of the aisle, climbing ropes hung neatly arranged like prairie rattlesnakes in vivid coils of red, orange, and teal.

The teal rope appeared to be a match to the length at the crime scene. Rita snapped a series of photos of the packaging with its specs.

A store clerk padded over, his shoulder-length hair tucked beneath a cap and yellow neoprene shoes on his feet.

"Hey," Rita said, pointing down. "I've been thinking about getting those."

The clerk glanced down at his feet. "Barefoot shoes? They're sick." He flashed a smile. "Feels like walking barefoot, but without stepping on rocks or freezing your toes off." He lifted a foot, flexing it. "Takes some getting used to if you wear regular shoes, though. First week, my calves were on fire." He looked at Rita's boots. "Are those steel-toed?"

"Not steel, reinforced rubber." She bent to press a thumb into the toe, then straightened abruptly, reminded of her full bladder. "Though I wear steel toes for search and rescue."

"Ah," the clerk said with a knowing nod. He wiggled his yellow-clad toes. "These are way comfier."

"Part of the uniform?"

"Nah, got 'em with my employee discount. They're in the next aisle."

Rita eyed them. "On a concrete floor, do you find they provide ample support?"

He glanced at his feet again. "Eh. Some days I swap 'em for camping slippers. You ever tried those? Like quilted puffer jackets for your feet. Super sick. I can show you a pair if you like."

"I'm actually here about this climbing rope." Rita lifted one of the coils from the wall. "I need to find out who bought this."

The clerk lifted his brows. "Oh, yeah?"

Rita looked him in the eye. "Can you help me with that?"

He shuffled his yellow-clad feet. "Not sure I know how to do that."

"Can you run the SKU in your system?"

He tilted his head. "Mmm…I mostly help people find stuff. Computers aren't really my vibe."

"Can I talk to the manager?"

The clerk bobbed his head. "Yeah, good call. Lynette's the one to ask."

"Great. Where can I find her?"

"She's off today."

Rita sighed. "I'll take her contact info."

The clerk adjusted the rope in his arms, pulled out his phone, and held up the screen. Rita entered Lynette's number into her contacts.

"Thanks," she said, pocketing her phone. Then asked: "So, the slippers. Do I find them in Camping Equipment or Weatherproof Outerwear?"

Chapter Twenty-One

From behind the black leather upholstered steering wheel of the BMW, Rita hit send on an email to Lynette McGuire, the manager of Casper Sport. Then she got out and hit the fob to lock the vehicle as she walked across the street and up the block.

Outside the bank, Stu and Vic were hanging out.

Rita paused. "Hi guys," she said. "Loitering as usual?"

"What do you care?" Stu said, chortling. "Y'ain't no cop no more."

"Anymore," Rita said.

"Huh?" Stu said.

Vic elbowed his friend. "Your grammar, man. It's shit."

Rita raised a brow. "Since when have you been interested in grammar, Vic?"

He stood straighter. "I been going to community college."

She gave an approving nod. "Good to hear. That'll serve you well."

Frowning, Stu and folded his arms. "What's it to you?"

"Yeah," Vic said, copying Stu's posture. "'*Serve you well*'—that sounds like some corporate bullshit."

Stu lifted his chin. "Sounds like pro-police bullshit to me."

Rita rolled her eyes. "Except I'm not a cop anymore, remember?"

Stu shook his head with dismay. "APEX won you over, huh?"

"All nice and cushy in your corner office," Vic said. "Must be real nice working conditions."

Stu spat on the sidewalk. "Boring as fuck."

Vic elbowed Stu again. "That's why she got to come downtown and hassle the likes of us."

Rita sighed. "I didn't move to APEX for the working conditions. I did it for triple the pay."

Vic sniggered. "Yeah, right."

Rita gave him a dirty look. "I worked hard negotiating that salary." Although she didn't mention the negotiations had been made over five-star hors d'oeuvres at the Faculty Club.

Vic stuck out his chin. "Well, why *are* you working on a Saturday?"

"Yeah," Stu said. "Salary can't be that good if you're working overtime."

"I'm not working overtime to pay my bills, you dimwits," she said. "It's a homicide investigation. Cops don't sit on warm bodies or hot leads."

They hung their heads. "Suppose so."

Rita scowled at them. "Of course, suppose so. If Stu was murdered, Vic, you'd want me to work around the clock to find out who was responsible."

Vic shifted on his feet. "Well, I think the circumstances would depend."

This time Stu elbowed Vic. "Hey!"

"Oh, good grief," Rita said. "You two are giving me a backache."

"Backache?" Vic said. "We're actually giving you a *headache*."

Stu sniggered. "Baby-brain's making her stupid."

Rita cut him a look. "I didn't come downtown to harass you."

"It's not a backache," Vic said, tilting his head with conviction. "It's a pelvis ache."

Rita stopped rubbing her hip. "Are you studying obstetrics?"

Vic stood another inch taller. "It's what my baby-mama said."

Rita blinked. "You have a baby-mama?"

Solemn, Vic nodded. "I got two of 'em."

"How did I not know this?" Rita asked.

Vic perked up. "You wanna hear about my kids?"

Rita waved a hand. "Another time. Thinking about my own is about all I can handle these days." She nodded at the two of them. "Good luck in your courses, Vic. Good-bye, Stu."

Stu dipped his head. "Bye, Sheriff. I mean, Mrs. Jonas."

"Call me Jonas," Rita said. "I'm not a Mrs."

They ducked their heads in agreement but said nothing more as she walked up the block to the Bighorn Bean. Its wrought-iron sign creaked over the door as Rita stepped in, out of the wind. She rubbed her hands together in the welcome warmth, her mouth watering at the aroma of freshly roasted coffee. Dr. Roseberg's voice replayed in her mind, recommending steamed milk.

Carol sat by the window, a half-eaten pastry on her plate and a coffee mug in front of her. Judging by the tightness in her expression, she was holding onto the last threads of her patience.

Rita gave her a wave as she strode up to the counter.

"Peppermint, chamomile, or lemon?" Skyler said.

Rita grimaced. "I'm not in the mood for herbal tea."

Skyler glanced at her watch. "It's after five. And you and I have an agreement."

Rita grunted. "I'm pretty sure my agreement's with Dr. Roseberg. But fine. Surprise me."

Skyler grinned. "I won't disappoint you. And good job kicking your coffee habit."

"Thanks," Rita said, grim. "I need something to eat, too, please, if you got any baked goods left at this time of day."

Skyler winked. "I can always scare up a snack. I'll bring your order to the table."

Rita hesitated, then paid and thanked Skyler, and joined Carol.

"Carol," she greeted as she sat down.

"Rita," Carol responded evenly. "How's the baby?"

Rita exhaled through her nose. "I find it interesting how people have stopped asking how I am."

Carol's eyebrows lifted. "I beg your pardon?"

"Everyone asks about the baby," Rita said. "Even Stu and Vic."

"Well, I don't know Stu and Vic," Carol said, "but I think you're very fortunate to have so many thoughtful friends. I can't say I ever did. Folks didn't throw baby showers for their girlfriends like they do nowadays."

Skyler arrived with a teapot and mug, plus a new sleeve of saltines.

"Sorry, no baked goods," she said. "But the tea's real nice."

Carol eyed the crackers. "Still morning sick?"

Rita tore open the packet and munched through three at once. "No."

She poured the tea, then lifted the mug to inhale the steam. "Lemon," she said to no one in particular.

"It's lemon-lavender!" Skyler called over from the counter.

Rita sipped. Then gave the barista a thumbs up.

Carol sniffed. "I didn't think you were one to drink tea."

"Doctor's orders," Rita said. The crushed crackers had turned to paste between her molars, and she worked her tongue to pry the sticky wad loose. "I've cut back on coffee."

Carol smirked. "I find that hard to believe."

"Sometimes I indulge in black tea. It has a lot less caffeine than coffee."

Carol fluttered her eyelids. "Well, I certainly wouldn't know." Then she indicated the corner of her mouth, while fixing her eye on Rita's. "You have some crumbs…"

"Thanks," Rita said, brushing them away before sampling the peanut-butter bar. "Mostly I've been enjoying London Fogs. Have you tried Bergamont? This girl, Haleigh, got me into tea. She tried to sell me her prenatal vitamins."

"Those are very important," Carol said.

"Yeah, but when I researched the brand, I found out it was an MLM."

"An LMN?" Carol asked. "What's that?"

"A multi-level marketing company," Rita said. "Basically, a pyramid scheme."

Carol continued to gape at her. "Pyramid?"

"Like all those home-selling parties you hosted when I was a kid?" Rita gave her a good-natured smile. "You've bought enough storage containers and scented candles to help lay the sturdy base of a pyramid."

Carol crinkled her nose. "I'd prefer you don't make sexual slurs at my expense."

"Never mind," Rita said, pulling out her phone. She flipped to the photograph of the mysterious woman standing with Otto. "Do you know who this is?"

Carol took Rita's phone and peered at the image, holding the screen close to her face. "Well, it's Otto, of course." Then she passed it back to Rita.

Rita took a patient breath. "I'm asking about the woman."

Carol handed back the phone. "I wouldn't know."

"When did Otto go to California?" Rita asked.

Carol's expression remained neutral, but her eyes flicked, ever so briefly, to the side. "As far as I know, he didn't."

Rita followed the glance. Carol's phone sat on the window ledge, recording. She snatched it up and hit stop. Carol lunged for the device, but Rita pulled back.

"You've got to be fucking kidding me," she said. "What the hell do you think you're doing?"

Carol squared her shoulders. "Ever since that argument at the campground, my followers have been very invested in our relationship. It's important for them to see our repair and resolution. Though I'm gonna have to edit out that stuff about those LMNO triangles."

Rita stared at her. "You're serious?"

"You're angry?" Carol countered.

Rita's jaw tightened. "Isn't it obvious?" She stood, scooping up her sleeve of crackers. "This is a complete violation of my privacy."

"You always were a brat," Carol said, her voice hardening. "Running off when things don't go your way."

Rita turned. "Well, at least I learned from the best."

Carol's fists clenched. "I never should have come back."

"Nope," Rita said.

Then she strode out of the cafe, breezing past the community news bulletin board in the foyer. Her eye caught on a familiar pattern: A pentagram with an M. The very same carved into Teddy Lake.

She crossed to the bulletin board and tore down the poster advertising an upcoming Moon Meetup. Listed below was a telephone number.

Rita stepped outside and dialed the number. It immediately clicked over to voicemail. Although she couldn't place it, Rita recognized the female voice, speaking in soft tones: "Please leave your name and number and we will contact you with details for the next Moon Meetup."

Rita disconnected, considering the implications. Then she went back inside.

Carol looked relieved, but Rita ignored her and walked over to Skyler. She showed her the flyer.

"Do you know who posted this?" she asked.

Skyler nodded. "It's Carly's group."

"Carly's group? Is she home?" Rita asked, gesturing to the apartment upstairs.

Skyler shook her head. "No, she's probably at work."

"Where's that?"

"In the strip mall," Skyler said. "Where the old Cactus Creek Cosmetics was."

"Thanks," Rita said, walking past Carol again and heading outside. The wind gave her cheek a cold slap, and she dove into the crossover, grateful for its warmth.

Arriving at the strip mall, she parked in front of Kimmy's place, formerly called Cactus Creek Cosmetics. A new sign read: Carly's Crystals. Below, red letters on a white banner declared the shop *Now Open!*

Rita tried the door handle, but it was already locked. A sign in the window listed the hours, stating that the store closed at 4:30 p.m. on Saturdays and would reopen at eleven on Sunday.

She returned to her vehicle and dialed Carly. The call rang through, but Carly's voicemail was full.

With a sigh, Rita shoved the phone back into her pocket and leaned against the driver's seat. When had everything changed? Carol had painted her van. Kimmy was gone. Carly was selling crystals. And Vic was taking classes at the community college.

She'd been so caught up at APEX, she barely recognized Still.

Chapter Twenty-Two

RITA FLUSHED the toilet for what felt like the twentieth time that day. She padded out of the downstairs half-bath and into the living room, where Cash appeared to be asleep in the bed.

Until he opened one eye.

"Do you have to wear those?" he asked.

Rita glanced down at his T-shirt and blue boxer shorts she was wearing. "Hope you don't mind, but my pajamas are getting tight."

"I meant those zeppelins on your feet," he said, propping himself up on an elbow.

She sat on the edge of the bed. "I love my new camping slippers." She lifted a foot. "They're very plush." Then she kicked them off and nestled under the duvet beside him. "Like puffer jackets for your feet."

Cash gave her a sidelong look. "Are you here to stay now?"

"Until the next time I have to pee. Which is already more times than I can handle. I can't imagine what it'll be like in my eighth month."

"Are you going to put the slippers on every time?"

"I don't know. Maybe. Why?"

"They're kind of loud when you walk."

"Loud?" Rita scoffed. "I'll admit they're a little whispery. But that's because they're quilted. Like a puffer jacket."

Cash grunted. "You already said. But I wouldn't call them whispery. More like squeaky. I don't want to dream about mice." He shuddered. "Or rats."

"They're squeaky?" Rita echoed. "No, my boots are squeaky. My slippers are…swishy."

Cash exhaled. "Maybe I should start sleeping with earplugs. The constant toilet flushing is already tough, and once the baby comes, it might be smart to be used to them already."

Rita blinked at him. "Are you serious?"

"About sleep?" Cash said. "Always."

"I mean about the earplugs."

He hesitated. "Y-yeah?"

Rita frowned. "You realize we'll be doing the opposite, right?"

"The opposite? What's the opposite of earplugs? An ear horn?"

"A baby monitor."

Cash groaned and rubbed his face. "Right. Well, I'll start sleeping with a pillow on my head." Then he pulled Rita's pillow onto his head.

She punched the pillow. "Fine. As long as you know you're on the night shift."

He popped out his head, sticking out his tongue.

Rita reclaimed her pillow, hitting him with it before returning it to her side of the mattress. "I'm putting you on baby-duty seven nights a week."

"Deal. If that means I don't have to get up to go to work."

"I don't think you should expect to be sleeping in, either." Rita wrinkled her nose. "Sounds like babies are a lot of work."

Cash laughed. "Sounds like?"

Staring at the ceiling, she blew out a breath. "I got as much experience as you, buster."

Cash matched her sigh. "Why are we doing this again?"

Rita rolled over and gave him a peck. "Because we did the other thing."

He nabbed her lower lip with his teeth and moved a hand to her breast. "By the other thing, do you mean…"

"Sorry, Cash," Rita said, rolling away. "My ultra-sensitive boobs aren't in the mood. And honestly, neither am I."

"You feeling queasy?"

She shook head against the pillow. "My meeting with Carol didn't go well."

"Ah," he said with a nod. "I heard about that."

Rita frowned. "You did?"

"Word around town was it got a little messy."

"How the hell do you hear the word around town when we live way the fuck out here?"

He shrugged. "I got my own meeting lined up for tomorrow, by the way."

Rita softened. "With your dad?"

A muscle tightened in his jaw. "With the man himself."

"It's hard talking to parents at this stage of life," Rita said. "I really appreciate it."

"Sure," Cash said. "Do I get another kiss?"

"Definitely." Rita kissed him again, letting her lips linger. "And good luck."

"Thanks," Cash said. "I'm sure I'll need it."

"I can come with you," Rita said, "if it would help making the question an official request?"

Cash set his jaw. "I think it's best if I go on my own."

"Fair enough," Rita said. She kissed him again, then turned out the lamp and put her head on the pillow.

For a moment, Rita watched the shadows dance across the ceiling as the wind rattled the bare branches outside. Then sleep pulled her under, and when she woke what felt like minutes later, it was already six a.m.

Her bladder urged her to the half-bath, where she quickly relieved herself. Afterward, she drank a full glass of water, hoping to wash away the persistent headache that seemed to reappear whenever she wasn't constantly hydrating.

Tiptoeing upstairs to the closet while Cash still lay asleep, she pulled on her black uniform and noticed with a frown that she couldn't fasten the bottom two buttons of her shirt. She tucked the shirttails into her pants and adjusted her belt, tightening it one hole beyond where she'd worn it yesterday.

Looking in the mirror, she smiled and patted her belly. "You're making yourself known now, baby."

She left the house quietly, grabbing a bottle of orange juice and a cereal bar on her way out.

At APEX, she waved to Gord at the guard gate before parking and heading inside, offering a quick wave to Ginny at the front desk.

Inside the conference room, Craig was sitting in his usual spot in front of the computer, but this time, he wasn't watching footage. He was reading a newspaper.

He held up the *Casper Chronicle*. "We made the front page," he said.

Rita took the paper, which was folded in half. The advertisement she'd placed looked good, taking up the lower half of the front page. It was asking for information about Teddy Lake. She skimmed it, checking the details. "Looks good," she said, handing it back.

But then, her eyes flicked to the top half of the page. The headline made her jaw drop: *Satanic Killer Strikes Still.*

"What the hell is this?" she muttered, scanning the article. It described a man's body found with its head replaced by that of a mule-deer shoulder mount and pentagram carved into its belly (including a diagram). It further mentioned that the body was found at APEX.

Growling, Rita slammed the paper down on the table. "Jesus Christ, who the hell leaked all this?"

Craig raised his hands defensively. "Not me."

Rita shot him a hard look. "I haven't even informed the victim's family yet. Lucas doesn't know."

"Shit," Craig cursed. "I can call Lucas."

Rita shook her head. "No. Just keep an eye on your phone, please." She paused, collecting her thoughts. "In the meantime, can you call the local rental car agencies in Tampa? See if they have any records for Teddy Lake?"

Craig frowned. "I didn't think he had a driver's license."

"Make the calls anyway," Rita said firmly. "And try the bus lines, too. We're looking for anything linking him between Tampa and here."

Craig rolled his eyes. "You're kidding."

"Look at this way," Rita said, her tone softening. "You get a break from watching more footage. You can use my office if you need some space."

"Got it," Craig said, getting up.

Rita returned to her car in the parking lot and drove to Jason's house, still thinking of it as Otto's. She parked in her usual spot but reminded herself to knock on the door instead of turning the handle.

A few minutes later, Lucas answered, his hair mussed and wearing sweats. "Hi, Ms. Jonas."

"I came by to let you know there's been a breach of information," she said. "I realize it's early, but I need to give you some more details about your brother's death."

The color drained from Lucas's face. "Um, okay," he said, stepping back and pulling the door open. "I guess you should come in?"

"Yes," Rita said, with a nod. She stepped inside, feeling oddly out of place. Jason's cleaning supplies smelled different than Otto's go-to Lysol products.

Lucas led her through the foyer and into the living room, where he stood by the large window, gazing out over the lawn. Patches of snow blanketed the yard like a frosted quilt, its delicate fabric dotted with the last Aspen leaves to fall.

"Have a seat?" he asked, his voice hesitant. "Um, I haven't made any coffee yet."

"It's okay," Rita replied with a smile. "I'm not drinking any. But would you like me to make some tea?" She smiled again, this time a little more warmly. "You know, I'll just grab us some water. Unless you'd rather have tea."

In the kitchen, Rita found Jason's dishes tucked in the cupboard across from the sink, where Otto used to store his canned goods. She filled two glasses and returned to the living room.

Lucas remained by the window, his posture stiff, his hands clenched at his sides.

Rita handed him a glass of water with a soft smile. "Have a seat, Lucas."

She chose the armchair closest to the window, the one Jason had said he liked for reading or napping. Rita took a sip of water and set the glass on the windowsill.

Lucas sat down on the sofa, his fingers interlaced and

resting on his knees. His knuckles were white from the tension in his grip.

Rita paused before speaking, her gaze steady but heavy with the words she was about to say. "I'm sorry to inform you that your brother's body was disfigured."

Lucas's breath hitched, his face paling as the reality of her words sank in. "I know. You mentioned…his head. It's missing."

"That's right."

"Has it been found?" Lucas's voice was tight, taut with a desperate hope.

Rita shook her head, a lump in her throat. "Not yet, but we're working on it." She exhaled, gathering her strength. "There was…something in place of his head."

The color drained from Lucas's face. "What?"

"A shoulder mount."

Lucas frowned. "What's that?"

"A taxidermy deer's head," Rita said. She splayed her fingers like antlers. "With a full rack."

Lucas shook his head. "But…how?"

Rita was familiar with the victim's tendency to ask for the details when receiving bad news, as if better understanding the situation could supply enough logic to mitigate the horror.

"The deer's head was removed from its mount and attached with a rebar," she said.

Nodding, Lucas's eyes glazed over. "Okay."

"That's not all," Rita said.

Lucas looked up at her. "Okay," he said by way of an invitation.

"There were markings carved into his torso," she said.

Lucas's lips peeled back in a sneer. "Jesus fucking Christ, what happened to him? What were these markings?"

"A pentagram," Rita said, "and the letter M."

He blinked at her again in succession. "That's why you asked me about the letter M."

Rita made an affirmative sound, then asked, "Do any of these symbols have any meaning to your brother, a star, an M, or a stag?"

Lucas took a moment to think, though Rita suspected he was simply trying to process the shock. A minute later, he shook his head, his eyes moist with tears. "This creepy stuff, it doesn't mean shit to him or me. Told you, Teddy liked to have some beers, shoot the shit, chat up the girls. But the only kind of rack he liked…"

His voice twisted into a bitter laugh, which became a sob.

"I'm sorry to have to give you this information at this time, when we are still conducting our investigation," Rita said. "Again, I apologize for the early intrusion, but I didn't want you hearing about this from anyone else, and it's splattered all over the front page of the paper today."

Luke nodded, swallowing back his emotions. "I get it, it's okay."

"Take it easy today," Rita said. "If you want to order in some pizza, call The Shaft and you can ask Lacey to put it on my tab."

Lucas nodded. "Thanks, that's real nice. I will."

Rita returned to the crossover in the driveway, then dialed the number for the paper before starting the engine.

The automated directory kicked in, and she punched in the exchange for Blaze Wright.

"Rita," he said, his tone friendly.

"Who gave you that information about Teddy Lake?"

Blaze's voice stayed cool. "I always protect my sources."

"Well, the timing of that article next to my ad makes it look like I told you."

"I can't help that," Blaze replied. "I don't direct the layout department."

"Don't pass the buck, Blaze," she shot back. "You can forget any future favors."

Blaze chuckled. "You never give me favors anyway."

"Take that back," she said, "I was fucking generous telling you about this case."

"Well, you got a bad case of the Karens," he said, "and I can't imagine that's good for your baby—"

Rita hung up before she could regret saying something that would prove he wasn't the only one in Still County who could eviscerate with words.

And besides, he was right. She didn't need the baby hearing her lose it the way she'd grown up witnessing Carol lose hers. She rubbed her belly, remembering how Carol's outbursts had always unsettled her.

Damn Blaze Wright, anyway. She slammed her hand against the steering wheel, then pulled out of Otto's driveway.

Her stomach rumbled loudly. She headed downtown and parallel parked out front of the Bighorn Bean.

She pushed open the teal door and spotted Jason standing in line. Before she could stop herself, she walked up to him.

"Are you responsible for this?" she demanded, waving the newspaper in front of him.

Jason snatched the paper from her hand and read the headline, his face flushing a deep red. He shoved it back at her. "Of course not. And I'm offended that you'd think so. You know I'd never leak information."

Rita raised an eyebrow. "Did you see who wrote it?"

Jason met her gaze squarely. "Blaze Wright, of course.

But I know better than to talk to him about an active investigation."

"Sometimes things can get murky. I've overshared with Cash, too."

Jason's jaw tightened. "Well, if you must know, Blaze and I broke up weeks ago."

Rita's tone softened. "I'm sorry to hear that. I didn't know."

Jason's voice remained hard. "Of course you didn't. You don't know much about me these days."

Rita nodded. "It's true. But I know Otto's place looks good. Thanks for taking care of it."

Jason's posture relaxed slightly. "I like living there." He shifted on his feet. "If you really want to know, things were strained with Blaze for a while. I never shared anything with him, and it felt like I couldn't fully relax. It always seemed like the story mattered more."

Rita shrugged. "You have to admit, *our* job always comes first."

Jason met her gaze. "Does it?"

Rita let out a deep breath, touching her belly. "I don't know." She turned to leave. "See you around, Jason."

"Your paper," he called after her.

"Keep it," she said, her voice flat.

As she pushed open the door to leave, Jason called out again. "You didn't order a coffee."

"Damn, you're right," Rita said, pausing in the doorway. "And you lost your place in line."

She turned and walked out, letting the door close behind her.

Chapter Twenty-Three

RITA STEPPED up to the door of Carly's Crystals, still closed, and peered through the glass. Beyond a hanging display of dreamcatchers, she saw a shadowy figure in the back of the store. She waved and the figure waved in kind, moving closer.

Rita straightened as Carly unlocked the front door, the wind chime tinkling.

"Hey, Rita," Carly said, wearing a paisley maxi-dress and her bobbed hair in spikes.

"Congratulations," Rita said, taking in Carly's new look as much as the store's decor. She suspected Carly had added a few new piercings since their last meetup for ribs at The Shaft, but she said nothing, instead pointing to a security camera. "Kimmy's cams are still working, I take it?"

"Yes. And I shoulda made friends with a cop sooner," Carly said, stepping aside for Rita to enter. "You're always looking out for me, girlfriend."

"Of course," Rita said. "As a kid, I ran the Safe and Sound Club check-in system for latchkey kids. I don't remember much, but Dad said we used colored paper in the windows to show we got home safe."

Carly's eyes misted. "It's cool your dad was around to tell you about your little life."

"Yeah," Rita said, her gazing at the massive Tree of Life poster pinned behind the cash desk, its emerald leaves woven with intricate Celtic knots. "For a long time, I thought of him as an anchor, tying me down to this place. But now…I'm starting to see he was a harbor to return to. And the choice was mine all along."

Carly frowned. "Your choice?"

"Between Otto and Dale." Rita chewed her lip. "It was never about Still. For so long, I thought I was choosing between the two loves of my life. But coming back to Otto made me realize, if I'd figured out Cash was the one for me in the first place, I could've stayed close to both my leading men all along."

"It's funny what feels like home, in the end. When I first left Jeff, I was so anxious to get out of Wyoming. But now that he's gone, well, that urge has faded." She glanced around. "I used to work in such a dark environment. But now I love the way the light reflects of the snow and bounces off the ceiling." She pointed to some faceted crystals hanging in the front window. "Later in the afternoon, when the sun is low, those prisms fill this place with miniature rainbows."

"I'll come by some afternoon to check that out," Rita said, her gaze roving along the shelves of shimmering stones and ceramic figurines. "You look right at home here."

Carly glanced around. "It's a good little set-up. Like your apartment. Not too much, not too little. And everything in working order. Kimmy left it real nice."

"It's definitely a step up from the purple walls and cracked vinyl recliners."

Carly grimaced. "Those chairs were heavy as fuck and cost a shit-ton to haul out of here. And the walls, don't even get me started on how many cans of primer I used."

Rita waved a finger at the walls draped in patterned tapestries. "You painted all this yourself?"

Carly put her hands on her hips and craned her neck to look around. "Sure did. Still purple, but not so electric. It's called Celestial Mauve."

"Looks bigger than the nail spa ever did," Rita said. "And it smells good in here. Couldn't even tell it was painted. Unlike my place."

"Patchouli," Carly said, her gaze staring away.

"And where'd Kimmy get to?" Rita asked. "I didn't know she was thinking of leaving town."

"She left her husband and moved to Albuquerque."

"Why?" Rita asked. "What was wrong with him?"

"Nothing, I don't think," Carly said. "But Kimmy met a finger fetishist online and realized she could never again be happy if she wasn't with him. And since I was able to take over the remainder of her lease, she was able to get a nail salon opened up there. I hear she's doing real well."

"Wow," Rita said. "If you're talking to her, please pass on my regards."

"Sure will," Carly said, her own fingers fidgeting. She blushed. "I hope it's not TMI, telling you about Kimmy's finger fetishist. I never really know where to draw the line with folks who aren't in the sex industry."

Rita gave her an encouraging smile. "Are you okay?"

Carly flinched. "Of course. W-why?"

"You sound nervous."

Carly blew out a breath. "I just want this place to be

successful. My last business venture didn't exactly turn out very well."

"I assume you're referring to the Rawhide Revue?"

Carly nodded, twisting her fingers.

"Those problems were related to Jeff," Rita said.

Carly blew out a breath. "You're right. I only doubt myself 'cause I never got anything out of that investment." Carly snorted. "Except a whole lot of PTSD."

"Well, it looks like you got enough stuff around here to heal that," Rita said, glancing around at the bowls of stones. "Sorry, I hope that didn't sound insensitive. I know you believe in all this metaphysical stuff."

"It's physics, all right," Carly said. "And you should believe, too, Rita. Whole state of Wyoming's on some kind of special rock or another." She picked up a deep green chunk. "Take jade, for example. Nephrite's found right here in Wyoming."

"Beautiful," Rita said. "Reminds me of glacial streams."

"Jade increases your psychic powers."

"It does?" Rita looked around again. "There's a lot in this place. You must have some potent powers by now."

Carly laughed. "It's not like I can read my customers' minds or nothin.' But you communicating with your baby could be amplified."

Rita looked down at her abdomen. "With a rock?"

Carly nodded and placed the rock against Rita's belly button. "It's what they say. 'Course I haven't had a baby, so I don't really know."

"Well, it's a nice idea," Rita said.

"Here, you take it," Carly said, putting it in Rita's hand.

Rita lifted her palm to study the piece of jade. "This thing better not lead to another breach of information."

Carly laughed. "Crystals can't be informants."

"Good," Rita said, pocketing the stone. "All the same, don't sell any to Blaze Wright."

"Is he a dancer?"

"Got the right name for it," Rita said. "But he writes for *The Casper Chronicle*." Then she pulled out the pink flyer with the pentagram. "I came by because I've seen these around town. I heard you hung one at The Bighorn Bean. Can you tell me about the meetup?"

Carly's smile tightened. "Are you thinking about going?"

Rita pointed to the pentagram encircling the capital letter M. "I'm more interested in this logo. Did you design it or see it somewhere else?"

"I made the star with the hoop," Carly said. "It's something I drew a few months ago. For a while I thought about getting it as a tattoo, but then when I conceived the moon meetings, I realized I just needed to add an M and it would be perfect for my brand."

"So the M stands for Moon Meetup?" Rita clarified.

Carly nodded.

"And what is the Moon Meetup?" Rita asked.

Carly squared her shoulders. "A gathering of women."

"What do you do?"

Her fingers twitched. "Talk about spirituality. Manifest Dreams. Divine the future."

"Divine the future?" Rita lifted a brow. "How do you do that?"

"We read oracle cards, Tarot, Spirit Guides, that sort of thing. It's about getting wisdom from the cards to help make better decisions, which lead to better outcomes in the future."

"That guy I dated in New York, Dale, he had a grandmother who read tea leaves."

"Did she read yours?" Carly asked.

"She did," Rita said, chewing on her lip. "I haven't thought about it for a while, but she did tell me something significant."

Carly's eyes widened. "Will you tell me?"

Rita let out a nervous laugh. "She said I was gonna be a mom."

"Nice." Carly said, grinning. She spread her hands. "See?"

"Back then, I thought she was full of crap," Rita said, "because Dale had a vasectomy with his ex-wife. But now, with things the way they are, I'll be thinking back to that night, trying to remember what else she said."

Carly crinkled her nose. "That's why it's wise to always record a reading. Or at least take notes. So you can look back on it, years later."

"I've never been good with paperwork," Rita said. "How many people are attending these meetings?"

"Usually about half a dozen of us," Carly said, her fingers fidgeting again.

Rita took out her notebook. "I'll need all their contact information, please."

Carly shifted her posture. "Um, okay. I'll work on that."

"How often do you meet?"

Her gaze skated away. "Weekly."

"Regular meetings?"

"Yes, Friday nights." Carly forced a giggle. "Gives a chance for the hubbies to have a night blowing off steam, while us ladies do our thing."

"Do you meet at any other times?"

"Sure," Carly said, adjusting a stack of journals. "On an as-needed basis."

"As-needed spirituality?" Rita clarified. "Can you give me an example?"

Carly flapped a dismissive hand. "Oh, you know, different organic factors."

Rita frowned, trying to understand. "Like—?"

"Like the cycle of the moon." Carly set her jaw. "Full moons can be pretty wild night for some folks."

"As a cop, I'd have to agree," Rita said. "Though I could say that about a lot of nights, like Christmas and Halloween. Whereabouts do these Moon Meetups take place?"

"Here." Carly flicked her hand towards the center of the shop. "We push back that display unit and set up folding chairs. Doing it here instead of my place means I can claim the utilities as a business expense."

Rita used her pen to point to a security camera. "And safer."

Carly's smile twitched. "I suppose so."

"Do any men come to the Moon Meetups?"

Carly's jaw tensed. "No, they're not invited."

Rita pulled out the mugshot of Teddy and showed it to her. "Do you recognize this man?"

Carly took the page and looked closer. "Sure, I read about him in the paper. Fucking diagram of a star with an M cut into him looks a lot like mine." She looked at Rita. "Shit, Rita, that's what brought you here, isn't it? My logo connects me to this dead guy. But I'm telling you, it's just a coincidence. Whatever kink the killer's into, it ain't got nothin' to do with me."

Rita nodded. "I'm following all leads. Any chance Teddy Lake wandered in here as a customer?"

Carly studied the mug shot again. "I danced for a lot of guys in my time," she said, "and it sure is hard to tell them apart, you know? Which is a real bitch when you gotta check out a lineup, because in my line of work, that happened more'n once." She handed back the mug shot. "But, no, I don't remember anyone like him coming in the shop."

"Have you had any suspicious customers lately? Anyone especially interested in the occult? Or your shop specifically? Or you?"

Carly took a moment to think. "No. To be honest, business is slow. Mostly a handful of repeat customers, usually the same two dozen women who were at my grand opening." She twisted her fingers. "Do you think someone's coming after me? Or one of the ladies in the group?"

Rita squeezed her shoulder. "We both know this could be serious. But I'm hoping the killer's simply copied the imagery from the poster and not crossed your path. After all, posters are all over town."

"And in Beaumont."

"And bound to stick in people's minds. I like to think the carvings in the body are a distraction. Like the deer's head. Do you have any thoughts on that?"

Carly pulled a book from a shelf. "Deer are prominent messengers from the spirit world to ours." She consulted the index, then flipped to a page. "References here to Buddhism and Hinduism and Celtic mythology. Some Native American traditions say the stag offers guidance and protection during life transitions."

"Like death," Rita said. "How *apropos*."

Carly closed the book and shelved it. "And birth." Then she flinched as a shadow passed by the front window.

Rita craned to look. "I think a customer's waiting outside."

"Jesus," Carly said, putting a hand to chest, "I'm on edge. I'm still getting over being married to Jeff." She touched a stone hanging on a chain around her neck.

"That's why I wear tiger's eye, to keep me feeling grounded. Like I don't got to run no more." Crossing to the cash counter, she waved through the window to the customer waiting outside the shop. "I'm late opening. I haven't even got all the lights on yet."

"I won't keep you any longer," Rita said, moving towards the door. "Stay sharp, okay? You're good at looking out for yourself. But…you know I'm always here if you need me to drive by?"

Carly swallowed. "Sure, yeah, of course."

Rita met her eye. "Even though I'm at APEX, I'm still around town."

Then she stepped outside, saying hello to the waiting customer before climbing into her crossover.

Rita checked her phone. A message had come in from Ruby Joe. She sighed. Conducting a homicide investigation on a Monday morning wasn't exactly the ideal time for a family chat about lineage.

But the first words of the message had caught her attention: *Official biz, don't ignore…*

Chapter Twenty-Four

As Rita opened the heavy wooden door to The Shaft, a warm aroma of burgers and ribs wafted around her. Her mouth watered at once.

She stepped inside, letting the door close behind her. She paused in the foyer, her eyes adjusted to the dim lighting. Then her gaze swept the room, which was relatively empty at this time of day.

At the bar, Chester sat eating bacon and eggs. As soon as he spotted Rita, he pushed up the brim of his cowboy hat so she could fully appreciate his scowl.

"Don't tell me the security footage has got extra-terrestrials in it, now?"

"I'm here to talk to Ruby Joe," Rita said, strolling past him a few stools to where Ruby Joe was chatting with a customer. She noticed Rita and closed off the conversation.

"Should we talk in your office?" Rita asked as she approached.

Ruby Joe nodded toward the back of the restaurant. "It's quiet," she said. "We can take a booth in the back."

Rita fell into step beside her in, a thick silence prickling between them. Ruby Joe slid into a corner booth and folded her hands on the table. Rita sat opposite.

Bypassing pleasantries, Ruby Joe said, "That guy in the paper…"

"Teddy Lake," Rita supplied.

"That's the one," Ruby Joe said. "He was in here the other night. Thursday. I remember him 'cause he was drinking like it was Friday. He was the rowdiest clown in the crowd."

"Was he picking fights?" Rita asked. "Or partying with anyone in particular?"

"He wasn't the fightin' type or the flirtin' type, not that it made him any less of an asshole," Ruby Joe said. She glanced back at Chester. "At first, he was sitting with the guys from the Gas-N-Go."

"Who was here from the Gas-N-Go?" Rita asked.

"Don, the mechanic who's been working there forever, and that new kid. That cute little gas jockey. Don't know his name. Looks barely old enough for beef dip, let alone beer."

"Were they drinking, too, like Teddy?"

"Oh, no," Ruby Joe said. "Don comes in for the eats, like you do. And the kid was just along 'cause Chester was dropping him off home later that night. Guess the kid gets around on a dirt bike, which ain't so easy with the weather changing."

"Was Teddy sitting with them?" Rita asked.

"For a while they were talking, heads bent close like they were sharing a joke. But then that Teddy fellow started getting loud. Real obnoxious."

"Do you know what about?"

"He was high about some kind of racket he had going on. He was in a real good mood, maybe too good. We were making moves to kick him out when he left on his own."

"Did he leave with anyone?" Rita asked.

"Not that I saw," Ruby Joe replied. "Though I know he didn't drive off, 'cause Paulie tried to take his keys. But he said he didn't have a car."

"So you're not sure how he got here?" Rita asked.

"Nope," Ruby Joe said, shaking her head. "While Paulie was having a word with him, I sent Wayne to check for out-of-state plates anyway, 'cause this guy was wearing a USF hoodie and cap."

"But nothing?"

"We know most of the regulars' rides, and Wayne didn't see any vehicles he didn't recognize."

"And it was Paulie who interacted with him?" Rita asked.

"Hey, Paulie." Ruby Joe gave a sharp whistle and a thin man in a Hawaiian shirt appeared around the corner and approached the table.

"This is Paulie," Ruby Joe said, sliding down the booth to make room for him.

Paulie settled into the booth with a smile and nod.

"Do you remember Teddy Lake coming in Thursday night?" Rita asked him, showing Paulie the mug shot.

"Sure do," Paulie replied. "Saw him walk in already liquored up, then practically crawl out a couple hours later. Shortly after six."

"Did he arrive with anyone?" Rita asked.

Paulie shook his head. "No. He said someone at the Gas-N-Go told him this was the best place to grab a snack. Though I don't recall him ordering no dinner. Just eating some nuts while he chugged a pitcher of our IPA on tap. Ended up sitting with the Gas-N-Go guys when they showed up a while later."

"What time did Ruby Joe talk to you about taking his keys?"

"About half-past eight," Paulie said. "But when I asked for his keys, he said he wasn't driving. And that I didn't need to throw him out 'cause he was headed out anyway. I asked him where he was going."

"That's protocol, if they're inebriated," Ruby Joe inserted.

"What did he tell you?" Rita asked.

"Said he was staying in Still for a while," Paulie answered. "He didn't appear to have no jacket, and it was gettin' real cold. 'Course I was concerned, but he was also a bit of a jerk, and we wanted the guy to go on his way." He paused, moistening his lips. "Shit, Sheriff, I was worried about that kid drinking too much or getting too cold from exposure. And look at what happened to him. He was someone's son."

"It's a tragedy," Rita agreed quietly. "Thanks for answering my questions, Paulie."

"No problem," Paulie said, getting up from the booth. "I only hope some peace comes to his family."

As he walked away, Ruby Joe slid out of the booth to follow him.

"Mind if I ask you another question?" Rita asked.

"I'm not sure what else I can tell you about him," Ruby Joe said. "Paulie dealt with Teddy more than I did."

"I actually have a personal question," Rita said.

Ruby Joe stiffened.

Rita pulled out her phone and swiped to the photo she'd taken of Otto and the woman in Hollywood. "Do you know who this woman is?" she asked, showing Ruby Joe the screen.

Ruby Joe looked, then shook her head. "No."

"Do you know why Otto went to L.A?" Rita asked.

Ruby Joe shifted in the booth. "Maybe you should be asking Carol these questions."

"In case it's not common knowledge," Rita said, her jaw tight, "my conversations with Carol usually don't go so well."

Ruby Joe surveyed Rita. "I heard about a commotion at the Bighorn."

"A commotion caused by Carol," Rita said with a head shake. "Look, Ruby Joe, I can't make you tell me about my past if you don't want to. And thank you for reaching out about Teddy."

Then Rita walked away from the table. As she passed Chester scraping up the last of his miner's breakfast, she paused.

She pulled out the mugshot and showed it to him. "Do you know this guy?"

Chester kept his eyes on her. "You said you weren't here to ask me no questions."

"I changed my mind," Rita said, ruffling the paper in his face.

Chester's gaze skidded over to the image, then snapped back to Rita. "Yeah, he was in here the other night, asking a bunch of questions about town that none of us could answer."

"When you say 'none of us,' can you tell me whom he spoke to that night?" Rita asked.

Chester chuckled. "Hell, he talked to everyone. I left before he shut up."

"What time was that?"

"Must've been shortly after eight. Had to drive Jesse home by nine o'clock. Kid's got a damn curfew, which means I can never schedule him for night shifts."

"Well, thanks for your help, Chester," Rita said, heading for the door.

Then stopped when Ruby Joe called her name.

She turned to see the older woman emerging from the hallway that led to her office. In her hands, she held a small book bound in burgundy vinyl.

"I'm fucking tired of family secrets," Ruby Joe said.

Rita retraced her steps across the pub, meeting Ruby Joe in front of the bar.

"Six months after you were born, " Ruby Joe said, "Carol left Otto. For the first time. And then Otto disappeared. He was gone a whole damn month. I figured he went after her, but he never admitted it. Maybe that's when he wound up in California."

Rita's stomach tensed. "What do you mean 'the first time'? I thought she only left once, when she walked out on both of us for good."

Ruby Joe let out a dry, humorless laugh. "Oh, hell no. Carol was always coming and going. One foot out the door, even when she was still in town." Her grip on the photo album tightened. "I always knew she was bad news. And I told Otto that. When he came back, I ripped him a new one for disappearing on his baby. Then I warned him, if Carol ever came crawling back, he shouldn't take her back in." She scoffed and shook her head. "But he was in love."

Rita let out a breath. "Hard to imagine Dad being sentimental."

Ruby Joe snorted. "He told me his love life was none of my damn business."

Rita couldn't help but smile. "Considering you make everyone's business your business, right down to their cholesterol count, I can imagine how that went over."

Ruby Joe's mouth twitched, but the humor didn't reach her eyes. "We fought. And that's when he told me I wasn't his sister anymore."

Rita's throat tightened. "I'm sorry. That must have hurt."

"I'm most sorry I lost all that time with him."

"We can't get that back."

Pain flickered in Ruby Joe's eyes. "All because of Carol." She exhaled sharply. "When she left the second time, for good, I tried to reconnect with Otto."

"But…it didn't stick?"

"I figured his pride got in the way," Ruby Joe said. "I tried to give him the benefit of the doubt. Have patience. But he still didn't want nothing to do with me." Ruby Joe held out the book. The cracked gold script on the vinyl cover read *Photographs*. "Not much in here," she said gruff. "But what's here is very precious."

Chapter Twenty-Five

RITA SAT in the driver's seat of the crossover, the photo album resting heavy in her hands. She ran her thumb over the cracked gold script lettering before flipping it open.

The first image was familiar: Carol sat propped against pillows in a hospital room, her hair damp, swaddling a newborn Rita in her arms. Otto stood beside the bed, smiling, though his posture was rigid. Rita had seen a copy of this photo before and had always assumed a nurse had taken it. But now she had to think it had been Ruby Joe.

She turned the page. The next photo showed Rita at six months, propped up on a sofa, chubby fingers curled into a fist. *First time sitting up* was written on a tiny label stuck to the back of the snapshot.

Then, Rita at seven months, an unsteady stance against a coffee table. *First time pulling herself up.*

Eight months, a wide, gummy grin, hands covered in mashed carrots. *Solid food.*

Nine months, clutching Ruby Joe's fingers, one foot hesitantly raised. *First steps (almost!).*

Ten months, two bottom teeth peeking from her smile. *First tooth!* Or technically, in this case, teeth.

Another snapshot showed Rita hugging a stuffed rabbit. Rita touched the image. She had a vague remembrance of Pom-Pom, which she'd slept with until kindergarten. Mostly because Pom-Pom was very effective at muffling the sound of her parents shouting after she'd gone to bed.

Another snapshot showed Rita walking unaided, arms outstretched. Ruby Joe's note read: *First time walking alone.*

For a year, Otto's sister had documented every milestone with a devoted determination, tucking detailed notes inside the plastic sleeves. She had been as present for these moments as Rita's own two parents had been.

The next picture showed Rita in a highchair, a single candle flickering atop a cupcake on the tray. Paper decorations dangled from an overhead light just out of frame. Carol sat at the table, her face lit up in laughter, while Otto sat beside her, fists resting on the table, his gaze not on Rita but on Carol.

Rita paused. How had she never noticed before how tense her father looked? She'd always thought of Carol as the angry one.

Then the album shifted. The baby pictures tapered off, and suddenly, Rita was older—a toddler, then a small child. As she flipped pages, the flood of images dried up.

By adolescence, there were only a handful left. No posed portraits, only candid snapshots. Rita at a summer festival, glancing away mid-conversation. Rita at The Shaft during a retirement party, distracted by something off-camera. Rita on Main Street, watching a parade float pass by.

A strange feeling crept up Rita's spine. For the first year of Rita's life, Ruby Joe had been *there*, cataloguing every moment that mattered. And then, slowly, as if someone had shut a door, Rita's aunt had faded into the background, watching from a distance. Recording from the outside. A witness to a life she hadn't been allowed to raise.

Rita swallowed and closed the album. She reached for her phone.

And felt the stone in her pocket. She pulled out the jade, rubbing her thumb over it. It was cool. She pressed her it to her temple, taking deep breaths. How could she prepare to bring a child into the world when the echoes of her own childhood still lingered unresolved? It felt as though the past and the future were colliding inside her, each demanding attention in ways she wasn't sure how to balance.

She returned the stone to her pocket and pulled out her phone and called Cash.

His voicemail picked up with the usual automated message: *"I'm driving right now. Leave a message."*

Rita disconnected and dropped her phone onto the passenger seat, then blew her nose into a tissue.

Her phone buzzed with a text notification. It was Cash: *Sorry I missed your call, you OK?*

Rita wiped her eyes, then sent back a thumbs-up emoji. *Something came up about my childhood*, she typed. *It can wait. Where are you?*

Rest stop 87, Cash replied. *On my way to see TG.*

Drive safe, Rita returned. She'd forgotten about his visit to Tom. *Talk to you later.*

Cash replied with a series of X's and O's, and Rita pocketed her phone.

She drove to the SCSO and parked in the loading zone. Pushing through the front door without pausing to acknowledge Jason and Candace, she breezed through the bullpen on a beeline for Mary Lou's desk.

"Did you know about it?" Rita asked, her voice sharp.

Mary Lou spun around, her silver hair swishing with the motion. "Know about what?"

"That both my parents abandoned me when I was six months old."

The color drained from Mary Lou's face. "Sure," she said, her voice low. "But it wasn't like I was holding a secret…it's only that no one really talked about it."

"Why not?" Rita pressed. "What difference did it make after Carol left, anyway?"

"Your dad's gone. Water under the bridge."

"Where did Otto catch up with her?" Rita persisted.

"Don't know," Mary Lou said. "Otto liked to keep his business private."

"You don't say?" Rita said, screwing up her nose.

"He came back alone and didn't say nothing about being away. Just took up caring for you again. It was another three months after that that Carol came back. If I remember correctly, she left when you were about six months old and came back right before you turned a year. In fact, I seem to rightly remember her throwing a birthday party. She must have come back for that express reason."

"Pardon me if I can't appreciate the sentimentality of that," Rita said, her jaw set.

Mary Lou bobbed her stack of hair. "I understand."

"Who looked after me during that time?"

Mary Lou was quick to respond. "Mostly Ruby Joe, and a couple local families when she needed a break."

"Like who?" Rita asked.

"Walter once," Mary Lou said. "But that was before he'd married Winnie and was a bit of a live wire."

Rita cringed. "Jesus."

"And the Briggs a couple times," Mary Lou added.

"The Briggs?" Rita said. "They both died of alcohol poisoning before I went to New York."

"Yeah, they were friends of Carol's."

"But how were they fit to take care of me?" Rita asked. "Dean had been a serial DUI offender. Otto told me the stories over the years."

"Well, hell, Rita," Mary Lou said, "the folk around here were trying to do the best they could, helping out Ruby Joe and her brother who got himself into a spot of trouble."

"A spot of trouble," Rita said. "Is that what I was?"

"You know I don't mean that." Mary Lou tipped up her nose. "I was referring to Carol. Trouble followed that girl wherever she went."

"Hey, hey, hey," Jason said, walking in with his hands in the air. "Sounds like things are gettin' heated in here."

"Sorry for the disturbance," Rita said wryly. "I just came in to ask Mary Lou something personal."

Then she turned and left, the door banging behind her.

Rita scuffed down the steps and dropped into the BMW with a sigh. Driving too fast, she crossed town to APEX HQ.

In the conference room, Craig bent over his phone, thumbs swiping.

"How's it going?" she asked, taking a seat at the board table. "Any calls on the hotline?"

Craig dropped his phone and craned his neck to stretch. "No. And no trace of car rentals or bus tickets for Theodore Lake, either."

"And you pinged his phone?" Rita asked.

Craig leaned back in the chair and stretched his shoulders. "Last time it gave off a signal was early evening on Thursday."

"Off the local tower?"

Craig nodded. "Yep. But now there's no signal, so it's likely out of power or turned off."

"Thanks for tracking down the details," Rita said, getting up from the table. "I'll check in with you later."

As Rita pushed through the glass door of the conference room, Craig's phone rang behind her. She paused.

Waving his hand at Rita, he mumbled a few "uh huhs" into the phone. She came back through the door and took a seat again at the table, this time beside him.

Craig scribbled onto his notepad.

Asking to be excused for a moment, Craig muted his cell phone and turned to Rita, his eyes bright. "This couple thinks they picked up Teddy hitchhiking."

"Transfer it to my direct line, please," Rita said, heading out the door again and riding the elevator to her office.

"Hello, this is Rita Jonas with APEX L.E.O. Thank you for calling in with this information. I'm going to be recording our call. May I have your names, please?"

"My name's Doug Wallace, and my wife, Michelle, is here with me on speaker phone."

The Wallaces answered a series of questions as Rita collected their personal information. Then they explained that their son, who lives in Casper, had recognized the victim's name and connected it to the hitchhiker they'd picked up.

"Please tell me everything about meeting Teddy Lake," Rita said.

"We picked him up at the Kansas-Missouri border," Doug said, "and dropped him off in Julesburg, Colorado. We were headed to Denver."

"Approximately how long was he in your car?" Rita asked.

"About seven hours too long," Michelle said.

Doug gave a dry chuckle. "We were relieved when we dropped him off. He was making us real uncomfortable."

"How so?" Rita asked.

Doug hesitated. "It wasn't anything specific…"

"He was too chatty," Michelle said. "Seemed odd for a drifter."

"Kept going on about his old man," Doug said. "Said he was a real hero but also a bit of a pirate."

"And he wouldn't shut up about some bit of hot information he had," Michelle added. "Something that would prove how smart he was, or something like that."

"Did he tell you where he was headed?" Rita asked.

"Cowboy country," he said. "We knew better than to pry, we were just trying to help out a lad."

"Do you remember what he was wearing?"

"Sure, 'cause he didn't look like no cowboy," Michelle said. "He was wearing sneakers and jeans, which I thought was odd for heading north."

"Teased him about his Bulls cap," Doug said, his voice tightening. "Said he needed something warmer."

"That's why we stopped in the first place," Michelle said. "We thought he looked real down on his luck, no bags and shoulders hunched against the cold. But once he started spouting off about that 'secret' of his … well, we wondered if he was delusional."

"Or maybe running from the law," Doug said. "We was real worried we might have helped out a criminal."

"Till we heard about what happened. Our son read us the article over the phone."

"We were real shaken up when we learned we'd delivered him in straight into hands of the devil."

"The killer didn't pick him up in Julesburg," Rita said. "He was seen alive in a pub a few hours before his death."

"No doubt he would've been safer had we kept him

with us," Michelle said, her voice shaky. "He might still be alive now."

"Or we might be dead," Doug said grimly. "That was some real Satanic stuff in the news. Maybe he was deep in it himself, could've done something like that to someone before. Or hell, maybe he even offered himself up as a sacrifice."

"Now why would he do that, Doug?" Michelle said. "He was real itchy over that secret of his. He was living for the day he could make good on his dad's memory."

Rita cleared her throat. "Thank you, Michelle, Doug. Your information has been very helpful."

"No problem," Doug said. "We like to help out where we can."

"Your heart's in the right place," Rita said. "But it's best if you two refrain from picking up any more hitch-hikers in the future."

Doug and Michelle made some agreeable sounds.

"If you remember anything else," Rita said, "please give me a call." She gave them the number for her direct line, in addition to using the hotline. Then she wished them a good stay in Denver and disconnected.

She got up to use the bathroom, before taking the elevator back down to the conference room. As she walked through the glass door, Craig was ending a call.

"Another tip?" Ria asked.

Craig nodded. "That was Donald Horgan from the Gas-N-Go. He says he saw Teddy Lake at The Shaft."

Rita nodded. "I have a feeling we'll be getting a lot of calls from patrons of The Shaft. Sounds like Teddy made quite a scene."

"Don said he'll be at the garage at nine tomorrow morning if you want to chat," Craig said. "Right now he's closing shop for the day and headed home."

Rita glanced at the time. "I'm closing shop for the day and headed home, too." She stifled a yawn. "I'll talk to him in the morning. But if any new tips come in, someone not at The Shaft Thursday night, let me know?"

"Ten-four," Craig said.

Rita bade him a good night, then left the conference room. Upstairs, she gathered her belongings, then returned downstairs where she said goodnight to Ginny before exiting the building.

Barely remembering the route, Rita drove home.

"For shame, Rita," she said to herself, mimicking Otto's rare but pointed scoldings. "You've got to stop working before you're so tired you'll fall asleep at the wheel."

She rolled down the window for the rest of the ride, letting the glacial air rush in.

Once home, she kicked off her squeaky boots and trudged into living room, ready to nosedive onto the bed, except the bed was gone.

The needlepoint bison stared back at her.

"You moved the bed?" she called out, her voice echoing against the freshly painted walls.

Cash's voice returned from the kitchen: "Yep. Bedroom's all set up."

Rita retraced her steps to the foyer to hang up her coat, the aroma of chili making her stomach growl. Then she entered the kitchen, where Cash sat at the table, watching something on his laptop.

"Thanks," she said. "Did you move the bed all by yourself?"

He nodded, gaze fixed on the screen. "Not many neighbors around. Besides, I had some pent-up energy after my visit to County."

"How did it go?"

Cash stiffened. "I couldn't do it," he said, continuing to stare at the tabletop.

"You mean you couldn't go in?" Rita asked, crossing to the table.

A shadow passed over his face. "I felt like a fucking idiot."

Rita gave his shoulder a reassuring squeeze. "Don't say that. It's totally understandable." Then she laughed. "Hell, look at how my conversations go with my mother."

Cash let out a small laugh before his expression sobered again. "That man messed me up as much as your mom messed you up. And I guess I still feel like I need space. So I can do a better job with his grandkids than he did with me, if I just keep him away."

Rita stayed quiet, unsure how to respond; they'd both lost the people they were closest to. She leaned down and kissed him on the cheek.

And froze when she saw the video playing on the screen. It showed her leaving the Bighorn Bean. Then it cut to Carol, sitting in her van, sobbing into the camera, reassuring her followers that she'd try again to repair things with her daughter.

"What the actual fuck?" Rita said, louder than she'd meant to.

"What gets me," Cash said, "is that for her to film this part in the van, she had to think about the lighting, roll down the window, set up a tripod, and adjust the focus. So how hard can she really be crying?"

Rita dropped into a chair. "It's bullshit, all right."

Cash lowered the laptop screen. "Sorry, but I had to see it. It's like a car wreck, I can't look away. But I didn't mean for you to see it." He glanced at the clock on the stove. "You're home earlier than I expected."

"Yeah," Rita said, "I'm bushed."

"Well, we can eat early and go to bed early," Cash said, sounding brighter. "Chili's been simmering all day while I lugged that mattress upstairs."

"Smells amazing and sounds amazing," Rita said, leaning across the table to kiss him again. "But I'll have to take a raincheck on an early bedtime." Rolling her shoulders, she blew out a breath. "I've got a meeting tonight."

Chapter Twenty-Six

"That was delicious," Rita said, kissing Cash on his tomato-stained lips. "You can never go back to being a mechanic, because then there'd be no one to cook for me."

His laughed, but his voice had an edge to it.

He stood up to clear the plates. "I was happy when you took the job at APEX. I thought it'd mean less stress for more pay. But I'm not sure that's the case anymore."

"This meeting is routine."

"At this hour? Last time, you got home pretty damn late."

"I'll talk twice as fast." She kissed his cheek. "Don't wait up for me."

He met her eye. "Take it easy tonight, huh?"

Rita nodded. "Always."

Out in the driveway, snow had already covered the fresh tracks she'd made only a few hours earlier. She cleared the accumulated drifts on the windshield and hood, then slid into the BMW, taking a moment to adjust the dashboard settings.

She pulled out of the driveway, bumping over the

rutted rural road before merging onto the freeway, heading north. Snowflakes swirled in the headlights, but she kept her focus on the center line.

She passed a handful of scattered ranches, their fences vanishing into the darkness, the distant glow of house windows flickering like stars. Visitors to Wyoming often called the high prairie lonely, but Rita had never felt that way. Out here, she could breathe.

Unwind.

What the hell had she been thinking, moving to New York?

She shook off the thought, gripping the wheel. Why was regret about running away from Cash welling up *now*?

It had to be the baby brain. People always talked about it. Pregnancy was making her soft in the head. And the heart. A tear slipped down her cheek, and she swiped it away.

This was definitely not the time to cry.

Taking a sharp right, she pulled off the freeway onto a rural road. The tires chewed over the gravel, vibrating her uterus.

"Hang on, baby," she said, taking one hand off the wheel to pat her stomach. "We're almost there."

An old barn loomed out of the snowfall, its corrugated metal siding streaked with rusted orange. Rita rolled through the gaping doorway and parked inside. Broken machinery pitted by rust leaned against the back wall.

She got out, the scent of aged metal and dry hay catching in her throat still feel emotional as hell.

She rubbed her hands together for warmth and took a seat on a dry straw bale arranged in a rough circle. Snowflakes drifted through a hole in the roof, melting on her parka.

In the distance an engine rumbled. Rita turned as

headlights slashed through the darkness. Jason's Kia pulled in. He parked, and a moment later, the passenger door opened.

Mary Lou climbed out.

Rita's stomach tightened. Her gaze snapped to Jason. "What the hell is she doing here?"

Jason sighed, his face tight with frustration. "I couldn't stop her."

Mary Lou straightened, her beehive as rigid as her spine. "That's right," she said. "I made him bring me."

Rita folded her arms. "Why?"

Mary Lou huffed, her breath misting. "Because I knew something's going on between the two of you." She shot Jason a look before turning her gaze back to Rita. "You're a pair of rotten liars."

Jason wiped a sheen of sweat from his forehead. "Mary Lou's right, I'm a terrible actor. I don't like lying."

"No one's got integrity like you, Jason," Rita said. She gave him a quick hug. "You doing okay?"

Jason frowned. "Not really. I found some things moved around at my place. Asked Lucas, but he said it wasn't him. Have you been by lately?"

Rita shook her head. "No."

"Changed the door code again," he said, "hoping to narrow the suspects. But someone seems to know another way to get in."

Headlights cut through the dim barn as a black Ford F-150 rolled in and came to a stop. The door swung open, and District Attorney Hunter Green stepped out.

Hunter spotted Mary Lou and scowled. "Why the fuck is she here?"

Mary Lou folded her arms. "I want to know what the hell is going on."

Hunter shot a look at Rita.

"We didn't invite her," Rita said. "But Mary Lou practically knows everything anyway."

Blowing on his hands for warmth, Jason said, "Yep."

Hunter stood firm, shoulders squared and hands in his pockets, as though the cold didn't touch him. After a long pause, he muttered, "I suppose it's better she knows than blunders and reveals it."

Mary Lou's eyebrows knit together. "Why does everyone keep talking about me in the third person when I'm standing right here?" Her eyes narrowed at the DA. "And it's not my style to blunder."

Hunter sighed. "All right, you can stay." He dropped onto a straw bale, resting his elbows on his bent knees. "We're looking into Title Six allegations against the governor."

Eyes bright, Mary Lou sat on a bale beside Jason. "Bribery?"

Hunter nodded. "There's been some suggestion that the governor owned the land APEX is built on. If that's true, there's a conflict. He could have had a direct financial interest in the real estate deal."

"Well, that I didn't know," Mary Lou said. "I always thought it was one of those parcels no one officially claimed, people were squatting, hunting, running cattle on it."

"The original paperwork is missing from the land titles office." Hunter spread his hands. "Hence the suspicious circumstances of the deal."

"All we've found is the corporation number from the 1970s," Jason said.

Mary Lou turned to Rita, her gaze sharp. "So that's what you're doing at APEX, digging into dirt on the governor?"

Rita nodded, then glanced at Hunter. "I've got nothing

to report tonight, other than I don't think Teddy Lake's death has anything to do with APEX."

"Except some concerned citizens are hell-bent on making a connection," Hunter said with a scowl. "Thanks to the splashy front page of the *Chronicle*."

Rita straightened. "Leaks aren't coming from my office."

Hunter made a sound in his throat. "SCSO isn't your office anymore."

Jason shifted on the hay bale, his gaze darting between them. "This is just temporary, isn't it?"

Rita flicked a glance at him before looking back at Hunter. "How much longer do you want me there?"

Hunter exhaled through his nose, considering. "I don't want to pull you out before the election. We need to give it more time."

It wasn't the answer Rita was hoping for, but she kept her mouth shut and nodded. Jason mirrored her reaction, his jaw tense.

"Keep me informed," Hunter said. "And we'll meet again in two weeks."

He got up, crossed the barn in long strides, and climbed back into his Ford. The engine echoed through the barn, then the truck rolled out and vanishing into a swirl of hot exhaust.

Rita coughed. "Well, that's that."

"Well, Jesus," Mary Lou said, throwing up her hands, "why the hell did you think I couldn't handle that information?"

"I had to keep the circle as small as possible," Rita said, getting up from the hay bale. "Angela's smart. If I didn't make it look like I left the SCSO for personal reasons, she'd sniff out the real one in a heartbeat."

A touch of color crept into Jason's cheeks. "Which is why Rita and I were always 'at odds.'"

"You mean, why you put up with Rita being an absolute ass," Mary Lou said drily.

"Aren't you funny?" Rita said, her voice equally dry. "We're only pretending we're mad at each other." She slapped Jason on the back and he coughed. "Old pals, like always."

Jason recovered his breath. "I'm damn happy to hear you're not actually mad at me. 'Cause it sure feels like you are."

Forcing a smile, Rita shrugged. "Well, I'm kind of annoyed about Deputy Watkins."

Jason frowned. "Why?"

"I think the station needs more experience."

Jason bristled. "What you're actually saying is I'm not experienced enough to mentor her. Which is a really a shitty thing to say about me, not her."

"You're right," Rita said. "I'm sorry." She rolled her shoulders against the cold. "I'm bitter being at APEX, in case you couldn't tell. Deputy Dillard requires a lot of supervision. My boots squeak and my office chair sucks and the sofa is useless. The snack cart's okay, even though it's no replacement for your lemonade, Mary Lou." She kicked at the loose straws of straw on the ground. "At least I like the Beemer."

"My point exactly," Jason said, glowering. "Here I am finding my feet as Sheriff and training a rookie, while you're kicking back."

"Hold up," Mary Lou said, stepping between them. "Is this gonna be another go-around about the helicopter ride to the Faculty Club? 'Cause if you two are gonna go sideways, I ain't goin' along with y'all."

"Thanks, Elvis," Rita said, rolling her eyes. "Initially,

we tried to involve you. But Hunter wanted to keep things locked down. He knew Angela would sniff out the truth unless I made a big enough scene about leaving the SCSO. Which is why I went out of my way to brag about my fancy-pants interview with Angela."

Mary Lou grinned. "Helicopter, my ass. I thought that was a bunch of bullshit."

"Actually, the helicopter was real," Rita said. "And the pay raise. I negotiated that salary, you know."

Mary Lou chewed on her thoughts for a moment. "For the record, I don't much like secrets, neither. Especially the ones about your childhood, Rita."

Rita blinked. "How do you mean?"

"I wasn't meaning to hold back on you, all those years," Mary Lou said, snowflakes catching in her silver hair. "I just...I wanted to protect you from the painful truth." She pulled Rita into a firm hug. "I'm real sorry."

The gathering flakes on her jacket melted against Rita's cheek as she stayed locked in Mary Lou's embrace. She glanced back at Jason, who looked as relieved as she felt.

"Thank God that secret's out," Rita said. "Keeping secrets is the only thing I hate more than guessing."

Chapter Twenty-Seven

RITA'S PHONE VIBRATED, yanking her from sleep. She reached out in the dark, knocking the lamp. Her phone hit the floor with a clatter.

"Shit."

Cash bolted upright. "What's happening?"

"I can't find the moving box," Rita muttered.

"That's because there's a bedside table instead," Cash said, his voice gravelly. "What time is it?"

"Twelve-fifteen," Rita said, detangling herself from the covers. "You can go back to sleep."

Her phone buzzed again, alerting her to its position on the floor. Flipping it over, she swiped open the screen. Mary Lou.

Rita answered. "Everything okay?"

"Jason needs you," Mary Lou said, then rattled off an address in one of Still's older neighborhoods, a few blocks behind Main Street.

"I'll be there in ten."

Mary Lou clucked her tongue. "Lord knows why you two moved so far out of town."

"I'll press the pedal to the metal," Rita said. "Be there in seven."

With another disapproving *tsk*, Mary Lou hung up.

Rita tossed her phone onto the bed and ducked into the closet. She yanked on a sports bra and a pair of APEX-issued sweats, then slapped on a ball cap, threading her hair through the snapback opening. Then she grabbed her gun and ID and stepped out of the closet.

Snatched up her phone, she pressed a quick kiss to Cash's forehead and hurried downstairs. Coat, boots, keys. Ten seconds later, she was out the door.

She took the rural roads fast, tires humming over the frost-crusted pavement. She traveled quickly through the darkened streets, not a single other vehicle in sight as she weaved through the empty streets.

The address came into view. It was a sturdy white bungalow with charcoal shingles and matching painted shutters, its facade illuminated by the headlights of two SCSO vehicles in the driveway. A dusting of fresh snow covered the roof and porch, while more flakes drifted through the beams of light, vanishing into the tangle of shadows cast by the shrubs in the front yard.

A woman's scream tore through the cold air.

Rita got out of the crossover and scanned the yard, a sharp wind nipping her neck. What she'd first thought was a cluster of shrubs was actually a person curled on the frozen ground, held tightly in Jason's arms. Ten feet beyond them, a uniformed deputy bent at the waist. It was Watkins, retching into the snow.

Jason looked up and met Rita's eye. She jerked her head toward the open front door and he gave her a tight nod.

Rita flicked on her flashlight and drew her gun, advancing toward the house with measured paces. The front door stood open, the soft glow of a lamp lighting the foyer.

She stepped carefully, the cracked concrete pathway slippery with frost and lined with overwintering plants, their bare, brittle stalks poking her calves as she passed.

She stepped onto the front porch and a sharp, chemical sting filling her nose. Bleach, thick and overwhelming. And beneath it, the scent of something fouler.

Blood. The liquid glistened across the tiled foyer floor, a slick expanse of blood creeping towards the lip of the door.

Her gaze swept the entrance area for footprints or fingerprints. The front door jamb and handle were wiped clean, and no tracks led in or out. A mop and bucket propped against the doorframe suggested the killer had taken the time to erase any evidence of their presence.

She leaned forward and sniffed the mop water. The pungent whiff of bleach burned the back of her throat.

Steeling herself, Rita stepped inside, her breath slow and steady. Opposite the living room archway entrance, arterial spray streaked the wall in chaotic arcs, dripping onto the baseboard and pooling along the hallway. A single lamp burned in the living room, casting a dappled glow on the blood-slick floor.

Whoever had done this would have been covered in blood and would be taking a long hot shower. If they weren't still on the premises.

Announcing herself with weapon raised, Rita rounded the archway and froze.

A man sat slumped on the couch. But something was wrong with his head—aside from the acute depression, and bloody bone fragments matting his hair. The skull was positioned at an impossible angle, displaying the partial tattoo of a knife.

It was Teddy Lake's head.

And across the body's bare chest, a pentagram had been carved deep into the flesh, the letter *M* gouged at its center.

Rita swallowed hard, pushing back bile. "Fuck."

Blood had soaked into the couch's fabric, staining the cushions and drizzling onto the area-rug, where it spread like blooming poppies. A TV remote lay soaking in the puddle.

The living room walls, including a series of framed watercolor landscapes, bore more erratic sprays of blood, while the coffee table (and beers) were lightly misted. Blood also spotted the lamp shade with a grotesque constellation, casting leopard spots of light around the room.

She cleared the house room by room, the scent of bleach and blood lingering throughout the bedrooms, full bath and ensuite, dining room, and kitchen. The hum of the refrigerator lent an eerie sense of normalcy, as though life ought to be carrying on within the house.

But the kitchen, like the other rooms, was empty aside from an aquarium of tropical fish, oblivious to the nearby carnage as they glided through the softly bubbling water. She cleared the laundry room, then returned to the hallway.

There was no sign of the man's missing head.

Wiping sweat from her own forehead, Rita re-entered the living room, taking in the details she had missed in the initial shock.

On the coffee table, two glass beer bottles sat side by side. One was half-empty, the other untouched. A wrench-shaped bottle opener lay beside them. A fine red mist coated everything.

Whoever had done this had been comfortable enough with the killer to offer a drink.

Rita stepped carefully around the blood and moved back outside. The woman on the lawn was now in Candace's arms, trembling, while Jason stood a few yards away, phone pressed to his ear. Rita waited until he hung up before closing the distance.

"Forensics?" she asked.

He slipped his phone into his jacket. "They're on their way."

"You got an ID on him?"

Jason nodded. "Donald Horgan."

"The mechanic at the Gas-N-Go," Rita said.

He nodded again.

"I had a meeting scheduled with him tomorrow." She glanced at her watch. "Or rather…this morning."

Chapter Twenty-Eight

"From what we can tell, the killer entered only the living room and the kitchen, specifically the broom closet," Tilda said. She and Rita stood near the open kitchen window, where the crisp scent of fresh snow drifted in.

"Aside from the mop and pail, is anything else out of place?" she asked.

Tilda shook her head. "Don't think so, although we'll need the victim's spouse to confirm that. The killer even put the empty bleach bottle back in the cupboard, like a good houseguest."

Footsteps sounded in the hallway outside the kitchen, then Dylan Bruce poked his head into the kitchen.

"On my way now," he said. "We've got Horgan's body and Lake's head packed up to go."

"Given the presence of Teddy Lake's body parts at both crime scenes," Rita said, "I'll presume we're dealing with the same killer. And not a copycat who chanced upon Teddy's head."

"Almost certain," Bruce said. "The blade patterns look

identical to me on first glance, but even more so the directional cuts in the pentagram. On Teddy's body, the star began on the bottom left, traveling to the top, with the knife turning and cutting downwards for the right-hand spoke before crossing back up to the left pectoral muscle. This pentagram follows the exact same directional flow." He flashed her a smile. "It'll all be in my report."

"Thanks," Rita said as Bruce disappeared down the hallway. Then she thanked Tilda and returned outside.

At the foot of the driveway, Jason stood talking with Deputy Watkins. She nodded fervently as she listened. Then Jason spotted Rita. Excusing himself, he turned and approached.

"What a scene," he said, blowing out a breath.

"Yeah," Rita said, matching his sigh. "And as incomplete as my scene out at APEX, given Don's missing head."

Jason ran his hands through his clipped hair. "This scene screams 'serial killer.' Is this some kind of twisted pay-the-head-forward game? Are we gonna find another body wearing Donald Horgan's head next? Maybe it'll turn up on a stag's body."

Rita scoffed grimly. "I wonder if Carly has an oracle deck that can answer these questions."

Jason gave her a look. "Huh?"

"Never mind." She crinkled her nose. "Only wishful thinking."

"Wishes," Jason said, his voice hollow. "If only those were a part of this profession. Earlier you said you planned to meet Horgan this morning?"

She nodded. "He was one of the witnesses who saw Teddy Lake at The Shaft."

"Maybe Don figured out Teddy was the thief," Jason said. "Maybe he caught him at the garage, caught him in the act. Maybe the angle grinder wasn't the only thing stolen. Maybe it was an accident, or——"

"But then who killed Donald?" Rita cut in.

Jason exhaled hard, rubbing a hand over his face. "Right. Fuck. I'm tired."

"Me too," Rita said. She gripped his shoulder. "But you're doing great. Need a hand with anything?"

Jason shook his head. "Think I got it covered, thanks. Watkins is doing great, too."

"First murder victim?"

He gave a sober nod.

Rita matched it. "Wish I had some saltines to offer. They really helped Craig the other night."

"You still feeling rocky?" Jason asked.

"Nah. Just hungry all the time, is all. Crackers became a habit."

"There are worse habits to pick up."

"Like wishful thinking," Rita said. "You know where wishing leads."

Jason winked. "To Neverland?"

Rita grimaced. "It leads to guessing."

Jason rocked on his heels. "Damn slippery slope."

Rita laughed. "If you've got everything covered, I'm heading to Casper Hospital to talk with Donald's wife. Let's touch base later and compare notes. It's obvious now our crime scenes are linked, seeing as I've got Teddy's body on my plate and you've got his head on yours."

This time Jason laughed. "You sound like Henry the Eighth."

"Then I'd better drop the act," Rita said, "since Mary Lou won't allow any other monarchs in the station."

She gave him a wave and crossed the street toward her crossover. Just as she reached for the door, something made her pause. A familiar vehicle.

"No shit," she muttered, striding forward.

Footsteps pounded behind her. She glanced back. Jason was jogging to catch up.

"Don't tell me…" he said.

"Yep," Rita confirmed. "It's Blaze."

Jason's fists clenched. "Well, I sure as hell didn't tell him." He strode past Rita. "Go on, get out of here!"

Blaze lowered his camera but didn't move. His dark hair was neatly combed despite the early hour, although a shadow of stubble crept along his jaw.

"I'm not going anywhere," he shot back. The cold had reddened his nose and cheeks, while Jason's complexion burned with fury. "You can throw me out of your life, you can throw me out of your shitty-ass trailer, but you can't throw me out of this public neighborhood. Besides, I won't be the only one out here with a camera soon." He gestured toward the cars lining both sides of the street. "Neighbors are gonna wake up in minutes, and they'll be posting pictures from their phones."

Jason stepped forward, hands fisted. "This may be a public street, Blaze, but listening in on the scanner—"

"Hold up," Rita said, pressing a hand to Jason's shoulder. "Take it easy, Sheriff. I'll handle him. You've got a hundred things to get back to. Or at least Watkins to check on."

Jason let out a growl, then turned on his heel and stalked off.

Rita snapped her gaze back to Blaze. "If you want to keep having a working relationship with me," she said through clenched teeth, "your car better be gone by the time Jason hands off this scene and gets in his."

Blaze held her stare for a moment, then flicked his eyes back to the crime scene. He raised his camera again.

"Then I guess I'd better hurry up and finish. Do you mind stepping to the left? You're in my shot."

Rita grunted and strode back to her crossover.

In a nearby window, a curtain twitched. Blaze was right, dawn was breaking, and soon, the neighborhood would be awake. It wouldn't take a front-page story for word to get around Still County.

Chapter Twenty-Nine

"I'M SORRY, Lana Horgan is sleeping right now," the nurse at the receiving desk said, her words polite, though her voice carried the weight of exhaustion. "We've given her sedation, so we're not expecting her to wake up just yet."

At the mention of sleep, fatigue pulled at Rita's eyelids. She glanced at the clock above the nurse's desk, framed by a grid of whiteboards filled with shift schedules.

She rubbed a hand over her face. "You got a spare bed?"

The nurse paused, considering, then cocked her head. "Help yourself to what you can find in the hall."

Rita stepped away from the U-shaped desk and turned the corner, following the sterile hum of overhead lights down the hallway. The place was alive with motion: nurses moving between rooms, doctors huddled over charts, and patients being wheeled past on gurneys. A gurney wrapped in blue hospital sheets sat unused tucked to the side of the bustling corridor. Rita kicked off her boots and lay down.

She rested her hands across her belly and took several

deep breaths until the buzz of hospital activity dimmed in the background.

But just as her eyes fluttered closed, the soft shuffle of footsteps nudged her awake.

"Your witness is awake now," the nurse said, her voice carrying the same calm urgency as before. "Room 219."

Rita groaned softly, rubbing her eyes as she sat up. "That didn't take long."

The nurse glanced at her wristwatch, a crease forming between her brows. "You've been sleeping for two hours, Sheriff, I mean, Ms. Jonas."

"Right," Rita said, adjusting the flattened bun at the back of her head. "Where's the bathroom?"

The nurse smiled and pointed down the hall before heading back toward reception.

With a sigh, Rita slid off the gurney, her boots squeaking across the vinyl floor as she made her way to the bathroom.

She washed her hands and splashed cold water on her face. Then she dried her hands and checked for messages, before stepping out. She opened the latest text from Cash.

Everything going OK?

Rita typed back: *Interviewing witness, at Casper Hospital now. APEX HQ next.*

She stared at the screen for a moment, awaiting Cash's response:

But you left in the middle of the night.

Rita smiled and replied: *Had a long nap in a busy hallway. May have drooled on the pillowcase.*

He responded with a laughing emoji and then: *See you later. Tacos tonight.*

Rita's smile faded as she typed: *Day 1 of a homicide investigation. Don't count on me.*

Cash didn't respond with an emoji this time. Instead,

he gave the message a thumbs-up. Rita stared at the screen, wishing he'd sent a heart instead.

Biting her lip, she silenced her phone and shoved it back in her pocket. She'd do well to let go of any more wishful thinking.

Rita left the bathroom and rode the elevator to the second floor. She entered Room 219, where Lana Horgan sat propped up in bed, her head resting against thin blue pillows as she gazed out the window.

As Rita approached, Lana turned her head, swiping at her eyes, red as fire, grief burning through her.

"Hello, Lana," Rita said softly, stepping closer to the bed. "I'm—"

"I know who you are, Sheriff Jonas," Lana her voice cracking. "Tell me what's happening. Who did this to Don? Oh, God…"

"I'm working on it," she said. "With Sheriff Perry at the SCSO. I work at APEX now. We're all working together to find answers."

Lana nodded, wild-eyed.

"Do you feel up to telling me about what happened?" Rita asked.

Lana nodded. Then wept.

Rita sat in the visitor's chair by the bed, drawing closer while allowing time for Lana's tears to fall.

Several minutes later, Lana's sobs subsided. Her ragged breath filled the room, the air laden with a pain that had nowhere else to go.

"I appreciate you taking the time to talk with me," Rita said, her voice gentle. "I know it's not easy." She pulled out her notebook and phone. "I'm going to record this, okay?"

Lana nodded, her eyes hollow. "I don't understand who would do this." Her voice was thick with disbelief. "He's such a nice guy. He's got lots of friends. He doesn't even gossip. He wasn't involved in anything crazy. Helps out a lot of people. He's a real good mechanic, you know. Always does a good job at the garage, even though he doesn't like how Chester can be a creep. At least the guy pays his employees well. Knows he's dependent on them, that's why." She scoffed, and her throat cracked with a sob. "I'm dependent on Don, too." Her shoulders shook and she hugged herself. "I don't mean financially. I work, too. But I mean the other way. He's my everything, you know?"

Rita got up and fetched a fresh blanket from the closet. "I'm going to put this around your shoulders, okay, Lana?" she said, returning to the bedside.

Lana nodded as Rita draped the blanket around her shoulders.

"Do you have family in town?" Rita asked.

"Don's mom's here in Still. She's got Parkinson's so she lives up at Heritage Park. But his dad's passed and his sister works on cruise ships. She's based in L.A. when she's not at sea."

"And what about yours?" Rita asked, filling a plastic cup from a two-liter bottle of water on the bedside table. She passed it to Lana.

"My folks live up in Michigan," she said, taking the cup. "I met Don when we were both in a wedding party." She sipped some water, then grimaced as though it were painful to swallow, and set aside the cup. "Moved to Wyoming for him, been together twenty-nine years."

"Do you have children?" Rita asked.

She blew here nose into a tissue. "Having a family wasn't in God's plans. So we do lots around the church, you know, helping with service and such. And of course he loves anything to do with cars."

"And what about you?" Rita asked. "What do you like to do?"

"Bookkeeping. I help out Chester a bit, preparing paperwork which he can take to his accountant. I'm also treasurer on church council, do the books for the preschool that rents the basement."

"And how about off-hours?" Rita asked. "When Don's watching car races?"

"At this time of year, I pour a bath and read romance novels." The corners of Lana's lips lifted slightly. "In the summers I drive around collecting old furniture, mostly at flea markets, then paint and resell it at The Vintage Barn in Beaumont."

"A good reason for you both to drive pickups," Rita said.

Lana's smiled faded. "Don always kept me in nice trucks."

Rita paused to moisten her lips. "Can you tell me what happened last night?"

Lana nodded. Collecting herself, she blew her nose again. "I was out."

"What time was that?"

"I left the house just before eight."

"Where did you go?"

Lana shifted in the bed, avoiding Rita's eye. "It's kind of private. But in the circumstances, I suppose Carly won't mind if I say." She returned her gaze to Rita's. "I was at a Moon Meetup."

"I've seen the posters," Rita said. "What did you do there?"

The blush returned to her cheeks. "Oh, we do astrology readings and things like that." She gave a shaky laugh. "Some folks say it's woo-woo."

"Did anything unusual happen at the meeting?" Rita asked.

Lana's flush deepened. "Nope. It was real nice. It's a bit

of a social time, too, you know? Last night, someone brought seven-layer dip." She started to weep again. "It was delish."

"Who attended?" Rita asked.

Lana hesitated. "Do I have to say?"

"Yes, please, for the sake of the investigation," Rita said.

Lana nodded and picked up her phone, the pink color draining from her cheeks. Her thumbs moved with surprising swiftness, given the trembles that still wracked her limbs.

Then she passed the phone to Rita. "This is the group in my Contacts. Everyone's there." Her gaze flickered away. "I never thought I would do this. We all swore to secrecy."

Rita looked at the screen of Lana's phone, which showed a list of names and numbers, including Carly's. There were eight names in total. Rita took a photo with her own phone to later cross-reference with Carly's list, then passed back the phone back to Lana.

"Thank you," Rita said. "Could you please explain the secrecy? I understand metaphysical activities go on at these meetups. But what else attracts members to this group? Are there any Satanic leanings?"

Lana laughed, then seemed shocked by the sound and took a sip of water. "I know why you asked that, Sheriff," she said, pulling the blanket tighter. "It's 'cause of what… what happened to Don. To his chest." She gagged. "That horrible star…"

She broke off, sobbing, the blanket slipping from her shoulders. A moment later she calmed again, and Rita pulled up the blanket again.

"I'm sorry to ask these questions," Rita said. "I wish

there was a way to find out more without you having to relive what you witnessed.”

“Witness,” Lana said, her voice hollow. “These women you’re asking me about … it’s not because we’re Satanists. They’re my witnesses, aren’t they? My alibi. I wouldn’t harm Don, if that’s what you’re asking.”

“I’m following every thread of a question,” Rita said.

Lana nodded, chewing on her lip and picking the hospital blanket. “It’s a group for survivors.”

“As in cancer survivors?”

Lana’s fingers released the blanket. “For survivors of domestic abuse.”

“I see,” Rita said after a pause. No wonder Carly had looked so nervous the other day, concealing the true intention of the meetup.

“Not that Don ever laid a hand on me,” Lana added, her words hurried. “I was one of the volunteers that helped Carly support the attendees.”

“What was your role as a volunteer?” Rita asked.

“Bookkeeping,” she said.

“There’s a need to track expenses?”

Lana nodded. “Sometimes we pay for hotel rooms, if someone needs to get away for a night. Once we paid for a martial arts trainer from Casper to come in teach us some self-defense moves.”

“What do the other volunteers do?” Rita asked.

“Amanda’s real good with health and nutrition, so she organizes to-go bags with non-perishables and always brings a good meal to the meetup. And I know Carly’s hoping to have a lawyer join us too sometime. Of course, Carly’s the one who pitches in the most. She’s real generous with her time and energy, that’s for sure. That woman’s on a mission.”

Rita felt for the piece of jade, in her uniform pocket,

reassuringly solid and cool to the touch. "What time did the meetup end last night?"

She thought for a moment. "I think we'd all cleared out of there by ten or ten-thirty."

"Is that typical?" Rita asked.

"We meet Mondays because it's real easy for people to remember. You know, Monday, Moon-day?"

"Carly said there's a regular meeting on Friday."

Lan's fingers plucked the blankets. "We meet different nights of the week."

"I was also referring to how late it runs," Rita said. "Is ten-thirty normal?"

Lana nodded. "Carly tried to end meetings at nine-thirty. But it always runs overtime."

"But you didn't find Don until midnight," Rita said.

At his name, Lana's breath quickened. "After the meeting, I drove one of the women into the Casper Women's Halfway House. That's another way I volunteer. If anyone needs a ride, I'm available at any time. One of the perks of being married to Don is he's always got me the best set of wheels he can give me. It was snowing, and I got top-of-the-line tires. I didn't have to be up early today and I knew Don"—her voice tightened—"would still be wrapped up in the race. So I was happy to take her. But if…"

"Yes?"

"If I had come home earlier, well, I would've been able to help."

Her voice shattered and she collapsed into tears again. Rita leaned forward to refill the cup of water. When she had recovered her breath, Lana took a sip.

"Was Donald expecting any company last night?" Rita asked.

Lana shook her head. "Not that I knew. Sometimes he had buddies over to watch the race with him. But being a weeknight, he planned to have an easy night at home, light on the beer."

Rita shifted in the vinyl chair, wondering if Lana had noticed the beers on the table when she'd discovered her husband.

"How long has the group been running?" she asked.

"Carly started it a couple months ago. At first it was just word of mouth and real quiet, but then folks started asking about it. We figured it'd be less suspicious if we posted about it all around town. Then the men folk would just think we're getting together to read the Tarot cards and talk crystals. You know some women wear them in—" She gestured to her groin. "You know."

"I didn't know that," Rita said, "but that doesn't surprise me about Carly. Did you know Don had plans to speak with me this morning at the garage?"

Lana nodded. "Yeah. He wanted to talk to you about the fellow that was on the front page of the paper. Teddy something. I remember 'Teddy' 'cause it's cute."

Rita took out the photo of the mugshot of Teddy Lake. She showed it to her. "This man?"

Lana nodded. "Yep, that's him. Donald says he met him at The Shaft. Chester likes to take out the mechanics for end-of-the-week drinks on Thursday 'cause it's cheaper than Friday."

"TGIT," Rita said. "What else did Don tell you?"

Lana thought for a moment. "Nothing, really. He told me Teddy Lake was drunk as a skunk. Blathering even louder than Chester, apparently. Don also said one of the gas jockeys was with them—Jesse, I think."

"Was that unusual?" Rita asked.

"Don suspected he's underage. But Jesse needed a ride that night. His dirt bike probably broke down again. Don often fixes it so he can get around town. It's hard for

Chester to get kids to work for him, 'cause he's pretty far out of town."

"Did Don mention what Teddy was talking about?"

Lana shook her head. "Something about his father being a cop. Some kind of legacy he left. Don said the guy wasn't very coherent. But he wanted to answer the information request. He'd told Jerry and Chester, and Jesse, I suppose, to call the hot-line, too."

"Thank you," Rita said, turning off the voice recorder. "I'll let you get back to sleep."

"No." Lana said with haste. "I mean, I'm tired, but …" She let out a shaky breath. "How am I supposed to ever sleep again?" Her hands trembled as she pressed them over her face. "Every time I close my eyes, I see Don. On the back of my eyelids, it's there. What happened to him…or what was left of him. Oh, God…"

Rita rested a hand on Lana's shoulder. "I know," she said. "Images like that don't fade easily." A beat of silence passed. "I still see mine."

Lana swallowed hard, her breath hitching.

"Victim services will come by," Rita continued, her voice tender. "They'll help you through this. None us have to do anything alone."

Chapter Thirty

Rita stepped out of the elevator as Ginny came around the corner with her snack cart.

"Good afternoon, Ms. Jonas," she said brightly. "I just finished my rounds, but seeing as you're back, I have your monthly tab here."

"Thanks," Rita said. Reading the tally, her eyes widened. "How's it possible I ate this much in one month? They're just snacks."

Ginny gave her an encouraging smile. "It's because you're in the second trimester," she said. "My cousin ate like a bison."

Rita grimaced. "Is that a lot of salad?" She pulled out her phone and sent an e-transfer to Ginny. "Paid," she said, then dug through the cart, selecting a banana, packet of salted peanuts, and a chocolate bar. "Start me a new tab, please?"

Ginny recorded Rita's selection, then rolled out with a wave.

Rita opened and bit into the chocolate bar as she crossed to the mini sink. She filled the electric kettle and turned it on. She threw out the wrapper, then she sat at her desk. Tearing into the packet of nuts, she ate them by the handful while checking her email inbox.

Skipping past Hunter's, she opened one from the manager at Casper Sport.

The manager introduced herself as Shelley Rodgers, then went on to explain that an update in their inventory system ten months ago had reset all sales information at that time. She could track transaction amounts but not the specific barcode.

She also explained that they hadn't put any more rope on the floor, and their inventory records showed that no new stock of that rope had been placed on the floor during the past few months. Customers didn't typically buy rope for outdoor climbing in those lengths during the winter months, and it was not unusual for the stock not to move until after the snow melt.

Rita replied, acknowledging receipt of the information and thanking the manager. The kettle turned off with a click. She got up, selected an herbal teabag (ginger peach), and filled a mug with boiling water.

A knock on the door drew her attention. She turned to see Craig standing on the other side of the glass, his expression expectant. She waved him in.

Craig entered and sank onto the sofa, eyes bright with excitement. "Heard about the murder last night. I was listening to the scanner."

"We found Teddy's head," Rita said, lowering herself into her chair.

Craig nodded. "I heard it was…"

"Placed on the beheaded body of Donald Horgan? Yep."

Craig's face paled. "Did the…how did…"

"If you're asking about head trauma, it appears that

yes, Teddy died from being struck by a series of heavy blows."

He licked his lips. "And was it…"

"Disturbing?" Rita nodded. "Every bit as what we saw out here at APEX." She blew out a breath. "Only in a different way. A lot more blood in an enclosed space. And the head was arranged kind of…" She hesitated, lifting her hands in an attempt to demonstrate. "Basically sideways."

Craig let out a strained belch. "Jesus fuck."

"In time, you get used to these kinds of things," Rita said, sipping her tea. She squeezed her eyes shut and reopened them, pushing away the image of Donald Horgan's living room. "Sort of."

She raised her mug. "Want some? Ginger's a charm for settling the stomach." She picked up the banana. "Or some banana? Also great at soaking up stomach acid. Turns out, there are quite a few similarities between treating morning sickness and typical nausea." She waved the banana at Craig. "You know what I recently learned?"

Craig leaned forward, resting his elbows on his knees. "No, what?"

She pointed to the bottom of the banana. "I always thought this was the ass end." She shrugged. "Growing up, that's what my dad called it. But it's actually the top." She rotated it so the stem pointed downward. "I always thought the stem indicated the upright position. But actually, this is the correct way. Bananas grow upward in clusters." With her other hand, she mimicked the shape of a bunch, fingers curled. "And that means the banana is meant to be opened from this end."

Craig squinted at it. "Really?"

Rita nodded. "I'll show you." She flicked open the tip with her thumbnail, peeled back a couple of inches, and bit off the end. "It's how monkeys open them. I'm telling you, you're never gonna open bananas the same way again."

Craig stared at her for a moment in silence. Then he said, "So it sounds like we're dealing with a serial killer."

Rita grimaced. "Or reciprocal killers, trading out body parts at one another's crime scenes."

Craig blinked at her. "Huh?"

She tossed the banana peel in the trash can under her desk. "Anyone else call the tip line?"

"Several folks phoned in, saying they saw Teddy Lake at The Shaft. Seems like half the town knows about his tear over at Ruby Joe's. Though no one interacted with him much, aside from telling him to move along."

"Anyone mention what he was chattering about?"

"Yeah, he was going on about his dad, the ex-cop. He recently died. Some witnesses seemed to think Teddy was struggling with the grief of that."

Rita's phone vibrated.

"Excuse me," she said, pulling it out and checking. It was Jason. "Gotta take this, it's Sheriff Perry."

"I'll catch you later," Craig said, stepping out and pulling the glass door behind him.

"Autopsy's tomorrow," Jason said. "You want to take it?"

"Course not," Rita said. "It's your jurisdiction."

"Thanks," he said, a smile in his voice. "Although it's your victim's head."

"But it's all yours from the neck down," Rita said. "I look forward to hearing about it."

She hung up and then headed for the bathroom. After she washed her hands, she studied her reflection in the mirror. Her bun had slipped again, looking as slept on as it had several hours ago. Puffy bags hung beneath her eyes, and she was pretty sure her breath could stop even Chester in his tracks.

She exited the bathroom and rode the elevator downstairs. Passing by the conference room, she wrapped her knuckles on the door and poked her inside.

Craig looked up from his phone, his posture indicating he'd probably been surfing.

"I'm on my way to interview a witness," she said. "I'll talk to you later."

Craig sat forward, putting aside his phone. "Can I come along?"

Rita shook her head. "I need you available to answer the tip line."

"Nothing's come in for a while," he said. "And the paper's been out for hours."

"Then you can continue looking through the security footage of Jim," Rita said. "There's got to be something we just aren't seeing."

Craig grumbled and pulled up to the conference table, tapping the keyboard to wake up the computer.

Rita stepped out and headed for the parking lot. She got in the crossover and drove to Carly's Crystals and parked in the back lot. Again, like last time, she bypassed the front door. She walked up to the back door and knocked.

It was opened a moment later by a slight woman with angular cheekbones and a pointed nose. Her tight curls were close to her head, turning gray at the temples. "Oh, hi, Sheriff Jonas," she said. "Can I help you?"

"Hi, Sherri," Rita said, recognizing the woman from her dental office in Beaumont (and her name on the list Lana had shown her). "I came to talk to Carly."

"Come on in," Sherri said, stepping aside. Cardboard

boxes filled the narrow back office. "We were expecting someone else, but I'm sure she'll arrive shortly."

Rita followed the dental technician into the storefront, where Carly was arranging pillows on a circle of aluminum folding chairs. A woman with dark hair worn in long braids was tapping a hand drum, while several other women hummed a haunting melody. Scented candles released their trapped fragrances into the air.

"Rita," Carly said, turning abruptly. "I wasn't expecting you."

"Are you having a Moon Meetup?" Rita asked, scanning the women who had gathered.

Carly nodded, drawing Rita aside. "It's impromptu."

"Yes," Rita said. "I would think most people are at work at this time."

Carly worried her lip. "Word's gotten around about Don Horgan. We're getting together to plan a meal train for Lana. And Lord knows what we'll do about cleaning up her place."

"There are specialists who can help," Rita said. "All things in due course. She'll appreciate visitors at the hospital. She doesn't want to be alone at this time."

Carly nodded, earnest. "We'll go as soon as we can."

"I've got some questions for you first," Rita said.

Carly's fingers twitched. "Uh-huh?"

"Lana told me the ways you really help the attendees here."

Carly flushed. "Shit, Rita, I'm sorry for not telling you." She swallowed. "Next to you, it's the only domestic violence support here in Still."

"I get it," Rita said. "You're only trying to keep attendees safe." She glanced around at the circle of women settling into the folding chairs. "And I'm not here to interview your membership."

Carly let out a sigh. "I only want to support however I can. Don sounds like a real nice guy, so we were also shocked." She paused, shaking her head. "Some of these women who come by…they live in real danger. Like I used to. But not Lana. Her marriage was solid, you know? But now she and me are both widows. It's so strange how things work out, huh?"

"None of us can predict," Rita said. "That's the only predictable part of life. Can you think of any reason that Lana might be targeted?"

"Lana?" Carly thought for a moment. "Do you mean, if she'd driven home instead of into Casper … that the killer …" Trembling, she twisted her fingers together. "Someone *couldn't* have wanted to hurt Lana. Maybe me—maybe there's trouble related to drugs? To Jeff's past? God only knows all the rackets he was caught up in, and he hasn't been dead all that long. I'm sure there're guys out there still wanting to cash in on what Jeff owed."

"I have no suspicions about drugs," Rita said. "Teddy Lake's from out of town. But I'll send out some feelers around Beaumont."

Carly nodded. "I'll keep my ear to the ground, too." Then she laughed. "I always do, even though Jeff's gone. I don't think I'll ever stop paying attention, the way living with him taught me to."

"Fair enough," Rita said. "But there is the possibility someone wanted to target the group, if not Lana personally."

Carly shook her head slowly. "Of course, someone might want to take revenge on us if we supported someone in leaving. But Jeannie was the first. And that was only last night. That's where Lana was when it happened. Jeannie's husband couldn't have known to exact revenge."

"Have you ever had any other trouble with the members' relations?"

"No," Carly said. "If I did, I would have hired security, and I know the best guys in the biz. Although there was this one guy that showed up on our second meeting. Not that he was anything I couldn't handle."

"Oh?" Rita said. "Why did he come?"

"He just wanted to crash the party because he saw the posters. Thought it was some kind of yoni steam or something. Wasn't related to any of the members."

"Do you remember his name?" Rita asked.

Carly thought for a moment. "Brent? Brad?" she said. "Can't say I remember his last name. He showed up in the tightest-ass jeans I've ever seen, and his shirt unbuttoned to his navel. I don't think he meant us any harm. A bit of an exhibitionist, I think, hoping we'd want some kind of plaything for the night. Thought we were a bunch of witches." She laughed. "So we hammed it up. I swept up a trail behind him, while the ladies dragged him out to the parking lot. Then I sent him on his way with a potion."

Rita raised an eyebrow.

Carly crinkled hers. "Not really, of course. I gave him a rose-water spray and told him to mist it on his, well, let's just say he was convinced it was a love potion. I told him he could have it on the house, but if he crashed another meeting, I'd call Sheriff Perry."

"I'm glad you're staying wary," Rita said. "I'll let you get back to your meeting now."

"Thanks," Carly said, still wringing her hands. "But now I can't help but think if I'd taken Jeannie to Casper myself, Lana might have been home in time to help Don."

"We can't indulge in wishful thinking," Rita said, reaching into her pocket. She rubbed the jade stone. "It won't help us get anywhere."

Chapter Thirty-One

RITA RETURNED to her office at APEX, settled in at her desk, and pulled up the latest email from the medical examiner. Attached was the toxicology screening report. She clicked it open, scanning the results.

Minimal traces of cannabis. Blood alcohol level: 0.09.

"Well, that makes sense," she said to herself, getting up to turn on the electric kettle, "given the eyewitness reports from The Shaft."

As the water began to boil, she mulled over what Lana had told her. Doug mentioned that Teddy had been talking about an old case of his father's. She selected a chamomile tea bag, dropping it into a mug before pouring the steaming water over it. And Don had reported Teddy telling people his father was an ex-cop, either retired or decommissioned. Rita didn't recall hearing that before, but was there something to it? Could that be why Teddy had come back to Wyoming?

She tugged the tea bag free and flicked it into the trash. Lucas had pointed out how unusual it was for Teddy to take up a bedside vigil for his father, considering they weren't especially close. Rita blew on her tea and took a tentative sip. What was it Lucas had said? That their father had been reminiscing, telling Teddy old case stories? She wrapped her fingers around the mug, letting the heat seep into her palms. Had Teddy picked up on some long-buried detail? Some essential clue to a cold case?

But if that were the case, why come to Still? Casper PD was his father's old stomping ground.

Rita sat back down, setting aside her APEX-branded mug before reaching for the landline. She hit speed dial for Casper PD, then navigated to the records extension.

"I'm calling to request a list of files for Sergeant Theodore Lake," she said.

"Lake was with Casper PD for over ten years," the administrator replied. "That's a lot of files."

"I know," Rita said. "I'd settle for a list of file types—or anything that stands out as unusual."

The administrator hesitated. "What exactly are you looking for?"

"I'm not sure yet," she admitted. "Before he passed, he shared some of his work stories with his son, who is now also deceased. I appreciate whatever package you can put together for me."

Then she headed downstairs, her boot soles chirping a steady tempo against the tile. At the front desk, Craig leaned in close, chatting with Ginny. As Rita approached, Ginny caught sight of her and turned back to her computer.

Craig, on the other hand, wasn't so quick to retreat. He glanced over his shoulder, saw Rita, and grinned. But the moment he caught her expression, his smile faltered.

Rita folded her arms. "Decided to man the phones with Ginny instead of the hot line?"

Craig coughed. "Just needed to stretch my legs."

"And I just need you to review the security footage," Rita countered. "There's fresh feed every day." She flicked a glance at the clock on the wall. "You can stretch your legs at lunchtime. In the meanwhile, do your job. Or I'll have to discuss your performance with Angela. And Angela already has a hard time remembering your name. I'm not sure she'll come up with many reasons to argue for your retention."

Craig bit back whatever he might have considered saying and trudged off in the direction of the conference room.

"I'm sorry for distracting him," Ginny said softly, still focused on her computer screen.

Rita rolled her eyes. "You're not distracting him, he's just distractible. But you are humoring him." She reached across the reception desk, plucking a fresh-baked cookie from the snack tray. "And he doesn't need any more encouragement."

Ginny nodded, twirling a pen between her fingers. "Okay, Ms. Jonas." Then she gestured toward Rita's cookie. "Is that chocolate chip?"

"Macadamia nut," Rita said, mouth full.

While Ginny updated Rita's tab, Rita headed outside and drove to the Gas-N-Go. Several vehicles were parked around the gas station, probably Blaze Wright's as well. In a poignant tribute to the beloved mechanic, fake flowers from the dollar store, carefully crafted homemade ones, and store-bought bouquets lay against the garage door, their vibrant colors out-of-season against the fallen snow.

Across the mourning crowd, Rita spotted Chester, talking to a small group of men at the front door of the storefront. When he saw her, he broke away from them and strode towards her.

"Jesus Christ, Rita, what's happening around here?" he

asked, running his hands over his head. For once, he wasn't wearing a ball cap, and his hair stuck up on end. His eyes were swollen and red. "That woman cop came by earlier and told me everything and asked me a bunch of questions, fucked-up questions, if you know what I mean."

"I'm sorry for your loss," Rita said. "The town is clearly moved by Don's passing."

Chester bobbed his head. "He was a real good guy," he said, almost choking on his words. "He didn't deserve that shit that happened to him. You gotta find this guy."

"Sheriff Perry with the SCSO is leading the investigation into Donald's death," Rita said. "I came by to follow up about Teddy Lake. I need to talk to the witnesses who saw him at The Shaft." Rita pointed into the crowd, where Jesse was waving people off to the side so a Camry could pull into one of the gas bays. "You mentioned Jesse was with you."

Chester nodded. "Yeah, the kid's as shocked as the rest of us."

"Take care, Chester," Rita said, moving towards the gas bays. She approached Jesse, his face tense with shock, and his long hair pulled back in a messy ponytail.

"Can I ask you some questions, Jesse?" Rita said.

Jesse nodded and gestured for Rita to join him at some picnic tables at the far end of the lot. An old dog food can containing cigarette butts was now filled with snow, turning it red with rust.

Rita pulled out her phone and showed him the mugshot of Teddy Lake. "I'd like to ask you some questions about Teddy Lake."

Jesse looked closer. "Okay," he said. "I was expecting you to ask me about Don."

"Do you have something to share?"

"Not really," Jesse said. "I just started here a couple

months ago. Only know him 'cause he works here. Though the gas jockeys and the mechanics keep different hours." He rubbed the back of his neck. "I mostly work afternoons, so the shop's usually closing up around the time I start."

"How would you describe your interactions with Donald?" Rita asked.

Jesse shrugged. "Seems like a nice guy. Yesterday afternoon he found the key to the station I'd lost. Didn't say nothing to Chester, just slipped it to me real quiet-like. I appreciated it, 'cause I didn't want Chester riding me again for being forgetful."

"Did Donald tell you where he found it?" Rita asked.

Jesse shook his head. "Nope."

"May I have it, please?" Rita asked. "Chester will understand."

Jesse looked unsure but he fished the key from his pocket, attached to a fishing float. The letters "GNG" were written on it in Sharpie.

"Thanks," Rita said, entering it as evidence. "And how about Teddy Lake? What can you tell me about him?"

"Saw him at The Shaft Thursday night," Jesse said.

"When you say you saw him," Rita said, "what does that entail? Did you meet him? Did you sit and have a drink together?"

"He was already drinking when we got there," Jesse said. "Was reeling around and talking a whole lot, telling the whole place he was gonna be rich. Some kind of secret he'd found out related to a police file back in the day."

"Did he tell you, or anyone, about the file?" Rita asked.

Jesse barked out a laugh. "He kept telling folk that if they bought him a beer, he'd spill the beans." Jesse laughed again, shaking his head. "Not that he needed another beer, he was drinking a pitcher all by himself. Chester told him to buzz off. But we left before he did."

"Chester mentioned you have a curfew," Rita said.

A pink flush flooded Jesse's neck. "Yeah. Chester complains it makes it hard to schedule my shifts." He shrugged. "But I'll have to quit if my mom doesn't approve of the schedule."

"So when you left the pub," Rita asked, "that was the last you saw of Teddy Lake?"

"Yep," Jesse said, straightening his spine. "In fact, the minute my butt was out of the booth, that guy Teddy dropped right into it, probably because no one else would give him the time of day. Anyways, he was chatting off poor Don's ear when me and Chester booked it out of there." Then Jesse stilled, a look of awareness coming over his face. "You don't suppose Don found out Teddy's secret and got killed for it, do you?"

Rita let out a sigh and gave him an obligatory smile. "I don't suppose anything."

Chapter Thirty-Two

RITA PULLED into the parking lot of the SCSO and parked beside the back door. Now that Mary Lou was in on the ruse, Rita felt at home again, in a way.

She entered the back door.

But she still didn't have an active security pass for the back door, so she walked around to front reception. Her hips ached by the time she strode into the bullpen.

Mary Lou sat working at her desk.

"You're the only one in?" Rita asked.

Mary Lou nodded, her tall stack of hair bobbing along. "Yep. Finally getting caught up on that paperwork, which is something you wouldn't know about."

"Ha, ha," Rita said. She held up the evidence bag with Jesse's key. "I need to use the evidence room. Got to send this key to Casper for processing. It may have been used by the killer to enter the Gas-N-Go."

"I'll do it for you," Mary Lou said, extending a hand. "It'll give me a reason to get my butt out this chair. I have to admit I don't get moving much in this weather."

"No, I can't imagine you want to ride your Harley these days," Rita said. "You bumming rides from the electrician?"

"Oh, I'm not dating Lucky no more," Mary Lou said. "Guess you didn't know I've taken up with the carpenter."

"You're not serious," Rita said, with a roll of her eyes.

Mary Lou spun around in her chair, arms crossed. "What's that supposed to mean?"

"Only that I've heard all the puns I can take," Rita said, "I don't think I'm in the mood for hammering, nailing, or talking about wood of any kind."

Mary Lou blew her lips like a horse. "Oh, go on you," she said waving a hand. "Second trimester is the horniest of all three."

"I heard Jason and Blaze broke up, too," Rita said, choosing to ignore Mary Lou's remark. "There's been a lot of change."

Mary Lou ogled her. "I'll say. How's pregnancy these days?"

Rita rubbed her belly. "Baby's been eating like a bison."

Mary Lou grinned. "Sounds like everything's going great."

Rita nodded. "Please keep telling me that."

"What is it?" Mary Lou asked with a frown. "Whatcha worried about?"

Rita chewed on her lip. "I can't help thinking about the hard parts coming up."

Mary pulled a grimace. "Labor."

"I was more thinking of the future-future," Rita said. "Like five years from now. Or ten or twenty."

Mary Lou pulled another face. "Sounds like catastrophizing."

Rita shrugged. "Sometimes I worry about this kid running away from me. Like I ran from Cash. Ran from the whole damn town."

Mary Lou leaned forward. "Well, that's because your parents ran away first. But if you stick by this kid, this kid'll stick by you. Look at Otto and you. He did right by you, minus a few secrets. And you came back to him when it counted."

"That's one way to tell the story," Rita said. "You could also say I ran away from New York, and Dale." She worried her lip some more. "Running all the time."

Mary Lou grasped her hand. "Maybe you're not running. Maybe you're just blowing, like the wind. The wind's part of this countryside, too."

"Carol's the breezy one," Rita said. She blew out a breath. "I'm like Otto, rooted in the high prairie."

Mary Lou winked. "Don't be so sure."

Then door to the front of the station opened and Watkins strode into the bullpen.

"Hi, Candace," Mary Lou said. "How'd it go with the door to doors?"

The deputy glanced sidelong at Rita, holding back.

"It's all good," Mary Lou said. "We're all looking for the same killer."

Candace gave a relieved smile and nodded. "I started with the neighbors on the south side," she said. "Everyone reported a normal Monday night. Real quiet, until Lana Horan came home." Candace said. "Then half the block came outside. Joe Peterson, he called it in, was the one who approached the residence."

"Don't tell me he entered the premises?" Rita asked.

"No, thankfully," Candace said. "But he collided with Lana Horgan when she fled the house. Said he startled the bejeezus out of her, is how he put it. He reported that she dove under a bush, continuing to scream. After he called 911, Joe Pederson told the other neighbors to go back inside, because the sheriff's office was coming to take care of matters."

"Any unrecognized vehicles?" Rita asked.

Candace shook her head. "No prowlers. Nothing unusual."

"How about earlier in the evening?"

Candace consulted her notes. "Simon Lee, neighbor on the north side, saw Don come home from work. Simon was pruning the hedges, and they chatted briefly about cutting down a shrub on the property line that wasn't likely to survive the winter. And another neighbor was out walking a dog when they saw Lana Horgan leave the property. Several of the neighbors noted that she was a committed volunteered in various capacities." Candace closed her notebook. "The Horgans were well-regarded in the neighborhood."

"Sure are," Mary Lou said. "Never heard a poor word spoken about either of them."

"I also traced Donald Horgan's path," Candace said, consulting her notes. "After he left work, he stopped at the rancher's pantry to pick up some snacks. He bought potato chips, beef jerky, and a six-pack to watch the race."

"Thanks for the info," Rita said. "I've also been meaning to follow up about your site-check at the Gas-N-Go. Jason said he'd follow up with you regarding whether the electrical cage was open?"

"He mentioned it," Candace said. "The cage was locked, no sign of vandalism." She flipped through the pages in her notebook. "I remember that the padlock's painted orange." She looked up at Rita. "I also took photos and can email those to you if you like."

"Thanks," Rita said. "Good job."

Candace smiled. "Thanks. Though I don't always feel like I'm doing a good job."

Rita met her eye. "How so?"

Candace's gaze slid away. "Well, I barfed at the crime scene. I'm not very proud of that."

"First homicide," Mary Lou said. "Anyone would do it."

Candace gave a nervous laugh. "I think I'd have dealt better with a gunshot wound."

"There was a lot of blood," Rita agreed. "I threw up at my first crime scene too."

Mary Lou turned with interest. "Oh, yeah?"

"Yeah," Rita said. "Lower East Side, small apartment, the height of summer. It reached 102 degrees that week."

Mary Lou grimaced.

"When we breached the door," Rita said, "we discovered the guy had exploded."

The color drained from Candace's face. "Exploded?"

"We were picking teeth off the ceiling fan."

"Well, fuck me," Mary Lou said with a whistle.

"Wasn't a full stomach in the place after seeing that," Rita said.

Candace's face went pale. Without a word, she spun around and bolted from the room. A moment later, the staff bathroom door slammed shut, followed by the faint sound of retching.

"Oh shit," Rita said, exchanging a look with Mary Lou. "I was trying to make her feel better, not worse."

A loud rumble sounded and the building trembled.

"What the hell is that?" Rita said.

Engine brakes squealed as she crossed to the front window, her own footsteps squealing.

A cherry-red semi-trailer had pulled up to the curb at

the front of the station, its chrome accents glinting like mirrors in the winter sunshine.

Rita looked over her shoulder at Mary Lou. "You expecting a delivery?"

Chapter Thirty-Three

RITA WATCHED through the front window as the driver got out of the cab and walked up the front steps to the station. With his snow-white hair, neatly trimmed goatee, and ruby cheeks, he was like Santa Claus gone rogue, trading a sleigh and his suit for a cab and a flannel shirt. The front door opened, and he entered the foyer with a swagger.

Mary Lou gave a low whistle and straightened, displaying her fringe-festooned bosom.

"Come on through," Rita said, calling into the foyer.

The driver looked into the bullpen where Rita stood beside Mary Lou's desk. He approached, removing his Aviator sunglasses. "I'm looking for the sheriff."

"Sheriff Perry's out," Rita said. "Can we help you?"

The man removed a piece of paper from his pocket and unfolded it to display the front page of *The Casper Chronicle*. "I have some information about this here fellow."

"Great," Rita said, pulling out the chair at Candace's desk for him. "Thanks for coming in. I'm Rita Jonas, Head of Law Enforcement Operations at APEX. I'm working with the SCSO on Teddy Lake's case."

"Pleased to meet you," the truck driver said, sitting. "I'm Abe Cunningham. I thought I should stop by, seeing as I gave him a ride."

Rita took out her notebook and flipped to a fresh page, then set her phone to record. "I'm going to tape our conversation," she said. "Where did you pick him up?"

"In Julesburg, Colorado," Abe answered. "He was hanging at the truck stop."

"And where did you drop him?" Rita asked.

"The Gas-N-Go at the south end of Still."

"That's about a five-hour trip," Candace said.

"I do it in seven and a quarter," Abe said. "I make several drops along the way."

"And when was this?" Rita asked.

"This past Thursday, when I was coming through the other way," Abe said. "I tell you, I had a hell of a shock when I rolled into town just now and saw the front page of the *Chronicle*. Not to mention everyone at the Bighorn's talkin' about it."

"Did Teddy tell you why he was headed to Wyoming?" Rita asked.

"Said he was headed this way to dig into a cold case. His dad had died and left him with some long-buried secret. Apparently, the old man had been a cop and had some explosive piece of intel."

"Did he tell you what that was?" Rita asked.

Abe shook his head. "Nah."

"Did you speculate?"

"I meet lots of folks who are trying to find answers," he said. "Sometimes they want answers to mysteries, sometimes passions, sometimes family trees. In Teddy's case, it sounded like he was trying to solve some old crime that his old man never cracked. Maybe he was one of them cold case enthusiasts. I listen to those podcasts when I drive. I always think most of them are fools to be digging up that past instead of getting on with the future."

He gestured toward Mary Lou's desk, where a framed photo showed her at Graceland half a century ago. "Of course, some things only get better with age, like the King's classics. Looks like you visited Graceland back when you were just a young lady, huh?"

Mary Lou dragged her eyes from Abe to look at her picture of Graceland. "1986," she said, her voice barely more than a whisper.

"I'm a fan, too," Abe said. "I visit every year."

Mary Lou's mouth opened but no sounds came out.

"I think she's trying to say that's impressive," Rita said.

Mary Lou nodded, her tower of hair shimmying. Abe's eyeballs tracked its undulations.

"You and Teddy were together for a lot of miles," Rita said, refocusing the truck driver's attention. "What happened along the way?"

"Well, besides talking about the cold case," Abe said, slowly drawing his gaze from Mary Lou, "there was a bit of a situation when we had lunch."

"Where was this?" Rita asked.

"We picked up some Subway sandwiches and ate on the road. But then Teddy pulled some booze out of his pack. I told him no drinkin' in my truck, just like I'd told him when I picked him up in the first place. But he took a swig anyway. Said he had to wash down the sub."

"Did he put away the flask after you asked?" Rita asked.

"Tried to make it look like," Abe said. "But the damn prick kept on stealing nips. Eventually, he got loose lipped and started saying he was following a money trail. That's how he got on to talking about his Pa's cold case. I told him I don't discuss no mysteries or histories with no one I pick up. I'd already told him that rule, too."

"Do you have a lot of rules for hitchhikers, Abe?" Rita asked.

"Mainly one," the truck driver said. "No dishin' any personal information." Abe counted on his fingers: "Riders can talk about games, books, movies, trucks, or sandwiches. But no need to be talkin' 'bout no other kind of shit."

"You run a tight truck, Mr. Cunningham," Mary Lou said, finding her voice.

"Hell, yeah," Abe said. "I'm doing these wayward wanderers a kind turn, no questions asked. All's they got to do is follow my law. After all, do they want a goddamned ride or not?"

"Indeed," Mary Lou said, sounding short of breath.

"Was Teddy meeting someone at the Gas-N-Go?" Rita asked.

"Nope," Abe said, "but he was confident he'd get a ride real easy. He had plans to visit the sheriff and his wife here in Still. Figured someone would be happy to give him a lift to the PD."

"Could you please repeat that?" Rita asked. "The part about the sheriff?"

Abe nodded. "Yeah, he said he was coming to visit the sheriff and his wife here in Still."

Rita glanced at Mary Lou, who looked as confused as Rita felt.

She returned her gaze to Abe. "Did Teddy give you a name for the sheriff?"

Abe thought for a moment, pulling on his goatee. "Teddy didn't yammer on 'bout so many details. Lots of big claims, like he was gonna be rich, thanks to his old man's secret. But no facts about the case. You can always tell a scheme by whether a guy has details, or not. Every so often some rider tells me about some genius idea he's got. And if he's got all the details lined up, that's when I know the sucker's onto something. 'Cause by my age, I've seen enough of them artists show up on-screen, or them inventors make some big bucks, to know that the recipe for their success was in those details." He tapped his temple. "But this guy, Teddy Lake, he didn't have no details. This rig can't haul shit from Corpus Christi to Klamath Falls if I ain't payin' attention to the details."

Mary Lou fanned herself. "You don't say?"

"So he didn't mention the name of the sheriff?" Rita confirmed.

Abe shook his head. "Didn't give no names or nothin'. And I got rules for myself, too, no prying."

"Good thinking," Rita said. "Although you might consider not picking up riders in the first place. So Teddy Lake gets out the Gas-N-Go. He didn't ask you to take him to the station?"

"Oh, sure," Abe said, "but I wasn't headed into town. I was unloading at Chester's and then headed for Beaumont. Besides, I was glad to be rid of the guy." Abe rolled his shoulders. "He was getting drunker by the minute."

"Did you notice Teddy talking to anyone at the Gas-N-Go?" Rita asked.

"I saw him approach one of the cars at the pumps. Reckoned he was asking for a ride. But the car drove off and Teddy cursed him out." Abe chuckled and shook his head. "Someone was either gonna pity that guy or punch him. By the time I was done unloading, Teddy was gone. I figured he'd gotten a ride."

"Thank you for coming in with this info, Abe," Rita

said. "It's very helpful." Rita gestured towards Mary Lou, who was standing as still as a statue and as pink as a piece of Carly's rose quartz. "Can you please supply us with your contact information?"

Puffing out his flannel-clad chest, Abe met Mary Lou's eye. "Be glad to."

Mary Lou was unusually speechless as Abe supplied his full name, date of birth, contact numbers, and address. Afterwards, Rita thanked him again, while Mary Lou gave the trucker a wordless wave.

"Well, this doesn't make any sense," Rita said when the door had closed behind Abe.

"What's that?" Mary Lou asked, still breathless.

"Teddy coming to Still to see the sheriff and his wife. He can't have meant Jason. Or me."

"Teddy's father might've assumed Otto was married."

Rita tapped on her lip. "Or Teddy's dad's story predates Otto's split with Carol."

"Teddy's dad also might've misremembered the whole thing," Mary Lou said with a shrug. "Maybe Teddy Lake was on a wild goose chase."

"True," Rita said. "I need to go make some inquiries. Please send me a copy of Abe's contact information?"

"Ten-four," Mary Lou said, setting her fingers on her keyboard.

"Thanks, Mary Lou." She glanced down the hallway that led to the lunchroom and staff bathrooms. "Tell Watkins to have a good one, okay?"

Then she gave Mary Lou a pat on the shoulder. "And I hope it goes well for you with the carpenter."

Mary Lou looked up from her computer screen, blinking. "I beg your pardon?"

"The carpenter," Rita said. "You have a date tonight."

"Oh, right." Mary Lou puckered her brows. "I'd forgotten about him."

Rita headed for the door. "Just keep things professional with Abe."

Mary Lou murmured something agreeable, but the words were lost beneath the squeak of Rita's boots as she stepped out of the station.

Chapter Thirty-Four

RITA ROLLED up Otto's driveway and parked in front of the porch, although nothing about it looked like Otto's anymore.

Gone was his favorite lawn chair, Cash's spare pair of work boots, and the potted hydrangea Rita had tried (and failed) to keep alive. She should have known better than to buy her father a plant.

Now, Jason's chic outdoor furniture with rainbow pillows was arranged to face the view, no matter the season.

She rapped on the door, feeling at odds to be knocking at the address where she once sneaked in through the bedroom window.

The door opened at once, Lucas Lake clearly awaiting her.

"Hi, Ms. Jonas."

"I've got some additional information about your brother's case," Rita said, stepping into the foyer. Even the inside smelled different, like lemon and evergreens instead of cigarette smoke and burnt coffee.

"Good," Lucas said, his voice dry. "Mom will be relieved."

"Let's get a drink before we talk," Rita said. "Do you prefer water or tea?"

"I already some boiled water for tea," Lucas said, his words hasty. "Can I pour you a cup?"

"Thanks," Rita said. She followed him into the kitchen and crossed to the cabinet to fetch a teabag. But instead she found a neatly organized rack of spices.

"Sheriff Perry has more spices than I know existed," Rita said, closing the cabinet again.

"Tea's kept in here," Lucas said, reaching past Rita to open a different cabinet. Like the spices, Jason owned a vast array, all neatly organized.

"They're arranged alphabetical," Rita said, "from bergamot to yerba mate."

"I've been enjoying the rooibos," Lucas said, setting two mugs on the countertop. At least Jason kept his mugs in the same cabinet as Otto had, next to the sink.

"Works for me," Rita said, grabbing two bags and dropping into the mugs. Then Lucas poured the hot water.

Rita picked up one mug. "Let's talk in the living room, where we have a view."

Lucas nodded, swallowing. Gripping the other mug, he proceeded into the living room and took a seat on the sofa. The steam from his mug curled around his head like set of ghost antlers.

Rita set her own mug of tea on the mantelpiece to cool and sat in the armchair by the fireplace. Then she took a deep and slow breath and moistened her lips.

"We've found Teddy's head," she said.

For a moment, Lucas hid his face, silent, his shoulders still. Then he looked up at Rita, his cheeks wet with tears.

"Thank God," he said. "Mom doesn't want to cremate him without it."

"I understand," Rita said. "Although we do need to keep the body for a while longer."

"Okay," Lucas said. "That's gonna be hard for mom."

"I understand," Rita said. "I expect the medical examiner's report will be death by blunt force trauma."

Teddy nodded. "Okay. Okay." He ran his hands over his head. "At some point in the future, I'll probably want to know how you found it. And where. But right now, well, could that be enough?"

Rita nodded. "Yes. We also have talked to some witnesses who picked up Teddy hitch-hiking."

Lucas sat up straighter. "Yeah?"

"He mentioned coming to Still to get rich, thanks to an old police case your father told him about."

"Oh?"

"He didn't mention this?" Rita asked.

"Never," Lucas said.

"He also said he was planning to meet with the sheriff and his wife."

"That's news to me."

"You ever hear him mention a man named Otto?"

Lucas shook his head.

"He didn't give any indication he was taking the trip when you saw him back in Florida?" Rita asked.

"I wasn't real close with my brother," Lucas said. "Like I said before, we had different lifestyles."

"And your mother said she didn't know anything about Teddy's plans?" Rita confirmed.

Lucas let out a shaky laugh. "Mom didn't know half the trouble Teddy got into. Thought he was a real golden boy. Couldn't do no wrong, even though I'd say that was his specialty."

"Life will be different without your brother now," Rita said.

Lucas nodded. "That's for sure." He let out a sigh. "I wonder if Mom will stop drinking now that the Theodores are gone. It'll only be the two of us at the holidays and I don't touch the stuff. But she also might hit the bottle harder, and then I'll lose her just like Dad."

"No doubt grief will demand an adjustment period. Counseling can be one helpful support, for the both of you, although I don't have contact information for any resources in Florida."

Lucas nodded. "I understand." Then: "If you have a minute, can I ask you about something?"

"Sure," Rita said. "What is it?"

"Jason was gone the whole night," Lucas said. "But I swore I heard someone in the house, moving around downstairs. Except I was too scared to check. But then I noticed something this morning."

"Oh?" Rita said. "What's that?"

"I'll show you," Lucas said, leading her back to the kitchen and through the back door that led to the rear porch.

Rita followed him outside, her boots creaking against the aging planks. Lucas rubbed his hands together for warmth, then pointed to a section of the porch where one of the wood slats had been pulled up, leaving a narrow opening.

"This is definitely unusual," Rita said, crossing to the gap. "Thanks for showing me."

She stooped, pulling out her phone and angling the flashlight into the dark recess beneath the porch. The latticework enclosed the cramped space, keeping the snow out and leaving the ground dry except for a few stray leaves that had slipped through the gaps. She squinted, scanning for anything out of place. Among the leaves, a yellowed scrap of paper caught her eye.

She glanced at Lucas, hovering near the railing. "Maybe someone retrieved something that was stored here."

She leaned in to collect the scrap of paper. She pulled it out, it was a piece of old newsprint. One side of the paper bore a fragment of a headline: *One Dead in DUI.* The other side showed part of a car dealership ad, the vehicle's style decades out of date. Rita slipped the paper into a small plastic bag and pocketed it.

Then she flicked off the flashlight and opened her messaging app. "I'll let Jason know."

Remind me when's your birthday? she texted.

A second later he responded: *Why?*

Rita typed: *I'll tell you more later, but need to reprogram the door code at your place.*

Jason gave Rita's message a thumbs-down and messaged: *That's a terrible code.*

It's memorable.

It's predictable.

Rita looked up from her phone at Lucas. "What's your birthday?"

He blinked at her. "October tenth."

"Ten ten," Rita said. "You cool if that's the new key code for the lock here while you stay?"

Lucas nodded and Rita texted the number to Jason.

That's too simple, he messaged.

Tough, Rita wrote back, *it's only until Lucas leaves.*

Then she put away her phone and smiled at Lucas. "Hopefully that will solve the problem. Though it's possible someone's coming through a window. I used to sneak in and out of the two front dormer windows over the garage roof."

"I'll make sure those windows are latched," Lucas said, opening the back door and retreating into the warmth of the kitchen.

"Perfect," Rita said, closing the door and locking it behind her. "You city smarts alone might outwit this small town prowler."

A shudder shook Lucas's shoulders. "Can't say I'm reassured, Ms. Jonas. My brother got murdered in this small town."

Rita flicked on the electric kettle, aiming for a reassuring smile. "I've got city smarts too, Lucas, but I was born and raised here. I can't promise anything, and I don't grant wishes, but I do make commitments. And I'm committed to finding Teddy's killer."

Lucas swallowed and nodded, then flinched when the kettle switched off.

"It's getting colder," Rita said. "Another cup of tea would do you good."

Chapter Thirty-Five

WHILE DRIVING across town to the Gas-N-Go, Rita's phone rang. She took the call hands-free.

"Hi, Craig. Find something in the footage?"

"Better than that," he said. "Fucking hotline's blowing up like Fourth of July."

Rita pulled over at the curb. "What's come in?"

"Abe Cunningham sent out a CB message to his fellow truckers to call in with info for a dead guy out of Florida." Craig consulted his notes. "This one guy, Harvey Barton, said Teddy had insisted they take a selfie together."

"Fast friends?" Rita asked.

"Harvey said he took the pic to get Teddy off his case. Hang on, I'll send it to you."

Rita's phone pinged and she opened the image Craig had forwarded. The selfie, somewhat blurred, showed Teddy Lake red-faced and grinning, while hanging off the broad shoulders of a trucker who, if Abe were to be compared to St. Nick, looked like a jacked-up version of Jack Frost.

"Harvey doesn't look so jolly," Rita said. "Although Teddy sure does."

"Harvey said Teddy was packing a flask and got lit like a Christmas tree," Craig said. "Apparently Teddy told Harvey that he didn't know it yet, but he was talking to a real rich son-of-a-bitch. And that Teddy promised to send him some cash for his trouble, once he got to Wyoming. He insisted they take a photo to commemorate the night they met."

Rita thanked Craig, then hung up and texted Cash, letting him know she wouldn't be home until late.

Then she got out of the crossover and entered the Gas-N-Go.

The bell over the door rang and Chester looked up from the ledger he was reading. Seeing her, he dropped the blue ballpoint pen and used both hands to rub his face, transferring ink from his fingers onto his forehead and cheekbones.

"Are you all right?" Rita asked.

"I'm fucking short-handed, that's what," Chester said. "Don's gone, of course, so I gotta clear the shop schedule. And of course Lana's not doin' the books so I'm trying to track all this shit. And I don't usually manage paperwork so it's like fucking alphabet soup to me."

"That sounds difficult," Rita said. "I'm here because I need to check the security footage of the date Teddy Lake came to town."

"You can go on back to my office," Chester said. "I got to man the counter here 'cause I'm down a jockey." He snapped the ledger closed and stuffed it under the counter. "You got to double-click the camera icon on the desktop, then select the folder. From there, choose a folder by week. The footage is organized into twelve-hour intervals."

"Thanks," Rita said.

In Chester's office, Rita sank into the vinyl chair, the cushion sighing as she settled. The desktop computer hummed on the desk, and she nudged the mouse to wake it up.

The tower ground audibly as the machinery woke up. As the screen flickered to life, she moved the mouse using only her fingertips, as its plastic surface, once white, was now gray and coated in a greasy slick.

She found what she assumed was the camera icon and double-clicked it. True to Chester's word, the files were labeled by date, each spanning from Sunday at midnight to the following Saturday at 11:59 p.m. The footage she needed was at the top of the list. She opened it and found the twelve-hour recording from Thursday night.

The files contained footage from four different cameras: one covering the back door near the electrical panel, the dumpsters, and storage sheds; another showed inside the mechanics' bays; a third oversaw the store's interior; and the last mounted over the front entrance captured a full view of the pumps.

Rita fast-forwarded, watching vehicles come and go, mostly pickup trucks, with the occasional sedan or crossover. Then she spotted Abe's truck pulling in, its chrome gleaming under the station lights.

It rolled into the lot, then turned and reversed to back up to the tire shed, the camera recording the music-note etching on the side-mirrors and the silhouettes of Elvis Presley, in his signature pose, on the mud flaps. As it backed up to the loading bay, the truck disappeared mostly out of frame.

A minute later, Teddy Lake cut across the camera's view, heading into the shop while Abe began unloading tires.

Four minutes later, Teddy reemerged, adjusting his ball

cap. He walked toward the only car at the pumps, a Chevy Malibu. Jesse stood by the driver's open window, processing payment.

Teddy approached and said something. The driver shook his head and Teddy flipped him off. Then he walked across the lot and sat at one of the picnic tables at the edge of the camera's view. Jesse finished up with the driver of the Malibu and the Chevy pulled away, then he walked over to the picnic tables, chatting to Teddy at a distance.

Rita tapped her fingers on the mouse. Jesse Levick hadn't told her about meeting Teddy Lake at any point before The Shaft.

She refocused on Abe, who had finished unloading and was climbing back into his rig. A minute later, he backed out of the lot.

Then Chester exited the shop, wearing his cowboy hat, and climbed into his pickup, parked near the picnic tables. He drove through the empty pump bays, momentarily blocking the camera's view of Teddy and Jesse.

When his truck cleared the frame, both of them were gone.

She rewound the footage and watched the scene several more times. But saw no further indication of which direction he'd gone.

Rita paused the footage, frowning. She switched between camera angles, fast-forwarding through the next five minutes. But there was no sign of Teddy. Or Jesse.

She returned to the exterior camera and watched in fast-forward until 6:30 p.m. when Teddy had been seen at The Shaft. Each time a figure entered the frame she paused the footage. Several vehicles came and went, and more often than not, the drivers were indiscernible. But nothing indicated Teddy had returned to the station, or had ever left in the first place.

Had Jesse taken him somewhere?

Rita compressed the files, labeled them, then emailed them to herself and exited the program. She walked to the front of the store. Chester was in the food aisle, checking expiration dates on cans of Spam.

"Is Jesse Levick at work today?" Rita asked.

"Nope," Chester said. "Why d'you think I'm so short-staffed? Fired him this morning."

Rita raised a brow. "Why?"

"Unreliable." Chester grunted. "Can't stay late when I need him. Rumor is he lost his key but won't fess up. And today? Late again. Another damn excuse about his dirt bike." He shot her a look. "As you know, Jonas, my business has taken a hit. I've lost angle grinders, mechanics, and now I'm losing my hired help."

"What kind of car does Jesse drive?" Rita asked. "Maybe even his license plate? I imagine a man like you is good at remembering those."

Chester chuckled, puffing up his chest. "You're right, I notice a plate or two. But Jesse don't drive. He rides a dirt bike."

Rita gestured toward the freeway outside. "On this stretch of road?"

"Sure does. Can't hardly keep up with the semis, but he rides real good."

"Safety, legality, and speed limits aside," Rita said, "his bike isn't street legal."

Chester shrugged. "How is that my problem?"

"You're right," Rita said. "I'm sure you didn't care how Jesse got to work, only that he showed up."

"Damn right."

"But you drive him home sometimes?"

"Sure. Gets dark early. Weather's turnin' bad."

Rita grinned. "So you do care."

Chester frowned. "Huh?"

"Never mind." Rita said. Then asked: "When you give him a ride home, how does he get back for his next shift?"

"If he leaves his bike here overnight, one of the jockeys usually picks him up."

"Does he leave his bike here often?"

Chester rolled around his eyes before answering, thinking. "Not usually. Only lately, since winter's settin' in. That's another good reason to fire him, would've needed more and more rides."

Rita held back a sigh. "I need his home address, please."

Chester snorted. "How the hell would I have that memorized?"

"Didn't you drive him home Thursday night?"

"Sure," Chester said. "Kid's got a goddamn nine o'clock curfew, which makes scheduling night shifts a clusterfuck." He tapped a blackened fingernail against the glass counter. "Like I said, I need employees who keep this place running."

"So where does he live?"

Chester waved vaguely. "Few blocks behind the bowling alley. Don't know the street name or number, I just turn when he tells me to. Couple of lefts, then a hairpin right."

Rita smiled patiently. "His address, please."

Chester let out a long sigh. "I'll have to check his employee records."

"They should be handy, since you terminated him this morning."

Grinding his teeth, Chester stomped into his office. Two minutes later, he returned with a sticky note, his mouth set in a firm line.

"388 Graff Place," Rita read aloud. Then she thanked him and left.

As she pulled out of the lot and headed toward town, she considered the possibility that Jesse had taken Teddy somewhere. Without a car, had they piggybacked on his bike?

Graff Place turned out to be a dead-end street with only four addresses. Bollards marked where the pavement stopped, and beyond them, the land had been claimed by a treatment plant.

Rita parked in front of Jesse's house, walked up to the door, and knocked.

A middle-aged woman answered, her disheveled ponytail and oversized sweatshirt at odds with the sharp, no-nonsense look she gave Rita.

"Hi, I'm Rita Jonas, Head of APEX Law Enforcement Operations," Rita said. "I'm looking for Jesse Levick."

"He's not home," the woman said flatly. "So you can buzz off."

"Are you his mother?"

The woman stiffened. "Jesse's my kid." She tongued her cheek. "Vicki Coogan's my name."

"Do you know where he is, Vicki?"

Vicki's brows knit together. "What's it to you? He ain't done nothing wrong. He might like a little freedom like the rest of us, but he ain't no lawbreaker. He's a real good kid."

"He's a witness in a murder investigation," Rita said.

Vicki's eyes widened. "It's that guy in the paper, isn't it? Teddy Blake? Jesse said he saw him hitchin' at the Gas-N-Go the other day."

"Teddy Lake," Rita corrected. "Did Jesse tell you what they talked about?"

Vicki tilted her chin up. "They didn't talk none. Jesse said he had the gall to ask a driver for a ride while Jesse was taking his payment. Apparently the driver blew him off. Doubt Jesse would've told him to buzz off. He's a real mellow type."

"I still need to ask him some questions," Rita said.

Folding her arms, Vicki looked her up and down. "He's at work."

"He's not," Rita said. "He was let go this morning."

"Like hell he was, you lying pig!"

Then Vicki slammed the door in Rita's face.

Rita sighed, standing on the stoop for a moment before turning and walking back down the driveway. She paused when something teal caught her eye among the leaves and broken branches beneath a large chestnut tree.

A tractor tire lay half-buried in the leaves, tied with a sawed-off length of teal rope. She walked down the driveway and up to the tree.

Tilting her head, Rita studied the sturdy branch overhead. The teal rope was gone, but faint grooves in the bark suggested where it had once been tightly wound. If the rope was as old as Tilda had said, chances were Jesse had swung on this tire as a kid.

Rita pulled out her phone and called Mary Lou.

"I need a favor," she said.

Mary Lou scoffed. "Hunter won't be pleased."

"To hell with Hunter," Rita said. "I need a search warrant for Jesse Levick's house. 388 Graff Place. That's Graff with two F's. His mother is Vicki Coogan."

"On it," Mary Lou said.

"I'll be waiting."

Rita hung up and leaned against the BMW, hoping her bladder could hold out.

Chapter Thirty-Six

THE SUNKEN SUN turned the sky brilliant blue, creating low-glare conditions that allowed Rita to view Vicki Coogan's oversized flat-screen TV through her front window, and through the crossover's windshield.

A young, artificially tanned couple with gleaming veneers and a pair of sledgehammers demonstrated how to dismantle maple-wood cabinetry and vinyl countertops.

Headlights swept across the windshield and Rita sat up, blinking against the shine. The SCSO truck parked, the engine cut off, and Deputy Watkins stepped out.

Rita popped open the door and climbed out. "Hi, Candace, thanks for coming by."

"Sure thing, Ms. Jonas," Candace said, hanging the station's Canon SLR camera around her neck. Then she grabbed the forensics kit and slammed the door shut. "Mary Lou sent Jason home."

"Is he all right?" Rita asked.

Candace nodded. "When Jason got back from the autopsy, Mary Lou sent him to bed."

"He was tired," Rita said, nodding.

Candace grimaced. "And queasy."

Rita exhaled. "That bad, huh?"

"Mary Lou sent him with a lasagna, too," Candace said. "It smelled really good."

"It'll be delicious," Rita said, suddenly salivating. "He's a lucky guy. That was nice of her."

"She made it for that truck driver."

Rita's eyebrows shot up. "Abe Cunningham?"

She nodded. "She gave Jason the leftovers."

Rita's stomach gurgled. "I could use leftovers right about now." She cocked her head towards Vicki Coogan's front door. "Let's get this done."

She and Candace marched up to the door of 388 Graff Street and knocked. Laughter from the sun-tanned couple filtered through the doorway, but no one answered.

Rita knocked again, then called out, "Police!"

The door flew open, and the laughter spilled onto the stoop. Vicki Coogan stood in the doorway, glaring at Rita.

"Why the hell are you still here?" Her gaze flicked to Candace. "You ain't even from the same station."

"That's right," Rita said. "We're working together. And we have a warrant to search the premises."

Vicki's eyes narrowed as she looked between them. "The hell you do."

Rita took a steady breath. "It's signed by the judge."

"Then let's see it," Vicki said.

Rita held up her phone for Vicki to read. "It's electronic."

Vicki squinted at the screen. "I ain't got no eyeglasses on."

"I can email you a copy," Rita said.

Vicki barked out a laugh. "Like I'm gonna give you pigs my email address!"

"We can wait while you get your eyeglasses?" Candace said.

Vicki scowled. "I don't got eyeglasses."

Rita glared at her. "Please step outside, Miss Coogan, so we can enter and conduct our search."

Vicki's eyes widened. "Step outside? Do you know how fucking cold it is?"

"We have a pretty good idea, standing out here," Rita said. "We need about an hour."

"An hour?" Vicki sucked in her cheeks. "I'm watching a show." Then she shoved past Rita, wearing slippers, she shuffled down the frosty steps. "Now I'm gonna have to go over to Tracy's to see the end of it."

"Excellent solution," Rita said.

"You're not only a pair of liars, but you're fascists," Vicki shouted, crossing the lawn to the neighbor's yard. "Lying fascist pigs!"

Then the neighbor's door slammed and the afternoon fell quiet again.

Rita threw Candace an encouraging smile. "That could have gone better."

Candace nodded. "Where do we start?"

"Here in the front yard," Rita said, waving her towards the old chestnut. She led Candace to the tire swing lying on its side on the ground. "I need to bag this rope for evidence. It would be helpful if you could hold the tire upright."

"Sure," Candace said, kneeling.

She propped the tire onto its side and Rita's fingertips worked at the knot. The rope's flexibility allowed for some give, but the bowline had been pulled taut from hanging for what might have been a decade. Fortunately, years of sun exposure and freezing temperatures had cracked the nylon fibers, making it easier to loosen. Rita dug in her fingers, prying at the loops until the knot finally gave way.

The rope slipped free of the tire, still curled in the shape it had held for years.

"Why don't you bag it and take it to the evidence room?" Rita said, standing.

"I appreciate the experience," Candace said, laying down the tire down again.

"Good," Rita said, striding toward Vicki Coogan's front door. "Let's go inside and get you some more."

The living room was a maze of sofas, side-tables, and towering stacks of magazines and unopened Amazon packages. On the floor, Dollar Store bags stuffed with plastic housewares and jumbles of clothing covered most of the carpeting. Overhead, cobwebs clung to lighting fixtures, forgotten or inaccessible, or both.

Candace coughed. "Musty in here." She cleared her throat. "Let's find Jesse's room and concentrate our search there."

"In here," Rita said, indicating a crooked bumper sticker on the door that read, *Follow Jesus—He takes the High Road*. A black Sharpie pen had changed 'Jesus' to 'Jesse' and a fluorescent green highlighter had turned the crucifix into the veins of a marijuana leaf.

Rita opened the door and stepped inside the bedroom. Candace followed.

Compared to the rest of the house, Jesse's room was clean, organized, and sparsely furnished. A twin bed, covered with a fleece blanket featuring a giant rainbow-striped hemp leaf, sat against one wall. A battered wooden dresser, a worn bedside table, and a single-door closet completed the space. Grateful Dead posters papered the walls, each one aligned with its neighbor along the top edge.

"Smells like marijuana in here," Candace said, flipping off the Canon's lens cap and photographing the room.

Rita stepped out of the frame, crossing to the chest of drawers in the corner. "And antiseptic." She ran a finger along the top of the highboy, checking for dust. None. "Jesse doesn't exactly follow in his mother's footsteps when it comes to keeping house."

"No doubt," Candace said, snapping a photo of the closet interior.

Rita pulled open the top drawer and found a bong, an assortment of pipes, and enough lighters to out stock the Gas-N-Go. In fact, several looked like they had come from the store.

"He uses cannabis," Rita said. "In case you haven't figured that out yet."

"The scent of his clothes supports that hypothesis," Candace said, having placed the camera on the bed to sift through the hoodies in Jesse's closet.

"I'm glad you think in hypotheses," Rita said. "Because I don't do guesses."

Candace held up two hoodies in Rastafarian colors, both featuring hemp-leaf motifs. "No guessing here."

Rita opened the next dresser drawer: socks and underwear. "So far, just paraphernalia. No proof of possession yet." She closed the drawer and opened another, this one containing pajamas. She pulled out a pair of flannel pants patterned with Mickey Mouse smoking joints. "How old is this kid?"

"He's a man with a kid's heart," Candace said, her head popping out from the closet. "He's twenty-two. And there must be half that in Squishmallows in here."

Rita blinked. "You know Jesse Levick's age?"

"Sheriff Perry had me review all the Gas-N-Go

employee records. See if anyone had a history of lifting workplace property."

"And you remember Jesse's record?"

Candace nodded. "I'm good at studying."

"Jason was right," Rita said.

"About what?"

"Top of your class. You make a great addition to the team."

Candace blushed. "Thanks, Ms. Jonas." Then she held up a pair of fuzzy slippers shaped like bird feet. "My nephew has slippers like this. But smaller. He's eight."

"Are those duck feet or chicken feet?" Rita asked.

Candace looked closer. "Dunno." She glanced back into the closet. "This is just one of several pairs of animal-feet slippers. Mostly furry. But there's also a bright green frog pair. All of them size twelve."

"If you're checking any shoeboxes," Rita said, "be mindful of firearms. Sometimes people stash them inside shoes."

Candace stiffened. "Right." She returned the fuzzy duck feet to the closet and started searching the upper shelf.

Rita pushed aside the jumble of pajama pants, exposing a small stack of greeting cards, mostly from Jesse's father. None of the communications suggested a current sweetheart. She searched the last dresser drawer, only sweatpants and jeans, and turned to the bedside table.

No firearm. Not even a penknife. Only a couple of tire-pressure gauges and several pairs of fingerless gloves, though whether they were for smoking joints or pumping gas, Rita couldn't be sure.

She opened an envelope of glossy photographs and flipped through them. Each one showed Jesse with a middle-aged man who bore a clear paternal resemblance.

They stood arm-in-arm in various outdoor settings, by lakeshores, on the ocean, beside campfires, atop Ski-Doos.

The backs of the photos were marked in two distinct handwriting styles. Some read, "Me & Dad," while others said "Jesse," followed by his age. The dates spanned fifteen years, with every picture taken in either July or December. It was clear, Jesse saw his father twice a year and treasured their time together in the wilderness.

Rita replaced the envelope and picked up a Bible, only to find its pages hollowed out, filled with small Ziploc bags, containing trace amounts of cannabis flakes.

"Evidence of marijuana," Rita said. "But still no proof of possession."

She pulled out a large Rubbermaid tote and popped off the blue lid. Sorting through layers of seasonal outer-wear, aware that her hand might close on a firearm, she moved with caution. Her pulse slowed when she reached the bottom. No weapons. Just a fishing vest, an orange PFD, ski pants, a camouflage hunting jacket, and an assortment of utility hats.

She slid the tote back under the bed and stood as Candace emerged from the closet.

"Find anything unusual?" Rita asked.

"Between the quantity of stuffies and the Bob Marley T-shirts?" Candace shook her head.

Rita moved towards the bedroom door, pausing to look inside a wicker wastebasket.

"Shit."

Candace approached with the camera. "What is it?"

Rita stooped beside the basket. "Facecloth. Stained red. Maybe cocktail sauce, but I've been at this job long enough to recognize dried blood on linens."

Candace snapped a few shots before Rita entered it into evidence.

"Looks like we're searching the rest of the house now," Rita said.

Candace nodded and followed her out of Jesse's room.

The search of the kitchen, mostly stocked with electrolyte drinks and breakfast cereals, revealed nothing sinister.

Similarly, a search of the full bath and Vicki's cluttered bedroom turned up no additional bloodstains or marijuana paraphernalia, only an excessive amount of books, music CDs, and VHS tapes (despite no evidence of a VCR in the house), and a stack of forty-year-old celebrity magazines, still sealed in plastic.

In the small, single-car garage, they found helmets for various sports and mountain climbing gear neatly stored in labeled Rubbermaid totes.

"This has got to be Jesse's stuff," Candace said. "His outdoor gear is cleaner than the inside of his mother's house."

After returning the bins to their shelves, they exited the garage.

"There's a shed," Rita said, pointing to the backyard.

Carving a fresh path through the snow, Rita led the way to the shed. She pushed open the metal door, revealing a wheelbarrow and lawnmower buried in a tangled mess of rakes, brooms, and discarded sporting equipment, damaged skis, a torn tent, and a broken VCR.

"Looks like mother and son both use this space," Candace observed.

Something orange caught Rita's eye.

"Check it out," she said, pointing. On the cement floor lay an open padlock, painted orange, with a key still in it. "Who do we know that's missing a padlock?"

"That's Chester's for sure," Candace said.

"Can you get this sent on to Casper Forensics, please?" Rita asked. "I'm gonna talk to Vicki before I go."

"Ten-four," Candace said, bagging the padlock and key.

Then they exited the shed, shivering, and walked around to the front of the house.

As the SCSO truck pulled out, Rita crossed the lawn to the neighbor's house and knocked. The door opened to reveal a woman with cornrows, clad in a flimsy tank top that barely contained her ample chest.

"I'm Rita Jonas with APEX L.E.O. I need to speak to Vicki Coogan."

The woman turned her head and hollered inside, "Door's for you, Vick!"

"Don't tell me it's that pig again," Vicki called back. "She's a fascist."

The woman frowned, looking Rita over once more. "You a copper? You said you was…"

"Head of Law Enforcement Operations at APEX Incorporated."

The woman snorted and shouted over her shoulder, "You're right, Vick, it's a pig."

"Tell her I'm busy," Vicki Coogan returned.

"Busy doing what?" Rita asked. "Unless Vicki's on the toilet…"

"Her show ain't over yet," the woman said, checking her wristwatch. "Just be a couple more minutes."

"You'll both be arrested for impeding an investigation," Rita warned.

The woman's eyes widened. With a reluctant sigh, she dragged the door open wider. "Well, if you're gonna be that way about it…"

Rita stepped inside and the neighbor gestured to the first room on the right. The house had a similar layout to

Vicki's, but it felt more spacious without the clutter. Vicki sat on the sofa in the living room, eating a bowl of potato chips while watching her show.

"Hello again, Miss Coogan," Rita said. "I appreciate you taking the time to answer some questions."

"Fuck you, you fucking pig!" Vicki shouted, eyes fixed on the screen.

"As I explained to your neighbor," Rita said evenly, "you will be arrested for—"

"So arrest me!" Vicki spat, spraying chip crumbs.

Rita sighed. Then she walked around the side of the sofa and placed a hand on Vicki's shoulder.

"Vicki Coogan, I'm placing you under arrest for obstruction to justice. Please stand up and place your hands behind your back…"

Chapter Thirty-Seven

"Snow!" Vicki Coogan groaned as flakes drifted down. "I'm wearing goddamn slippers. And I haven't got a fucking jacket either."

Rita grasped Vicki's upper arm, guiding her across the neighbor's lawn. "Ever heard of camping slippers? They're waterproof, you can wear 'em inside and out. Might be useful for you."

"You can't just drag me around like this," Vicki spat, her eyes flashing. She pulled away. "What is this, some kind of fascist police state?"

"Stop resisting," Rita warned.

"Resisting? Ha! What's next, rounding up people who speak out against the system?" Vicki's voice rose in pitch. "Oh wait, that's already happening, isn't it?"

"I'm not arguing politics with you," Rita said, steering her toward the crossover.

Vicki stopped dead. "We're not riding in a squad car?"

Rita opened the back door. "This is my APEX vehicle."

Vicki peered inside. "It's a fucking limo."

"Not quite, but close."

"You been in a limo?" Vicki asked.

"Yes," Rita said. "Once. Overrated experience."

Vicki scoffed. "Bullshit. You're ungrateful."

Rita gave up on diplomacy. She grabbed Vicki's elbow and guided her into the backseat. "Get in. Now."

Vicki smirked. "Keep pushing me, and you'll only prove my point."

Rita shoved her inside. "What point?"

"That you'd rather silence dissenters than deal with what's actually wrong."

Rita pulled out the seatbelt. "And what's wrong?"

Vicki strained against the belt as Rita buckled it. "Fascism! On the rise. And you're doing your part, ain't you?"

Rita rolled her eyes and slammed the door. She walked around to the driver's side while Vicki continued to shout through the glass.

"Should never have sent you with the fucking evidence, Watkins," Rita grumbled to herself. "Could use some backup right now."

She popped the door and slid into the driver's seat.

Vicki growled. "You think locking me up is gonna solve anything?"

Rita fastened her seatbelt, then glanced in the rearview mirror. "We'll talk about it at the station."

Vicki pouted. "Talk? Ha! This is exactly what they want!"

Rita started the ignition. "Who's they?"

"The system, of course."

Rita pulled out of Vicki's driveway. "Which system?"

"The *whole* system," Vicki said, her voice raising. "It's rigged. The moment someone speaks out…"

Rita exhaled and kept her gaze focused on the road.

The drive felt like an eternity, but finally, they pulled up to the curb in front of the SCSO.

"...treat us like criminals for wanting a better world," Vicki ranted. "You think this is gonna stop me?" Then she glanced around. "Shit, you got a paper bag?"

"You feel sick?" Rita rummaged through the glove compartment. "Might have some crackers."

"I need to hide my face," Vicki said. "'Cause here you go again, pushing me around in public where everyone can see. If you want me to cooperate, put a bag on my head."

"It's an unmarked vehicle," Rita said, getting out. She opened the back door and unbuckled Vicki.

"I ain't no criminal," Vicki spat, "and I ain't gonna be paraded around like one."

Rita pulled the woman out of the backseat. "If you keep talking this loud, you'll likely draw a crowd from the Bighorn Bean."

Vicki bristled. "I can't wait to hear all the 'reasons' why you do this job. Maybe you'll even convince yourself you're doing the right thing."

Boots squeaking, Rita marched her up the front steps the station.

"I still don't see how locking me up will solve anything," Vicki said.

Rita pulled open the front door. "It'll solve the issue of your non-compliance." She nudged Vicki Coogan into the bullpen and up to Mary Lou's desk, where rainbow-colored file folders lay fanned out.

"Hiya, Vicki," Mary Lou said. "Haven't seen you since Susan's neighborhood BBQ." Her gaze flickered to Vicki's arms, cuffed behind her back. "Tough night?"

Vicki cocked her head towards Rita. "Wasn't 'til this one showed up."

Mary Lou glanced at Rita. "Charges?"

Rita opened her mouth, but Vicki spoke first:

"You really think you're doing the right thing? Locking me up for asking questions? For challenging the system?"

"You don't have to worry about that here," Mary Lou said, consoling.

"Oh, I get it, Mary Lou," Vicki flared. "You think you're above it all. You don't care what's wrong with this world, you just follow orders! You'll see, this is just the beginning!"

Rita sighed. "Argue all you want, but it won't change a thing."

"You can't silence me!"

"No," Rita said, her voice steady. "But if you keep talking like this, you'll be doing it in a cell."

"Fascist!"

Rita pulled up a chair for her. "We're here to talk about Jesse. Why don't you have a seat?"

Vicki tilted her chin, avoiding eye contact.

Rita looked at Mary Lou. "Talk some sense into her, please."

Then she strode toward the staff kitchen, boots squeaking.

At the sink, Rita braced her hands on the basin, taking deep breaths. After a minute, she filled a glass with water and drained it in one gulp. A glance at the cupboards revealed a dismal selection of canned baked beans, Mr. Noodles, and a half-eaten box of animal crackers. She grabbed the crackers, chewing mechanically. Stale, but not the worst option.

After tossing the empty box, she washed her hands and returned to the bullpen.

Glasses perched on her nose, Mary Lou was absorbed in her computer screen.

"Where's Vicki?" Rita asked.

"In old your office," Mary Lou said, eyes fixed on the screen. "She's ready to talk."

"Thanks." Rita crossed the bullpen. "I knew you'd sort her out."

"All in a day's work."

Rita stepped into the sheriff's office, closed the door behind her, and took a seat. She exhaled, missing the ergonomic masterpiece she'd ordered for the SCSO, now adjusted to Jason's height in her absence. With a few pumps of the seat pedal, she dropped it back down.

"Thanks for your cooperation," she said to Vicki, failing to disguise her sarcasm. She set up the voice recorder. "This interview will be recorded."

Vicki scoffed. "You call this justice? Just another way for fascists like you to control people. Go ahead and record, I don't care. I ain't telling you anything I don't want to, anyway."

"Your son is a witness in a murder investigation," Rita said. "And I'm concerned he might be missing."

Vicki's expression shifted. "Jesse? Missing? Since when?"

"Since he was fired from work this morning," Rita said. "And I've got two dead bodies on my hands. I don't want Jesse turning up as the third."

Vicki paled. "Well, why didn't you say?"

"When did you last see Jesse?"

"This morning, when he rode to work."

"What time?"

"Six-thirty."

Rita jotted down the time. "Did anything seem off?"

"Yeah," Vicki admitted. "His mood."

"How so?"

"He was damn happy."

"That's unusual?"

Vicki hesitated. "He's generally content, 'cause he—" She broke off, turning red.

"What is it?" Rita asked.

Vicki waved a hand. "All's I'm tryin' to say is, he's chill."

"I suspect he uses marijuana," Rita said. "But that's not my concern today."

Vicki nodded. "I didn't want to say nothin' incriminating." Her gaze skated away. "But it's true weed helps me sometimes. Medicinally."

"So you were saying, Jesse is generally content."

"Sure. But this morning, well, he seemed eager. Excited. Like he had some good news."

"He didn't mention what it was?"

"Nope."

"Any guesses?" Rita asked, going against her own creed.

"Not really. He was hoping for a promotion, his probation at the Gas-N-Go was ending. He wanted to work the store counter instead of pumping gas. It's real cold this time of year. And Jesse ain't got much meat on him."

Rita thought back to the contents of Vicki's kitchen; Jesse's diet wasn't doing him any favors. He could do with a few more meals at The Shaft.

"Did you hear from him at any point today?"

"Nope," Vicki said. "Figured he got to work since no one called to say otherwise."

"His manager, Chester, said he was late today. Any idea why?"

"Nope."

"Did Jesse tell you about losing his key to the Gas-N-Go?"

Vicki's eyebrows shot up. "Like hell he didn't! That wouldn't be good for his chances at a promotion."

"Did he mention anything about Thursday night at The Shaft?"

"He was home by nine, like he should be," Vicki said. "Otherwise, I would've whipped his ass."

"Why nine," Rita asked, "considering Jesse is twenty-two?"

Vicki shifted. "He helps inject my Copaxone."

"I see," Rita said. "He's helpful, your son."

Vicki's shoulders softened. "The world ain't built for someone who ain't at full strength every day."

"I can only imagine the magnitude of the million little things you need to do every day. Home must feel like a very safe place."

"Sure is," Vicki said, her gaze roving around the office. "I don't like to leave it much."

"Then we'll finish up quick so you can get home soon," Rita said. "Did Jesse mention meeting Teddy Lake?"

"Who the hell is Teddy Lake?"

Rita pulled up a mugshot on her computer screen. "His photo was in the paper the other day."

Vicki leaned forward to squint at the screen. "Don't read the paper. Never seen him. Never heard of him, neither."

"You didn't hear about the homicide around town?"

Vicki shrugged. "I don't go into town."

"Right," Rita said. "Well, thanks for your compliance, eventually. Mary Lou has some paperwork for you. Then I'll give you a ride home, since you're wearing slippers."

Vicki snorted. "I'd rather eat shit than ride with a fascist pig." Her gaze flickered to Rita. "No offense."

Rita sighed. "None taken."

Chapter Thirty-Eight

"Smells delicious," Rita said, stepping into the house and kicking off her squeaky boots.

Cash appeared in the foyer, sleeves rolled up to reveal his well-muscled forearms, a kitchen towel slung over his shoulder. "You must be hungry."

"I could eat a bison." Shrugging off her coat, she pulled the bagged scrap of newspaper from her pocket and handed it to him. "Check this out."

Flipping it over, he read both sides, then handed it back. "What is it?"

"Might not mean anything," Rita said, hanging her puffer coat. "Found it at Otto's place." She paused at the foot of the stairs. "My plan is to ask about it at the *Chronicle*, except I don't particularly want to run into Blaze."

Upstairs, she tucked the newspaper clipping in her bedside drawer next to the photo of Otto with the woman. Then she field-stripped her service weapon and locked it in the gun safe before changing into her APEX sweats. In the bathroom, she washed her hands and face, then went downstairs to the kitchen.

Cash had set the table with fried chicken, cheesy potato skins, and green beans.

"It's warm, I think," he said when she walked in. "Though definitely not hot." He poked at a potato skin. "Cheese is congealed."

Inhaling, Rita slid into a chair. "Who cares? I'm pregnant, if it's homemade, it's getting devoured."

She picked up a chicken leg and bit into it. It wasn't warm, it was cold.

"Just as I suspected," she said. "Delicious." She wiped her mouth with a paper napkin. "Although in future, you should feel free to go ahead and eat."

Cash gave her a look. "Why would I want to do that?"

She gave him one back. "So the food's hot."

He growled. "I didn't move in with you to eat alone. I'll wait until midnight if I have to."

"Well, I'm here now," Rita said, with an overly bright smile. "No need to wait till midnight."

"Yeah, there is," he said, running his hands over her shoulders. He kneaded her tense muscles. "Let's unwind a bit, first. Since the food's cold anyway." He bent over to kiss her neck. "I promise not to manhandle your breasts."

Closed her eyelids, Rita relaxed into his touch, until her phone rang.

"Ignore it," Cash said against her skin.

"I can't," Rita said, pulling away. "This is now a double-homicide investigation." She picked up her phone from the kitchen table. "Plus, I might have a missing person."

Cash stepped away from her and dropped into his own chair. "Busy start to the week. I was hoping we could talk tonight about which crib we're getting."

She swiped open the screen. "It's Jason, I'll be quick." She put the phone to her ear. "Hi, Jason, what's up?"

"Caught the burglar," he said. "You might want to come see who it is for yourself."

"On my way," she said, hanging up.

Cash frowned. "You're leaving already?"

"I'll take a chicken leg with me," Rita said, grabbing one from the serving plate.

"What's up ? Has your missing person been found?"

"Nope," she said, getting up from the table. "But it's not a body either, so I shouldn't be long." She kissed him, quick, brief, and headed for the foyer.

Mumbling a goodbye, Cash stayed in his chair, poking at a potato skin.

Rita's heart clenched. "See you soon," she called out from the foyer.

Outside, she started the SUV again, relieved the driver's seat was still warm.

Traffic was light as she crossed town and pulled up to Jason's house. Several interior lights were on, illuminating the place like a lantern.

She parked and hurried up the front steps. Snow had started to stick to the porch railings.

Lucas Lake met her at the door, eyes bright, gripping a baseball bat.

"Hi, Lucas," Rita said. "You okay?"

He screwed his hands around the bat, resting it against his shoulders. "I heard someone trying to get in." His words came out in a rush. "I was taking a nap in the guest room and I woke up to someone trying to open the window. It was dark already, so I didn't see who what it was. And by the time I even figured out what was happening and ran downstairs to turn on the lights, they were gone. Or so I thought. I called Sheriff Perry and when he pulled into the driveway, he caught someone leaving on foot." Lucas cocked his head, gesturing. "They're in the kitchen."

Rita nodded and followed him inside, keeping her shoes and jacket on. She stepped into the kitchen, and stopped short.

Carol sat at the table, hands cuffed behind her back. Her dyed blonde hair was mussed, and dirt smudged her newly plumped cheek. Jason sat beside her, looking exhausted, his own hair clotted with dirt.

"Thank God you're here!" Carol spat.

"Hi, Rita," Jason said.

Carol twisted toward him. "Now that she's here, let me go."

Rita turned to Lucas. "Carol's my mother. Feel free to go back to bed."

Lucas hesitated, gripping the bat. He glanced at Jason, then exhaled and leaned the bat against the wall. "Okay."

As he left, Rita pulled up a chair. She glanced between Carol and Jason. "Looks like you two had a bit of a tussle."

Jason inclined his head towards the driveway out front. "She took off running. I chased her down."

Carol narrowed her eyes at him. "He hit me like a linebacker."

Jason scoffed. "And for good reason. You would've run off without coming clean." He met Rita's gaze. "She parked her van in the bushes halfway down the driveway."

Rita frowned. "I still don't get why you broke in through the window."

"Because you changed the locks."

She crossed her arms. "Because Jason lives here now."

Carol sniffed. "I don't care who the tenant is. It's my house."

Rita snorted. "Hardly."

Carol tilted her chin. "I've got the will to prove it."

"I inherited the house," Rita said. "You inherited the sewing machine."

Carol blinked. "Well, if you're looking for a renter, why not me?" She nodded toward Jason. "Instead of running a boarding house for your colleagues?"

"It's not my house anymore," Rita said. "I sold it."

Carol's face tightened. "What? I never saw it listed."

Rita squared her shoulders. "It was a private sale between me and Jason."

Carol's gaze darted between them. "Without an agent?"

"Saving on commissions meant I could give Jason a better deal," Rita said.

Carol's face darkened to a deeper shade of purple. "So you sold it to him? Who isn't even family? What about me? You know I need a home."

Rita folded her arms. "No, I didn't know that. I thought you were happy as a clam, roaming around in your van. Isn't that why they call you the SilverNomad? Besides, Jason *is* family."

Jason nodded. "She's right, I'm a *bona fide* uncle." He shot Rita a sidelong glance. "Though I don't think clams roam."

Ignoring him, Rita turned back to Carol. "So why are you here, casing the house?"

Carol wrinkled her nose. "It's none of your business."

"Oh, I think it is," Rita said, through gritted teeth. "My town. My house. My friend. Not to mention, you scared the bejeezus out of Teddy Lake's brother."

Carol set her jaw. "I was looking for something. Something that used to be here."

Rita studied her. "Are you the one that pried up a board on the back porch."

Carol squared her shoulders. "I won't submit to your interrogation tactics, Rita."

"Um, okay," she said. "And what are you looking for?"

Carol shrugged. "You'd know it if you saw it."

Rita rolled her eyes. "Oh, for the love of—" She paused. "Is it the newspaper clipping?"

Carol blanched. "Newspaper?"

"In the space under the porch."

Carol shook her head. "I don't know anything about that."

Rita sighed. "I always know when you're lying. And you're not welcome back at the house."

Carol glanced between Rita and Jason. "Oh, come on now. Just give me a minute to look around. Now that I'm here."

"I can't allow that," Rita said. "This is Jason's home now. It doesn't belong to our family."

Carol let out a little sob. "It's just so hard…"

Jason rubbed his temples. "Oh, go ahead and look," he said. "I'm exhausted, and I really don't mind." He glanced at Rita. "If you don't."

Rita threw up her hands. "Oh, why the hell not?" She fixed her gaze on Carol. "Just be quick about it."

Jason got up and walked around the table to unlock Carol's cuffs. Without a word, she scurried out of the kitchen.

"Just leave Lucas alone," Rita called after her. "He's staying in the guest room."

Carol didn't respond as she headed into the foyer and yanked open the coat closet.

Rita looked at Jason. "Sorry about this."

"It's all good," Jason said. "But I gotta say, it's one hell of a way to get to know your mother." He leaned back in his chair. "Makes you think, doesn't it?"

"About what?" Rita asked.

"What made us the way we are," Jason said. "Our mothers have a lot of influence on us."

"Well, I'd like to think I'm nothing like Carol," Rita said.

Jason laughed. "And I'd say the same about mine. But that's what I mean by influence. They either shape us to be like them, or push us to be the complete opposite."

"Otto always used to say the apple doesn't fall far from the tree," Rita said with a sigh.

Jason shrugged. "Some apples roll all the way down the hill after they fall." He chuckled. "Some of us end up sprouting in altogether different soil."

Rita laughed. "New York was all downhill from this place."

Jason gazed through the kitchen window. "Funny thing is, your kid's probably gonna spend a lot of time growing up here too."

Rita felt tears creep into her eyes. She opened her mouth to respond, but her throat tightened.

Jason smiled. "Because isn't that my job as an uncle? I always liked obstacle courses as a kid, used to set them up for my sisters. I never met a kid who wasn't jazzed about an obstacle course."

Carol reentered the kitchen, empty-handed.

"Find what you were looking for?" Rita asked, recovering her voice.

Carol grunted.

"Now don't come back," Rita said, getting up. "Next time, Jason will charge you with trespassing." She headed for the foyer and Jason followed. "I'll walk you to your van."

Still silent, Carol followed them to the door. Rita bade

Jason goodnight, then stepped out with Carol as he softly closed the door behind them.

Rita let out a breath, looking up at the stars. The night was clear, a welcome respite from the flurries. Then she squared her shoulders and set off down the driveway, their feet crunching on the gravel.

"In here," Carol said, finally speaking. She stepped off the driveway and into the underbrush. Tire tracks had flattened the grass where her van was parked, hidden in the bushes. She pulled back some branches and moonlight bounced off the silver paint, reflecting like liquid metal.

"Nice paint job," Rita said, willing to compliment Carol's vehicle over her recent cosmetic updates. She wagged a finger. "Fancy decals."

"Thanks," Carol said. "If you were a subscriber, you'd have seen the new paint job. I posted several before-and-after videos."

"I'm sure you did," Rita said.

"I designed the logo myself using one of those free apps. I think it's the perfect blend of nostalgia and wanderlust." She dug in her coat pocket for the key. "All part of my brand."

"Your *brand*?"

Carol lifted her chin. "I've gained quite a following. My page gets a lot of traction."

"Thanks in part to me," Rita muttered.

Carol unlocked the driver's door. "I'll admit, videos featuring you get the most likes."

Rita stiffened. "Well, enjoy your wandering ways. You've always been transient."

Carol paused, throwing Rita a look before climbing into the seat. "That's not true. What about all the years I settled down to raise you?"

Rita scoffed. "Settled down? *You?*" She shook her head. "This from the woman who abandoned me. Twice."

Carol snorted. "Abandoned you *twice?* Who told you that?"

"So it's true?" Rita asked.

"I didn't leave you. Not the first time." She climbed into the seat and fastened her seatbelt. "It was Otto's doing."

Rita frowned. "I don't understand."

Carol gripped the door handle, pulling git closed. "He kicked me out."

Then she slammed the door and turned the ignition before Rita could respond.

Rita took a step back as the van's tires spun against the dirt, breaking branches. Then the wheels hit the driveway, spraying gravel.

A cloud of dust blurred the taillights as Carol disappeared into the night.

Chapter Thirty-Nine

A WAVE of homesickness washed over Rita as she smelled Mary Lou's coffee percolating in the staff room. It had never been as good as Skyler's, but always there when Rita needed it.

She walked into the bullpen, where Mary Lou and Jason sat around Candace's desk, steaming cups of coffee in hand. Jason looked up as she entered.

"Morning, Rita. You're right on time to go over the autopsy." He set aside his mug, which read, *'I like it hot &* *creamy'*, and hopped up. "I'll grab you a chair."

As he disappeared into his office, Rita glanced at Candace, whose pallor rivaled a leek's.

She clapped Candace on the shoulder. "You got this, Watkins."

Candace gave a stiff nod.

Jason returned, rolling a desk chair toward her. "Here's your ol' saddle, Jonas."

"Awesome," Rita said, dropping into it. "I've missed this baby." She lowered the seat with the lever, then she adjusted the headrest, lumbar support, and armrests.

"There," she said as the last clip locked into place. "Ready."

"Ready as a damn rocket," Mary Lou said. "You planning to blast off?"

Jason laughed. "She already did that when she went to APEX."

Rita stuck out her tongue at him. "Let's hear about the autopsy."

"Right," Jason said, tapping he stack of glossy photographs on the desk. "Do you want to start with Teddy Lake's head, or Donald Horgan's decapitated body?"

Candace stifled a burp.

Jason reached for a cardboard box stamped with the Big Horn Bean logo and set in the center of the desk. "Muffin? Sometimes having something in your stomach helps with the nausea."

Rita helped herself to two. "One hundred percent."

Candace belched. "No thank you."

"I'll start with Donald Horgan's body," Jason said. "Casper Forensics is close to certain that the victim was shot in the head. There's plenty of brain and skull matter on the wall behind him."

He displayed a close-up photograph of the victim slumped on a blood-soaked sofa. To the side of the body, a dark, starburst-shaped stain spread across the wall, embedded with fragments of bone and brain tissue.

Jason laid out additional photographs showing the living room walls and ceiling. "The blood spatter patterns on the walls also support this scenario."

He gestured to an image of the corner where the two living room walls met. A high-velocity spray of red droplets radiated outwards in a chaotic pattern. Another shot revealed the ceiling, where arterial blood had spattered in a thin arc, curling toward the light fixture.

"The bullet entered just above the right ear and exited near the left temple," Jason continued, flipping to another photo of the autopsy report. "The wound path suggests the gun was angled slightly downward, which is consistent with someone seated beside him pressing the muzzle to his head."

He tapped a final image, one showing a close-up of the victim's hands. "There's no evidence of defensive wounds or hesitation marks." He exhaled, placing the last photo on the top of the pile. "It would seem the killer sat beside him on the sofa, put the gun to his head, and pulled the trigger."

"What do we know about the firearm?" Rita asked, biting into a lemon poppy seed muffin.

"Nothing," Jason said. "No bullet found. And none found at the crime scene. So without the skull to examine, the hypothesis stops here."

"And what about the decapitation marks?" Rita asked through a mouthful. "Was it an angle grinder in this case, too?"

"Not an angle grinder this time," Jason said. "Different serration patterns, but we don't have an answer on that either yet."

"Got it," Rita said, sampling the carrot cream-cheese muffin. "And what about the carvings in his chest?"

"The lacerations of the five-pointed star and the letter M follow the same directional paths as the carvings on Teddy. Same handiwork, in that regard. But again, a different instrument was used."

"So it's all hands on deck, still looking for this head," Mary Lou said, snapping her chewing gum. "At least the whole family's working together again."

Rita couldn't help but smile. The urge to have a mug of Mary Lou's coffee intensified.

"Next, we'll examine Teddy Lake's head injuries," Jason said, flipping through the glossy prints. He selected a close-up image of the victim's severe cranial trauma and placed it on the desk.

Candace shifted in her seat.

"Before decapitation," Jason said, "Teddy Lake was first struck in the mouth with a heavy object. Something like a club. It shattered his teeth, as seen here." He selected another photo. "Fragments were found in his throat."

"Jesus," Rita said.

"Then the same object came down on his head," Jason continued, sifting through the pile for a different photo-graph, "as fragments of teeth were also found embedded in the skull."

Rita slid the muffin box towards Candace.

"It also appears that Teddy's head had been kept frozen," Jason said, "as there wasn't much decay."

Candace selected a muffin.

"I recommend the lemon-poppyseed," Rita said. "It's quite bland." Then she narrowed her eyes at the muffin she was eating. "Not sure what I think of this carrot affair."

"I love carrot cake," Mary Lou said. "In fact, I make a mean one. What's wrong with this one?"

"It has raisins *and* walnuts," Rita said. "Surprise me with soft, squishy things. Or surprise me with hard nuggets. But this business of having both isn't working for me." She took a swallow of her London Fog tea to clear her mouth. "What makes your carrot cake mean?"

"Pineapple juice," Mary Lou said.

Candace set down her muffin. "I'm not sure I can eat this. It tastes like stomach acid."

Jason cleared his throat and tapped the stack of

photographs against the table, aligning them into a neat pile. "If there aren't any questions about Teddy's head, we can move on to the crime scene forensics."

"I still got questions about Don Horgan's head," Mary Lou said. "He was my neighbor's mechanic for nearly twenty years. Solid guy, came and did some work at her place once to save her the cost of a tow. This isn't just any old head. It's a highly recognizable one. Not like Teddy Lake's." Mary Lou shook her own head, her silver bouffant like a halo. "And you're suggesting it's in someone's freezer, here in Still?"

"Could be in a freezer truck," Candace said, suppressing hiccups.

"Which is why you better be keeping things professional with Abe Cunningham," Rita said, cutting Mary Lou a look.

Mary Lou bugged her eyes at her. "It was only a pineapple cake."

Rita narrowed hers. "And lasagna."

Jason cleared his throat. "I love your lasagna, too, Mary Lou, but let's get back to the crime scene. It's confirmed that whoever was in the house used the bleach and mop to clean up their footprints. Lana Horgan confirmed that the mop and pail and bleach were all theirs. Fingerprints were lifted, all of them Lana's or Don's. Nothing else out of the ordinary was found at the crime scene."

"Seems like the killer knew where to find the cleaning supplies," Candace said.

"And that Lana would be away from the house," Rita added. "It wasn't a typical night for a Moon Meetup, so Don must have mentioned she'd be out."

Jason nodded. "That's it for the forensics update." He looked at Candace. "How's it going for you, Deputy?"

Candace burped and Jason swiveled his gaze to Mary Lou. "Why don't you go ahead, Mary Lou?"

"I went through the Horgans' phone records, both their landline and each of their cell phones. There were no incoming calls that night, perhaps because all their acquaintances knew Don was an avid fan and would be watching the race. And location tracking confirmed Lana was at Carly's Crystals, and then the women's shelter in Casper. They also confirmed she left shortly after eleven."

"Thanks," Jason said. He turned back to Candace. "Deputy?"

Nodding, Candace took a sip of coffee. "I spoke to all the employees at the Gas-N-Go, which totals six guys including Jesse. No one knew he'd been fired because Chester reported he'd left without saying goodbye."

"Suicide risk?" Jason asked.

"Unlikely," Candace said. "One of the jockeys, Rodney Potter, said Jesse was in good spirits. He had a secret he was excited about but had to wait a few days to share it."

"So he's got a big secret and leaves work without telling anyone," Jason said, tapping his pen.

"Chester also reported that Jesse had left his dirt bike behind," Candace said. "Chester found it around back where Jesse usually parked it out of sight."

"Shit," Rita said. "This ain't lookin' good for Jesse."

Chapter Forty

RITA WALKED into the conference room, where Craig sat in front of the desktop computer, slurping from a cup of instant soup.

She glanced at her watch. "Lunch hour already?"

Craig looked up and shrugged. "It's already eleven-thirty."

"But you probably had breakfast at nine-thirty."

Craig met her eye. "How'd you know?"

Rita set a cardboard Bighorn Bean box on the table. "Leftover muffins from the autopsy review."

Craig set aside his styrofoam soup cup and flipped open the lid. "Excellent." He grabbed a cranberry muffin.

"No one was particularly hungry," Rita said, taking a blueberry one. "Except me." She pulled out a chair and sat down. "How's it going with the calls?"

"No more truckers," Craig said. "Tips seemed to have dried up."

"That's to be expected," Rita said. Squeezing her eyes shut, she rubbed her temples. "After those autopsy photos, I need to get my mind off of this case."

"I've got a question for you," Craig said, chewing on his muffin.

Rita opened her eyes. "Oh, yeah?"

"How do you open a banana?"

Rita blinked at him. "I told you, the ass-end—"

"No, no, it's a joke," Craig said.

"Okay," Rita said with a shrug, "how do you open a banana?"

Craig grinned. "With a mon-*key*."

Rita couldn't help but smile. "Thanks," she said, " I needed that." She ran her hands over her head, then tightened her bun. "Everyone's funny these days. By the way, you hear if forensics got back to us on the padlock or washcloth from Jesse's house?"

"No word yet."

"Didn't think so," Rita said. She rested her chin on her hands. "I need to stare at Jim playing solitaire and eating a pizza pretzel. Well, today maybe not a pizza pretzel. Can I swap some time with the security footage while you run through some files for me?"

Craig perked up. "What kind of files?"

"Teddy's dad, Sergeant Theodore Lake, his records arrived from Casper PD. Mostly traffic stuff, but some thefts and B&Es. Skim for anything that stands out."

"Deal," Craig said, pushing the remainder of the muffins into his mouth.

"Came in a few minutes ago." Rita navigated to her email. "This link will take you to the files."

Then she handed him her phone and Craig took his soup to the far end of the conference table, away from the humming desktop. He propped up his feet up and leaned back in the chair to scroll through the files, sipping from the styrofoam cup.

Rita cleared her throat.

Craig looked up.

"Boots," she said.

"Boots," he echoed, lowering his feet and tucking them beneath him.

Rita turned back to the monitor and started scrubbing through the footage, speeding it up.

Over several days, Jim's routine played out like clockwork. Craig was right, nothing stood out. Same habits, same schedule. The man even used the bathroom at the exact same time every day. Either he wasn't stealing company secrets, or he had hidden it so well that—

Her eyes widened.

"Fucking hell," she muttered.

Craig glanced up. "What's that?"

"That's how he did it," she said, tapping the monitor. "How the hell did we miss this?"

Craig leaned forward. "Miss what?"

Rita switched to a different camera angle, tracking the suspect through the building. He wasn't acting alone, he was meeting someone.

"Well, I'll be damned. It was right in front of us this whole time," Rita said. "We've been watching the wrong person."

Craig blinked. "I have no idea what you're talking about. Who were we supposed to be watching?"

"Hang on." Rita pulled up footage from the previous month. Fast-forwarding through several days, she watched the pattern repeat.

"I need to check something," she said. "In private. Can you go upstairs to my office?"

Craig frowned, then got up and lumbered out of the conference room, dumping his soup cup in the trash can.

Rita swiped open her cell phone and rang Ginny.

"Hey, Ginny," she said. "Could you please swing by with your snack cart? I'm in the conference room."

While she waited, Rita scanned through another week's worth of tape. The same pattern, every time.

"Hi, Ms. Jonas," Ginny said, rolling into the conference room with the snack cart. "I just restocked the protein bars."

"Have a seat," Rita said, gesturing to a chair.

Ginny hesitated, confused. Then she released her grip on the snack cart and sat at the table. "Y-yes?"

Rita met her eye. "How long have you been involved in corporate espionage?"

Ginny's complexion turned white. "What?"

Rita drew Ginny's attention to the computer monitor, pointing to the time stamp on the paused footage. "Every Wednesday morning, you deliver Jim a pizza pretzel and coffee. The two items total four dollars and eighty cents. He passes you a five-dollar bill and tells you to keep the change."

Her gaze glued to the monitor, Ginny nodded but said nothing.

"I pay my tab once a month," Rita said, "which is typical, right?"

Ginny dragged her gaze to meet Rita's but stayed silent.

"Isn't that how it's done around here?"

Ginny pulled in her lower lip. "Um."

"But not Jim," Rita said. "He always pays using a five-dollar bill."

Ginny continued to chew her lip. "Uh-huh."

"May I see the bills, please?" Rita asked. "You should have four in your cash box for the previous weeks."

Ginny swallowed. "Um, I don't have them."

"That's right," Rita said. "Because…"

She moved the mouse, closing the current window and pulling up a different camera feed. She hit play. The footage showed Ginny rolling the snack cart back to the front lobby, where Martin met her.

"There," Rita said, pausing the video. "Martin buys a coffee and a pizza pretzel. Then he hands you a ten-dollar bill." She pointed at the screen. "And you hand him back Jim's five-dollar bill as change."

Ginny's words tumbled out in a rush. "I didn't know what was going on at first, Ms. Jonas, I swear! Martin asked if he could pay cash, like Jim, and I said I supposed so."

"It's unusual for employees to pay weekly with cash, isn't it?" Rita asked.

Ginny nodded. "Uh-huh. The first time, I didn't think much of it. But the second time, I noticed Jim had written something on the bill. I tried to read it, but Martin saw me looking. He told me not to worry about it, then he offered me fifty bucks a month in tips. He said he'd keep tipping me well if I just looked the other way."

Rita raised an eyebrow. "A tip, huh?"

Tears welled in Ginny's eyes. "Am I gonna lose my job?"

"Lose your job?" Rita echoed. "Trade secret violations can carry up to ten years in prison."

Ginny let out a shuddering breath. "I can't go to jail," she whispered. "I didn't know it was bad, Martin was always so nice about it. I was just doing what I was told."

"Doing something against policy," Rita said. "For money."

Ginny's voice rose in pitch. "I can't live in some cell. My parents will hate me. I'll miss my best dating years. And when I get out, no one will hire me. Or marry me. Or even be my friend! I'll be that girl who went to prison for screwing up her whole life over one stupid mistake!"

"Take it easy," Rita said. "I might be able to help you."

Ginny wiped her eyes. "Yeah?"

"If you do exactly as you're told," Rita said. "Which, let's be honest, you've already proven you're good at."

"I swear, Ms. Jonas." Ginny drew an X across her heart. "I'll do whatever I need to."

Rita held her gaze. "But if you take one wrong step…"

Chapter Forty-One

RITA CLICKED THE MOUSE, opening a live feed from the security cameras. Frame by frame, she watched Ginny go through her usual Wednesday lunchtime routine.

"She delivers the pizza pretzel to Jim, takes his five-dollar bill, and walks out to the lobby," Rita narrated. "Martin Middleton happens to be passing through, stops to pick up a coffee and a pizza pretzel, hands her a bill, and she gives him Jim's five as change."

On-screen, Ginny returned to her desk. But Martin lingered, leaning an elbow on the counter. He appeared to be asking her a question.

Ginny shook her head and tapped her temple, then pulled a bottle, probably Tylenol, from the drawer and gave it a shake. Martin shrugged and turned away, crossing the lobby to the sliding glass doors.

Rita stayed on the camera feed, watching the afternoon unfold. Jim remained at his desk. Ginny stayed at hers. Martin patrolled the guards by golf cart.

Then she called Cash. "Remember when you asked if you could be my new deputy?"

He chuckled. "What's up?"

"I need help with something, but I can't bring the SCSO in. And I don't trust anyone at APEX."

"Sounds interesting," Cash said.

"Can you pick me up at the office in ten minutes?"

"Cabbage rolls are already in the slow cooker. I'm on my way."

Rita stepped through the front doors of APEX and crossed the parking lot to the guard's hut.

Martin was returning the golf cart. He leaned out with a wave when he saw her.

"Hi, Ms. Jonas."

"Hi, Martin," Rita said with a smile.

"Can I help you?"

Still smiling, she shook her head. "No, just waiting for Cash. He's giving me a lift."

"Something wrong with the Beemer?"

"Nope, just an appointment. I'll pick it up in the morning." She pointed past him. "Here he is now. Have a good night, Martin."

Cash pulled up to the gate and idled. Rita walked around the side of the hut to the curb where's Cash's Dodge idled. She climbed into the passenger seat and gave him a peck on the cheek.

"Nice to see you, too," he said, leaning in for a kiss on the lips.

But she pulled away and buckled her belt. "Not too many public displays of affection. I made a show of saying goodbye to Middleton, and hopefully he idly watched me walk over here."

"Not really sure what any of that means," Cash said, putting his hands on the wheel, "but I figure I'll catch on quick, as the deputy."

Rita buckled in and pointed through the windshield. "Take that side road along the property, please."

"Sure thing."

Cash turned onto the less-traveled path. "What's going on?"

"This is where someone broke in the other night to dump the body, if suspending it from the trees and decorating it with a deer's head can be considered dumping."

Cash pulled over at a gap in the fence, where a neon-yellow rope stitched the ruptured chain link together. "Here, presumably."

Rita unbuckled and climbed out. Together, they approached the fence. She almost felt tempted to hold his hand, like she did when they went for weekend walks in the neighborhood or downtown.

"I've got all sorts of doohickeys," she said, gesturing to the taser, handcuffs, pistol, and everything else on her belt. "But I don't have a penknife."

"Allow me." Cash flicked open the pocketknife he carried in his back pocket and started slicing through the nylon twine. It took him a solid six minutes to cut enough loops free to pry back the chain link.

"You coming?" he asked from the other side.

"Baby and I don't fit through as easily as you, Daddy," Rita said, protecting her stomach as she squeezed through. She motioned towards APEX HQ. "This way."

Keeping to the trees, they made their way back toward the building, passing by the chemical storehouses and pump sheds. They hung back in a shadow and Rita pointed at the guard's hut.

"Middleton's coming off shift any minute now," Rita said, checking her watch. "He just finished his rounds so he'll be dropping off his keys and checking in with the guard before leaving."

A few minutes later, Martin emerged from the hut and headed toward his SUV on the far side of the lot.

"Let's go," Rita said.

They retraced their steps, climbing the hill and squeezing through the vent in the fence again.

"I'm driving," Rita said.

Cash tossed her the keys and they climbed in and buckled up. Rita cruised along the dirt track, returning to the main exit from APEX. She turned onto the asphalt and spotted Middleton's SUV a quarter mile ahead.

"Not much foliage for cover at this time of year," Cash said. "Guess we'll have to hang back."

"Clever deputy," Rita said. "Or else the son of a criminal mastermind."

"Funny."

"In all seriousness," Rita said, "you're right. It will be hard to hide. So I figured our best bet was coming in from a different road and hoping your vehicle blends in better than mine."

"Now you're funny," he said with a wink. "I got something to tell you."

Rita glanced at him. "Yeah?"

"That newspaper clipping you showed me?"

"Uh-huh?"

"Hope you don't mind, but I took a photo of it and sent it to Tom's lawyer, Alan Crawford."

"That surprises me."

Cash shrugged. "Figured if anyone could decipher it, he could."

"I'd agree with that," Rita admitted.

But before she could say more, Martin surprised her. Instead of driving into Still, he veered onto the freeway on-ramp. Rita hit the gas to merge behind him.

"Well, here we go," she said. "Headed to Beaumont."

But then, once again, Martin threw her off, taking an exit she didn't recognize.

"Keep going," Cash said, waving her on.

"What?" Rita asked.

"Trust me." Cash grinned. "I'm your deputy tonight, ain't I?"

Setting her jaw, Rita drove past the exit. "I'm trusting you."

"It's coming up here real quick," Cash said. He leaned forward, peering through the windshield. "See up ahead there? Where those antlers are nailed to the tree? Take that turn."

"No," she said, putting on her signal, "I don't see the turn. And I'm not sure I want to see any more antlers up a tree in this lifetime, especially if they're decorating a dead—"

"Here," Cash said, pointing.

Rita braked hard to make the turn. "Jesus, that was a tight one."

"Lots of little country roads around here that used to make sense before the freeway was widened," Cash said. "Take this one down to the bottom of the hill. It connects with the exit ramp."

As Rita pulled up to the stop sign at the T-section, Martin drove past her, then took a right.

Cash pointed. "There's our mark."

Rita took a right, then another, then saw the SUV pulling into the parking lot of a playground.

"Turn left," Cash said. "We can park behind the washroom block and not be visible from the parking lot."

"Perfect," Rita said, pulling up to the curb and turning off the ignition. "But why do I have a feeling you've done this before?"

"I only know this park because I took Heather's kids

here a few times," Cash said. He gave her a reassuring smile. "She needed a babysitter to take meetings with her lawyer."

"Of course," Rita said, avoiding his gaze and getting out of the car. She walked around the hood of the car to join him on the sidewalk. "Which way now?"

He waved her into a sloping grove of pine trees overlooking the playground nestled in the vale. A red tube slide and a yellow climbing structure stood out among the gathering drifts of snow.

Passing the playground, they climbed up the other side of the slope, entering a wooded area. From there, they had a clear view of the parking lot. Martin's SUV was parked nose-to-nose with a white Cadillac CT6. Both drivers' windows were lowered, snow drifting inside both vehicles.

Martin passed something small. While looking like an average drug deal, the goods were likely a thumb drive. Then Martin raised his window and left.

"Let's move," Rita said, heading back down the treed hill. She and Cash ran past the children's area and back up the other side of the slope.

"Shit," Rita muttered. "All this running makes me have to pee."

"Everything makes you pee," Cash said, out of breath.

They arrived at the Dodge and jumped in. Rita pulled away from the curb and made a U-turn to head back to the freeway. As she did, she spotted Martin's SUV pulling out of the parking lot. A minute later, the white car followed, moving at a slower pace.

"Get me the plate," Rita said, pulling onto the road.

Cash popped the glove box, pulled out a notepad, and rummaged for a pencil. He jotted down the number, then tore out the page.

The CT6 merged onto the freeway, but instead of heading toward Still, it took the exit for the interstate.

"Looks like we're going to Casper," Rita said with a sigh. "Better settle in."

But when they passed the second exit for Casper, Rita's heart sank—and so did her bladder.

"I have a feeling we're not going to Casper."

"Fuck, not Cheyenne," Cash groaned. "Not that I mind, bein' your deputy and all. But I was hoping to get you into bed early tonight."

"How unprofessional, Deputy Gabriel," Rita said with a wink. She had a lot of reasons to go to bed early, too, most of them related to sleep.

For several minutes they drove in silence, the rumble of the tires against the road and the dashboard fans the only sounds between them. The freeway stretched ahead, mostly empty, with only the occasional semis, sedans, and pickups passing by. Rita maintained a steady distance behind the Cadillac.

Then, the vehicle's turn signal blinked on, cutting through the darkness.

"Hold hope," Rita said. "Looks like they're turning off."

"For gas," Cash said, pointing ahead at the fluorescent sign for a Shell station.

Rita jacked the wheel, pulling onto the shoulder.

"Keep an eye on him," she said, unbuckling her seatbelt. "I gotta pee."

"Sure," Cash said.

Rita darted behind the car, yanked down her APEX-issue pants, and squatted. The cold night air nipped at her thighs, causing her tissues to tighten. She sighed, relaxing her muscles, and peed on the asphalt, shifting her weight on her heels to avoid splashback.

Then she scrambled back into the driver's seat, reaching past Cash to rummage in the dashboard for hand sanitizer.

"Is he still there?" she asked.

"Yep," Cash said, looking over her head through the windshield. But he never got out. Pulled into the full-service bay."

She located a small container and pumped some in her hand.

"He's paying now," Cash said.

Rita sat upright and pulled on her seatbelt as the Cadillac's taillights illuminated.

"It's go time," Rita said, clicking the buckle and pulling onto the freeway. She kept her speed low until she saw the Cadillac merge, then punched the gas to close some of the distance.

The miles ticked by and the sky deepened to indigo. To the west, the faint outline of the Laramie Mountains was barely visible against the darkening dome. Billboards whizzed past, floating rectangles in the gloaming. One advertised a cowboy museum, another promoted a truck stop famous for its pie. Campaign signs dotted the roadside, their slogans and smiles half-lit by passing headlights. Cattle fences stretched endlessly, interrupted only by the occasional gravel road leading off into the unknown.

Almost two hours later, the Cadillac finally signaled and took an exit.

"Thank God we're not going all the way into Cheyenne," Cash said. He looked around at a rolling hills dotted with juniper and ponderosas. "And you think we're rural."

"It's pretty out here," Rita said. "More pines than we have around our place."

"Long-ass commute for our Cadillac driver," Cash said. "Must be something good on that thumb drive."

"Must be," Rita said. "Seeing as they make this trip every Wednesday."

Rita followed as the Cadillac turned onto a quiet rural road, where sprawling historical ranches stretched across the rolling hills. Wooden rail fences, painted as white as the snow itself, traced neat boundaries around the estates, where stately homes and stables sat nestled in sapphire-blue snowdrifts.

At last, the Cadillac slowed before a grand mansion of pale stone, its roof white with frost. Wide columns framed the deep green double door. Its tall, rectangular windows glowed golden-yellow in the dusk.

At the base of the hedge-lined driveway, a security gate dusted with snow opened with a mechanical hum, and the Cadillac glided through.

Cash whistled. "Nice place."

"This is the governor's house," Rita said.

"No shit?"

"And you know something else?" Rita said.

"What's that?"

She parked the pickup behind a ponderosa. "I gotta pee again."

Chapter Forty-Two

"I SLEPT IN," Rita said, entering the kitchen and trudging straight to the refrigerator.

At the stove, Cash stood in a denim barbecue apron, flipping flapjacks. "Didn't think you were drinking coffee these days."

"Today demands an exception," she said with a yawn. She uncapped the jug of orange juice and filled a cup. "We didn't get home till past midnight."

Cash nodded. "I'm feeling it myself."

Rita took her cup to the table, where Cash had already laid out two place settings.

"Dig in," he said, flipping the last of the pancakes.

"Thanks, this looks amazing," Rita said, drizzling maple syrup over her stack. The dining room window framed the morning sky, peach-colored and cloud-streaked.

He turned around to face her. "I've already been hard at work today," he said with a grin, his teeth bright against his five o'clock shadow.

Rita sucked a drop of syrup from her fingertip. "Oh yeah?"

"You're not going to believe this," he said, striking a pose with his fists on his hips, "but I'm happy to report that Alan Crawford came through for us."

Rita cut into her flapjacks. "Oh, yeah?"

"He found the article linked to the torn newspaper clipping from Otto's house."

Rita stabbed a forkful of pancakes and shoved them into her mouth. "Oh yeah, these are good."

"Can you say anything other than 'oh, yeah'?" Cash asked.

"Sorry," Rita said with a smile, "I've only got two brain cells firing. But more are coming back online with every bite. Good work, Deputy Gabriel. On account of the flapjacks as well."

Cash grabbed his open laptop from the counter and set it on the kitchen table. "I've got it right here," he said, clicking twice before rotating the screen toward her.

She pulled the laptop closer, scanning the article while he returned to the stove. A black-and-white photo showed an accident on the highway. A uniformed officer stood in the frame, identified as Deputy Theodore Lake. Beside him was the motorist who was first on the scene:

Carol Jonas.

"What the fuck?" Rita said through a mouthful of pancake. She put her finger on the scroll pad and bumped up the photo to read the article.

LOCAL AUTHORITIES REPORTED that an armored truck transporting a large sum of cash to Elk Mountain Equity was involved in a fatal accident on the freeway late yesterday afternoon. The truck was traveling southbound when a severe storm, which had already caused widespread damage by toppling trees and power lines, turned deadly. A large tree fell across the highway directly in the truck's path, leaving the driver with no time to react.

The armored vehicle collided with the tree at high speed, resulting in extensive damage. The impact caused the truck's fuel tank to rupture, and it was engulfed in flames within moments. Tragically, neither of the guards inside the vehicle were able to escape, and both were killed in the subsequent explosion. Authorities are continuing to investigate the incident.

Rita's hands trembled, and she set down her knife and fork. "This is where the money came from," she said, her voice quiet.

Cash approached the table again, carrying the tray loaded with steaming pancakes. He set it down and rubbed a hand across Rita's shoulder blades, his touch warm through her T-shirt.

"1981," she said, pointing to the date. "Matches the age of the bills. Carol must have stolen it from the armored vehicle. And Theodore Lake Senior knew about it."

"But why didn't he say anything for all those years?" Cash asked.

"Because he likely stole money too," Rita said, scooping up another forkful of pancake. The syrup was rich and dark, but suddenly, it tasted like nothing. "And they kept it a secret between the two of them."

Cash untied the apron around his waist and hung it on the back of his chair, before taking a seat. "Until now."

Rita closed the laptop lid and pushed it aside. "Exactly. Whether he was delirious or guilt-riddled, he obviously disclosed the event when he was dying."

"And somehow he knew Carol was Otto's wife?" Cash asked.

Rita shrugged. "Law enforcement's a small world."

"So Teddy Lake came to Still to get the money," Cash said. "But how?"

"Maybe he planned to blackmail Carol," Rita said. "Teddy's research probably led him to Otto's obituary. And he assumed that Carol would still be living here."

His expression soured, as if the flapjacks had turned to ash. "You don't think … Carol killed Teddy, do you?"

Rita swallowed the last of her orange juice, its citrus sourness clashing with the syrupy sweetness on her tongue. "It's not easy to imagine."

She wiped her hands on her napkin, then unlocked her phone and dialed Carol. The all went straight to voicemail. Then she texted: *Call me now.*

For a minute, Rita ate her pancakes in silence, barely tasting them.

Then Rita's phone rang, and both she and Cash jumped in their seats. She snatched it up, but it wasn't Carol calling.

"Hi, Jason."

"Hi, Rita," he said, a note of tension in his voice. "You're not going to believe this."

"Try me," Rita said. "I've already heard that one today."

"Well, are you sitting down?" Jason asked, his voice still tight.

"Uh-huh," Rita said, "and eating my breakfast too."

"Well, I've got a whole bunch of people calling the station, making all sorts of wild claims."

"Uh-oh," Rita said. Her stomach clenched. "What do they say?"

"That something's happened to Carol," Jason said. "And that maybe her daughter killed her."

Chapter Forty-Three

"LET ME HAVE A LOOK," Rita said to Jason. "I'll call you back."

She hung up and reopened the laptop, her fingers moving quickly across the trackpad. Navigating to Carol's *SilverNomad* YouTube channel, she found a live stream still running. But instead of Carol's usual scenic vistas or rambling confessionals, the camera was pointed at the ground, a blurry patch of dirt and dead grass filling the frame.

"Cash, get a look at this," Rita said, scrolling through the flood of comments.

Carol, are you okay?

Pick up, Carol.

Someone should call the police.

Then, among the frantic messages, a darker comment stood out.

"'I bet that daughter murdered her,'" Cash read over her shoulder, his voice sharp with disgust.

Rita clicked back to rewind the recording.

The video began with Carol in the driver's seat, chatting to the camera as she guided the van down a rural road. She talked about her meeting with Rita at Jason's house the other night, acknowledging a reconciliation of sorts with her daughter.

Mid-sentence, she paused to take a left turn onto a narrow road lined with bone-white birch trees, then continued her monologue. A moment later, she passed a red barn with a collapsed roof, its broken beams jutting skyward like ribs.

"I know where that is," Cash said, tapping the screen. "That's Cowie Road, east side of town."

"What's down there?"

"State-owned land," Cash said. "A whole lotta sage-brush and a whole lotta wind."

"Then it's probably a good place to park her camper van," Rita said. "No Sheriff Perry showing up, telling her to move along."

On-screen, Carol pulled over and climbed out, phone in hand. She announced to the camera that she'd found her newest slice of heaven, the perfect quiet place to sleep beneath the stars. Or at least, park the van beneath the stars.

Her voice softened as she spotted something nearby—an owl's nest, or maybe a squirrel's drey, perched high in a crooked pine. She took it as a sign from her spirit guides, a reminder that home wasn't about a place but about the people we carry in our hearts.

"…And that's why I keep my family with me, always," she added. "Rita, if you're watching this, I—"

A scuffle sounded, then a gasp. The phone tilted, the snowy trees spinning past in a dizzying blur. Then the phone hit the frosty ground, followed by a sickening *thud*.

More scuffles.

A choked cry.

Then—

Silence.

"Shit," Rita breathed, shoving back from the table. "I gotta go."

"You're not going alone," Cash said, already moving toward the foyer. "I'll grab your keys."

"Fine," Rita said, knowing better than to argue. She sprinted to the half-bath, hands shaking as she fumbled with her belt, relieved herself as fast as humanly possible, then raced to the foyer.

Cash tossed her the keys and Rita caught them, shoving them into her pocket before jamming her feet into her squeaky boots. She grabbed her puffer coat but didn't bother putting it on.

Outside, the cold air slapped Rita's face as she bolted for the passenger side of the crossover. Cash slid behind the wheel, turned the ignition, and cranked up the heat.

Still hugging her coat to her chest, Rita called Jason.

"White Haven Road," she said into the phone. "Carol's at Whitehaven."

"Ten-four," Jason said. "See you there."

As Cash pulled out, Rita brought up the *SilverNomad* feed on her phone. The live stream was still running, but the screen remained unchanged, just a frozen, grainy patch of frozen dirt where Carol's phone had fallen.

Cash took the freeway, pushing the speed limit, then veered onto a quiet country road.

Sirens flared behind them. Rita kept her eyes on the side-mirror, watching the SCSO truck close in, Jason at the wheel, its blue lights pulsing against the darkening sky.

Behind him, Candace followed in the cruiser.

"We're looking for a silver vehicle," Rita said, scanning the trees. "She's painted it."

"Better for winter camouflage?" Cash said.

Then he pointed ahead. "There it is." A glint of silver flickered in the distance. "Every now and then, the sun hits it just right."

He flicked the turn indicator for Jason's benefit and pulled onto the shoulder, spraying gravel and chunks of ice.

"I didn't drive your ride as hard as you're driving mine," Rita said, trying for a joke.

But her heart felt cramped in her chest, with barely the space to beat. Now, with a clear angle, she could see Carol's camper van, nestled in the trees like one of Carly's crystals. Rita rubbed the piece of jade in her pocket.

The SCSO truck and the cruiser pulled in behind them, coming to a stop on the shoulder. Their sirens fell silent.

"Stay in the car," Rita said, unbuckling and climbed out.

Jason and Candace were already moving. Jason's jaw was tight, his eyes scanning the scene.

"Rita," he said with a heavy voice.

She met his gaze and nodded.

"There's her phone," Candace said, pointing to the ground a few feet from the van's front tire.

Rita darted forward to where the phone lay face-down in the dirt. She snapped a photo, then flipped it over. A hairline crack splintered across the screen, reflecting a fractured sky. She switched it off and set it back exactly where she found it.

"Check it out," Jason said, nodding toward the van. "Back tire's flat."

His hand went to his holster, and in an instant, Candace and Rita did the same. Jason moved first, approaching the side of the camper. He knocked, sharp and commanding.

"This is the Still County Sheriff's Department! Carol

Jonas, I mean—" He shot a glance at Rita. "She still go by Jonas?"

Rita licked her dry lips. "She goes by her maiden name, Platt."

Jason squared his shoulders.

"Carol Platt," he called, "if you're inside, come out with your hands up."

No response came.

Rita stepped closer. "Mom?"

The wind rattled through the trees, sending dry leaves skittering across the dirt.

Jason knocked again, louder this time. "Last chance! Open the door and step out!"

Still nothing.

He shot Candace and Rita a look, then signaled toward the side door. "Cover me."

Rita braced her weapon as Jason grasped the handle. In one swift motion, he pulled the door open, then jumped back.

Nothing.

He ducked inside, sweeping his flashlight through the dim interior.

"Clear," he called after a tense pause.

A minute later he stepped back out. "No sign of her."

"But there's signs of a struggle," Rita said, her throat tightening. She gestured to the ground.

They crouched, together scanning the dirt. Scuff marks crisscrossed near the van's door, like someone had been dragged or fought back.

"There's something damp here," Candace said, reaching out.

Jason touched the spot with two fingers, then grimaced. "Blood."

Rita's pulse roared in her ears. "Shit."

Jason straightened. "Spread out and look for evidence."

"Doesn't look like she was dragged into the woods," Candace said. "No broken twigs, no flattened grass."

But Rita had spotted a series of deep grooves in the dirt, leading away. "Another vehicle was here."

Jason followed her gaze. "And it's long gone."

He turned and bolted for the SCSO truck, grabbing the radio. "Casper PD, this is Sheriff Perry, requesting immediate assistance, possible abduction. Suspect vehicle unknown."

"I'll call Beaumont," Candace said, already dialing. "We need checkpoints along the freeway."

Jason shot her a thumbs-up as he relayed Carol's description over the radio.

Rita listened, but Jason's words blurred, an indecipherable hum of protocol and urgency. Her breath came shallow, each exhale curling into the cold. She tuned her face towards the fragile sunlight filtering through the trees. The ponderosas loomed, their resinous scent sharp and earthy, grounding her in the woods.

A hand touched her arm and she flinched.

"I told you to stay in the car," she said.

Cash draped her puffer around her shoulders. "You're cold."

Ria blinked at him. "I don't feel cold."

He helped her thread her stiff arms through the sleeves. Then he squeezed her hands. "Your fingers are frozen." He tugged her hand towards the BMW. "Come on, let's get you warm."

She shook her head. "I don't need to warm up." Her fingers curled around his. "I need to find my mom."

Chapter Forty-Four

"I appreciate the care and concern," Rita said, pulling into the driveway. "But I'm not taking the rest of the day off."

"You're allowed to take the rest of the day off," Cash said, unbuckling. "Given the circumstances."

"Given the circumstances," Rita echoed, "I need to pitch in."

"Jason's got it handled."

"I'm a cop, too."

Cash gave her a soft smile. "You're emotional."

"Understandably," Rita said. "Someone's taken my mother."

He squeezed her hand. "You're tired, too."

"Also understandable," Rita said. "I worked late last night."

Cash met her eye. "And you're pregnant."

Rita blew out a breath. "Not this again."

"I'm making sense, Rita," Cash said. "This isn't chauvinism. You're supposed to be resting. Maybe on desk duty. I hear Dr. Roseburg say it every time we go."

She frowned. "Thanks for the PSA, but I won't sleep until she's found." Then she softened. "I know my limits, Cash. I won't run myself ragged."

He searched her eyes. "Promise?"

She nodded. "Promise." Then she kissed him, a brief press of lips.

"Good," he said. "'Cause that's my kid you're transporting."

"'Transporting?' You sound awfully like your dad right now."

Cash blew out a sigh, his shoulders rising and falling. Then he leaned in for a deeper kiss, his lips warm and firm against hers. "Take care," he said as they broke away.

He shut the car door and Rita reversed onto the road. She gave Cash a wave, then shifted into drive, heading for Jason's house.

When she knocked on the door, Lucas Lake answered. At the sight of Rita, concern creased his brow. He stepped aside, holding open the door.

Rita stepped inside. "I've been following leads into why your brother may have come to town."

Lucas nodded, his silence expectant.

"Did your father ever talk about finding a large sum of money while he was policing in Wyoming?" Rita asked. "Roughly thirty years ago."

Lucas shook his head. "Not that I'm aware of, but my mom would be the one to ask about that."

"Please call her," Rita said. "More lives may be at stake."

Lucas fished out his phone and made the call. Rita heard it ring before clicking over to voicemail.

"She's been sleeping a lot since Teddy died," Lucas said, disconnecting then redialing. "I wasn't sure how she was gonna handle losing Dad, considering their shared grief over Brandi. But ever since Teddy—"

"Lucas?" A hoarse voice came through the phone. "I was taking a nap."

"Mom," Lucas said. "I have something important to ask."

"You got me on speaker?" Loreen interjected, her voice thick with fatigue.

"There's a police officer with me. She'd like to ask you some questions."

"Hi, Loreen," Rita said, "I'm Rita Jonas. I'm tracing some money that went missing over thirty years ago."

There was a moment of silence, then Lucas looked closer at the screen. "She hung up."

"Call her back," Rita said.

Lucas hesitated, then dialed. On the final ring before voicemail, Loreen picked up.

"Mom, please," Lucas said.

"What the hell is this? I can't even grieve my son without digging up the past?"

"The past likely has something to do with what happened," Rita said.

"Satan has something to do with what happened," Loreen shot back.

"This is to help Teddy," Teddy said.

"Teddy can't be helped!" Loreen flared. "He's gone. And that can't be undone!"

"Your cooperation is appreciated, Loreen," Rita said. "We can't bring back Teddy. But we can bring his killer to justice."

A long silence ensued. Then Loreen spoke, her voice bitter. "That money didn't do no one no good."

"So tell me about it," Rita said.

Another moment of silence followed. "He wouldn't

have kept it, if times hadn't been so hard for us. The medical bills had stacked up. Our youngest, Brandi, wasn't well, you know. Insurance wouldn't cover this or that, and our house was about to be repossessed."

Lucas nodded. "I remember how hard it was, Mom."

Loreen continued, as if he'd said nothing. "Theo came home one night, saying he'd found some money." She let out a brittle laugh. "Didn't believe him at first. But then he showed me the packets of bills. All crisp and new, bound in little paper sleeves. Said he didn't feel comfortable spending it in Wyoming. So, he quit his job at the Casper PD and we moved to Florida. But things weren't any better."

"Please explain," Rita said.

"Brandi died all the same," Loreen said. "And the debts still had to be paid."

Lucas hung his head, still holding the phone but hiding his face from Rita.

"I'm so sorry for your loss," Rita said. "No mother should lose children as you have."

For a long moment, Loreen Lake stayed silent, as did Lucas. Then she sniffled and said, "We paid off the debts. And gave Brandi a real nice memorial service. Even took the boys to Disney World."

Lucas looked up, a flash of happiness in his eyes.

"But Theo was a real wreck," Loreen said. "He felt guilty about taking the money, real bad. Started drinking, like he was trying to drown it all out. Felt like he'd betrayed his vocational calling."

"What else did he share?" Rita asked.

"If you're asking me where he got it," Loreen said, "he never did spill. Not even when he'd had too much to drink. Kept that shit locked up tight, like it was buried inside him."

"Did he ever mention a woman named Carol?" Rita asked. "Or a man named Otto? Carol and Otto Jonas?"

"Nope," Loreen said. "Worked real hard as a cop after that. In fact, work consumed him." She paused. "Well, maybe it was the drink. But I'd bank that it was the guilt that killed him, in the end. Not guilt over taking the money so much, but guilt over not being able to save his baby daughter."

A thick silence settled on the line.

"Thank you for sharing," Rita said. "I know this hasn't been easy."

Loreen gave a grunt, then she disconnected the call.

Shoulders tense, Lucas pocketed his phone. His gaze searched Rita's face. "Are you getting any closer to finding the killer?"

"Getting there," Rita said, pulling open the door. Snowflakes fluttered in on the breeze and fell at their feet. "And your mom's information helps, I now know Teddy's secret. He came to Still in search of a large sum of money, hoping there may have been more than what your father took to Florida." She exhaled, watching the pines sway in the restless in the wind, then looked back at Lucas. "If only we knew just how much your dad told your brother."

Chapter Forty-Five

BEFORE PULLING out of Jason's driveway, Rita sat behind the wheel, chewing her lip. She suspected Carol harbored another secret, this one about the money in Otto's safe deposit box.

Yet for all the secrets she possessed, Carol gave everything away on her YouTube page—her thoughts, her habits, her location. The answer to her abduction had to be there.

She navigated back to *SilverNomad* YouTube channel and clicked on the most recent video before the fateful livestream. The screen filled with Carol holding up a bagel, explaining the perils of driving on a 'donut.'

"Limit how much distance you travel on your spare tire," she said. "It's imperative that you replace it with a proper tire as soon as possible."

She concluded the video with a cheerful thanks to the 'friendly mechanic' on his way to deliver her a new one.

Rita froze. Someone had driven out to the bush to meet Carol.

She rewound, watching the video again. But no further

clues revealed themselves. She clicked the next most recent video, posted a several hours before the bagel episode.

Carol was behind the wheel again, answering comments from followers about her conversation with Rita at The Bighorn Bean. Rita was about to skip ahead when Carol suddenly glanced into the sideview mirror, her posture stiffening. She looked over her shoulder, then pulled onto the shoulder and got out.

For a moment, she vanished from view. Then she climbed back inside and addressed the camera.

"Wouldn't you know it? I got a flat tire." Her pearly pink lips smiled. "But you know me, I live independent and free. And you can bet I know how to take care of myself in a situation like this. If you don't know how to change a spare, stay tuned. I'll walk you through it."

Then she pulled the phone from its mount and stepped outside.

The camera wobbled as Carol moved to the back of the van and popped open the rear. Settling the phone in the back of the van, she dug for the spare.

Then the angle shifted as Carol propped the phone at a low vantage point outside the van, positioned to film her as she jacked up the van.

When she struggled to heft the ruptured tire into the back of the van, Rita's chest tightened with concern. Carol insisted she was independent, but was she entirely capable?

Below the video, comments flooded the screen.

"So helpful! I didn't learn this stuff growing up."

"My dad was never around to teach me, thank you!"

"This is why we love you, Mama C.!"

"You always get it done right, SilverNomad."

Rita paused the video, piecing together the sequence: First, Carol got a flat and filmed herself changing the spare. In the next video, she mentioned arranging a tire delivery. Then, in the livestream, she was waiting to meet the person bringing it.

Rita swiped open her phone and called Randy at Bighorn Towing.

"Hiya, Rita," he answered. "Hell of a situation up at APEX."

"You can say that again. I'm wondering if anyone called to change a flat today?"

"Nope," Randy said, "been real quiet. Most folks are on their recently balanced snow tires by now, so there shouldn't be too many flats."

Her stomach knotted.

"Thanks," she said, hanging up.

She started the ignition and rolled down the driveway, heading for the only other place in town that sold tires, the Gas-N-Go.

A few minutes later, she arrived at the station and parked near the picnic tables. More snow had accumulated on the can of cigarette butts. The lot was quiet, with no sign of Chester's truck.

Rita got out and approached Rodney, who was sanitizing the pump handles. He wore the same retro sunglasses, even though the heavy gray clouds threatened a heavy snowfall.

"Chester around?" she asked.

Rodney shook his head. "Ran an errand."

"Where to?"

He shrugged. "Dunno."

"When's he back?"

Another shrug. "Dunno."

Rita cocked her head towards the store. "You watching the counter?"

Rodney nodded. "Yep."

"I need to look at the security footage."

Rodney adjusted his sunglasses. "I dunno how to do that."

"I do," Rita said.

She crossed the bays to the convenience store, then pushed through the side door into Chester's office.

Perching on the edge of the chair, she tapped the mouse. The desktop flickered to life. A minute later, she was scrolling through security footage, until Carol's Silver Nomad pulled into view.

She climbed out of the driver's seat, her figure blurring as she moved around the back of the van to pump the gas, disappearing from sight.

Then Chester stepped into the frame.

He approached the van and dropped to one knee by the back right tire. Then he straightened and walked off, circling the pumps before vanishing near the picnic tables.

A couple minutes later, Carol climbed into the driver's seat and drove off.

Seconds after that, Chester followed in his pickup.

"Shit," Rita said, bolting from the office.

"Where does Chester live?" she ordered, running up to Rodney.

He blinked. "Dunno."

Rita clenched her jaw and pulled out her phone.

She messaged Ruby Joe: *Ever send Chester home in a cab? I need his address.*

Two seconds later, Ruby Joe responded with an address.

Tnx, Rita texted back.

She thanked Rodney, though she wasn't sure for what, then headed for her crossover.

While driving, she called Jason hands-free. "You still at Carol's camper?"

"No. Candace contained the scene," Jason said. "I'm back at the office."

"Can you meet me at Chester's house?" Rita asked.

"Ten-four."

Despite the tension in her jaw, Rita smiled. Working with Jason again felt right, like slipping into a comfortable pair of duty boots. No squeaky complaints, unlike working with Craig. Let alone Cash's complaints about her APEX-issue footwear.

She gripped the wheel and tore through Still's quiet streets, her pulse pounding in her ears. Taking a sharp turn onto Chester's street, she scanned the houses. The driveways. The sightless windows.

Nearing his address, she spotted his pickup. Her pulse quickened.

In the rearview mirror, Rita saw the SCSO truck turn onto the street. She pulled over and parked, glancing up at the house. The driveway showed signs of a patch job, leading to a detached garage set back behind the house. The garage door was open, spilling a jumble of salvage cars into the yard. Both the house and garage had well-maintained roofs, a sign Chester kept up with the essentials, even if the landscaping was neglected. The skeletal branches of a shrub leaned over the mailbox, as if its fingers were checking for a letter.

She exhaled, steadying herself, as Jason pulled up behind her.

Time to move.

Rita climbed out and checked her bulletproof vest. Jason met her at the curb.

"Hey, partner," she said, her voice feeling fragile in the frigid air. "Thanks for coming out for the entertainment tonight. Ready?"

He set his jaw. "Ready."

Rita nodded. Then forced a laugh, patting her abdomen. "Vest is getting snug."

Jason met her eye. "You okay? I mean, you're carrying more than a badge today."

Biting her lip, Rita rubbed her belly. "Yeah. Better than paperwork, right?" But her words wobbled.

Taking a deep breath, she looked up at the uneven blinds in the windows. "I'm pretty sure Chester's behind this."

Jason set his jaw. "Shit. I've known him since I was a kid. He'd taken over the gas station the summer I turned twelve. I was riding my bike out his past the station—"

"Jesus, Jason, on your bike? On the freeway?"

"I was on the shoulder."

Rita scoffed. "Still, you didn't value your life?"

"Anyway, I came across a dog that'd been hit. Couldn't walk. I put the dog across my handlebars and rode to Chester's to call the cops, like my mom taught us to do when we came across roadkill. But Chester said the dog was in too much pain to wait for the cops to come and shoot it. So he euthanized it with exhaust, then said he'd dispose of it along with his remains from his hunting trip." A shiver shook his shoulders. "Euthanizing animals is one of the things I don't like about this job."

"I haven't dealt with much roadkill," Rita said. "A lot of pigeons get hit in New York." She shrugged. "Although maybe not as many as you might expect."

"Worst for me was a cow, actually," Jason said. "It wasn't roadkill, but it was tangled up something fierce in a fenceline, trying to squeeze through. It had broken its neck. I still stop at that spot sometimes. There's a real nice view of the sunset."

Rita shook out her shoulders. "I'm gonna enjoy

tonight's sunset." She met his eye. "And so are you, Perry. We're gonna toast it together when we get this job done."

Then she raised her fist, knuckles turned towards him.

He bumped his knuckles to hers. "Deal."

Then they each took a steadying breath and fell into step together, just like old times, approaching the front door.

Rita knocked, her palms damp with sweat.

"Police!"

Silence.

She knocked and called again.

Still nothing.

Heart pounding, she tried the handle. It turned easily.

Swapping a look with Jason, they pulled their firearms. Then she pushed the door open and stepped back.

Jason stepped in first, clearing the foyer. Rita followed.

The air smelled of aged leather and wood polish. A wooden bench sat against one wall, cluttered with shoes and a folded buffalo-check jacket. Above it, a row of metal hooks held coats, scarves, and hats.

They took three steps into the living room—

And froze, caught under a dozen wide-eyed stares.

"Jesus," Jason said at the same time as Rita said, "Christ."

Every inch of space was filled with a taxidermic creature, each one frozen in a lifelike pose, their glass eyes staring vacantly at the room's visitors.

"Chester's hobby is more than a little…unsettling," Rita said, her voice tight with discomfort.

Jason's throat worked as he swallowed, his expression hardening. "Yeah. Not exactly my idea of a pastime."

Rita called out their presence again and they backed out of the living room, heading down the hallway.

Rita moved in step with him, then paused, pointing through the living room into the dining room beyond.

A collection of mule-deer busts loomed over the dining table, which was cluttered with crumpled junk food bags and small automotive parts.

She pointed. "That vacant space on the wall suggests a missing mount."

Wordless, Jason nodded.

They cleared the dining room, then the kitchen, and the laundry room. More car parts, although instead of smelling like motor-oil and sweat like Chester's general aroma, it reeked of bleach. A bundle of clothes soaked in the sink. A pair of steel-toed boots sat on the linoleum floor.

"Unusual place to keep your work shoes," Jason noted.

"Unless you're cleaning them." Rita picked up a red whisk-and-dustpan set, tipped over the left boot, and frowned. "The soles have been wiped down." She sniffed the grooves. "Smells like blood."

"Let's move," Jason said, leading the way back through the kitchen and down the hallway.

Rita's pulse thundered in her ears, her mind prepared to confront Chester at any corner, even though his vehicle was nowhere to be found.

They cleared the first room, a bathroom, filthy but empty. Then the guest bedroom, stocked with spare auto parts and more dead wildlife.

"What's with all these lifelike postures?" Rita asked. A taxidermied pronghorn's head, mounted on the wall, showed off its sharp rack, flanked by two coyote busts frozen mid-snarl. "Are those coyotes supposed to be hunting that pronghorn?"

A muscle tensed in Jason's jaw. "Looks like."

The master bedroom was equally cluttered, and

equally empty of life. In this space, there was only one stuffed critter, a beaver.

The ensuite, guest bathroom, and kitchen offered no life, and thankfully no DIY taxidermy.

They returned to the living room.

"You okay?" Rita asked. "You're looking a little green."

Jason wiped sweat from his brow. "This ain't like an autopsy."

"Definitely not," Rita said, eyeing another coyote lurking behind a bookshelf. She gestured to a flock of sage grouse mounted in mid-flight, wings spread as though taking off from the rafters. "Half of these critters are engaged in life-or-death struggles."

"Taxidermists mount 'em in action poses to disguise the damage," Jason said. "It's how they hide bullet wounds." He fanned himself. "Damn, I hate dealing with animal harm. How would Chester feel if someone took his head off and mounted it on a wall?"

Images of Teddy's and Don's heads flickered through Rita's mind. "Um…"

"And cats?" Jason said, his voice strained. He pointed to a mountain lion, mounted mid-pounce, claws extended and glass eyes fixed on invisible prey. "It's not right to stuff cats."

Rita's gaze skated over to a lynx perched on the mantelpiece. "The Egyptians did it."

He shot her a look. "Mummification is not the same as taxidermy."

Rita bit her lip. "You're right. Sorry." She smiled slightly. "At least it's like old times."

"You mean working together?"

"I mean me putting my foot in my mouth. And you being the bigger person about it."

Jason let out a short chuckle. Then his expression hardened. "Where the hell does he do all this taxidermy?"

"Let's check the garage," Rita said.

Stepping outside, she gulped in the fresh air. They quickly crossed the driveway and entered the garage, the scent of oil in the air. Navigating piles of old car parts, stacks of boxes, and abandoned tools, they began clearing the space.

"What's with the tarp?" Rita asked, pointing to an orange sheet draped on the back wall.

"Looks like it's covering an old engine block," Jason said, pulling it away from the wall and peering behind it. He extracted his head and looked at her. "And a door."

He pulled back the sheet and she joined him at the old wooden door. They traded a look and Jason gave a slight nod, silently signaling her to follow as he reached for the doorknob.

He opened the door and Rita called into the room. "Police! It's Rita Jonas and Sheriff Perry. Come out where we can see you!"

A muffled voice responded and Rita exchanged a look with Jason.

Then they stepped inside.

Chapter Forty-Six

"UNCLE JASON'S GOING FIRST," Jason said, stepping ahead of Rita into the dim room.

Drawing a breath, Rita followed him. Weak light leaked through the grimy windows, revealing a room that was a graveyard of abandoned hobbies, rusted automotive parts stacked beside boxes of new ones; broken bicycles; musty camping gear; hunting equipment; and taxidermy projects unlikely to ever see display, thanks to grotesquely overstuffed appendages.

Slow and steady, they advanced, with guns drawn.

They passed a mountain goat with misaligned eyes. "Remind me never to take up the hobby," Jason muttered, lip curling.

"How about hunting?" Rita asked, making a beeline for a chest freezer humming in the back corner.

Jason followed, throwing her a glance. "Baby okay?"

Rita reached the freezer. "Yep. Why?"

He patted the lid. "Just making sure everyone's ready for what might be inside this thing. I'll try to catch you if you pass out."

"Likewise," Rita said. "Though I'm more likely to puke."

Jason nodded. "Then you're holding your own barf bag."

Rita licked her lips. "Here we go then." She drew a breath. "Hold your nose."

Then she lifted the lid.

Nestled among the frozen venison chops and sausage links lay Donald Horgan's head. Unlike the meat, it wasn't wrapped and labeled. Frosted white eyeballs stared up at her.

Rita closed her own eyes and exhaled. "Jesus Christ." Then she remembered to shut the lid.

She slammed it down as a muffled voice called out. She jumped. "Don't tell me that head's trying to talk to us."

Jason turned around, gun up, scanning the room. "Sounds like it's coming from over there."

He gestured toward a queen-size mattress and box spring leaning against the wood-paneled wall. "Behind that."

They moved in, each taking a side. Peering around the mattress, Rita spotted something metal, dimly glinting.

"I think there's another door behind here," she said, pulling back to look at Jason. "Pretty sure I see a hinge."

Jason gripped the mattress and gave it a tug. It sagged in his arms. He adjusted his hold and grunted. "This thing is bagged out."

"I feel bad not helping," Rita said, rubbing her belly. "But my doc expressly told me not to move mattresses. Poor Cash had to haul ours upstairs."

Jason nodded, blowing out a breath. Then he pulled again, dragging the mattress away from the wall.

The muffled sounds grew louder.

Rita pressed her ear to the paneling. "Someone's banging on the wall."

Jason shoved the mattress into the corner, then reached for the box spring. "I got it."

Reluctant, Rita stepped back, her heart hammering louder with each passing second. Jason hauled the box spring aside.

She raised her weapon, steadying her breath. "We got a door."

Jason leaned the box spring against the wall, turned, and pulled his gun again. They flanked the doorway.

Rita met his eye. "You ready, Uncle Jason?"

"Ten-four."

She nodded, then called out, "Police! Open the door!"

A faint voice answered. "Rita..."

Rita's stomach dropped. "Mom?"

She darted forward, stepping in front of Jason's firearm, forgetting protocol. "Mom!" She grabbed the doorknob. Locked. She rattled it hard.

"Be careful, Rita," Carol's voice warned, shaky but firm. "He's got a gun."

Rita's grip tightened. "Get away from the door, Mom. I'm shooting the lock."

Carol's voice grew fainter. "I'm backing away now ..."

Rita counted a few beats to ensure Carol was clear, then fired.

The first shot obliterated the handle, sending splinters of wood and shards of metal flying. The second shot tore apart the locking mechanism and the door swung inward.

Rita lunged forward, the sharp scent of gunpowder stinging her throat.

Carol stood pressed against a worn countertop running along the back wall. Blood trickled from a gash on her forehead.

Rita ran to her, pulling her into a tight embrace. "Mom!"

Then she leaned back, gripping Carol's shoulders, scanning her face. "Are you okay? How's your vision? You dizzy?" She found Carol's wrist and checked her pulse. "Heart rate normal?"

Carol's teeth chattered. "There's a sick boy over there."

Rita released Carol and scanned the cold cement room. It was sparse, outfitted for the skinning and dressing of animals, a stainless steel sink, a stack of cutting boards, lower cabinets, and a pegboard holding an array of knives, hooks, and saws. A large metal trash can with a lid sat in one corner.

And a cot. A bundle of discarded bedding lay atop it. No, not bedding. A body. Barely moving.

She dropped beside the cot. "Jesse?"

Jesse lay with his head on a pillow, crusted with dried blood. His complexion was ashen, his breathing shallow.

"Jason!" Rita said. "It's Jessie Levick. And he's injured."

"Ambulance is already on its way," Jason said, lowering his phone. "I'll sit with him while you get Carol out of here."

Nodding, Rita led Carol out of the room and settled her in the farthest corner from the freezer. She unfolded two camping chairs and guided Carol into one.

"Tell me what happened," Rita said.

Carol rubbed her temples. "That fellow, Chester, called me the other day."

"Why?"

"He wanted to talk to me about some things from Otto's past, of all things."

"What kind of things?"

Carol wrinkled her nose. "Nothing personal. He wanted to chat about old police files and whatnot."

"What did you tell him?"

"I brushed him off, of course. How the hell would I remember anything about Otto's old cases? Besides, your father never really talked about work. Bottled it all up."

"He talked to me," Rita said without thinking, and Carol shifted, uncomfortable.

"Go on," Rita prompted.

Carol huffed. "Well, this Chester fellow was *quite* bothersome. He must have noticed the airbrushing on my van because next he reached out by leaving a comment on my YouTube page."

Rita raised an eyebrow. "What did he say?"

"That he didn't believe I was a nomad. That he thought I'd come back to Still County for good. And he knew the reason." Carol waved a hand. "Obviously, he just wanted my attention, like any other troll or opportunist. So I blocked him." She sniffed. "Anyway, I'd hoped ignoring him would be the end of it. But then this morning, I had to get gas."

"You were avoiding Chester," Rita said, "but you still filled up at the Gas-N-Go?"

"That's right," Carol said. "I go there so often I know all the kids. And I figured the chances of running into Chester were slim to none."

"Did you see him?"

"I only saw him pass by," she said. "He must've noticed my van, of course. But since he didn't stop to talk, I figured he got the message." She let out a bitter laugh. "Boy, was I wrong!"

"What happened next?"

"I got a flat," Carol said. "Happens from time to time

—life on the road. So I did what I always do. I keep a spare in the back."

"I saw the video," Rita said.

Carol brightened. "Did you? Good! You *should* learn how to change a tire. I don't think Otto ever taught you."

Rita gave her a tight smile. "I know my way around a vehicle. But I usually just call Randy. Like Otto did."

Carol lifted her chin. "Well, you're lucky to have such a capable and independent mother to teach you these things." She tilted her head. "And that video was *very* popular, by the way. You wouldn't believe how many people don't know how to change a tire." She exhaled. "Actually, I might do a more detailed series. Maybe a video on what to do if you crack your oil pan on a speed bump or culvert—"

"I'd call Randy," Rita interrupted.

"My point exactly," Carol said knowingly. "But anyway. I couldn't drive around on a spare forever, so I called the Gas-N-Go to order a new tire." She hesitated. "I was hoping to talk to one of the younger attendants, but Chester answered."

Rita's stomach tightened. "And?"

"I was flustered at first, but I told him what I needed. He said nice things about my van, mentioned he just so happened to have the right tire in stock, and offered to send a kid to deliver it."

"And?"

Carol's spine stiffened. "I never saw him coming." She swallowed hard. "I woke up slung over Chester's back like a carcass, being carted into this room."

Rita clenched her fists, swallowing her own reaction. "Did he hurt you?"

Carol's hands shook as she pushed hair from her face.

"No. Other than shoving me in here, he hasn't laid a hand on me. But he's got a hunting rifle."

"Has he questioned you?"

"No."

"He wants to know about the money, Mom."

Carol flapped her applied lashes. "Money?"

Rita looked at her, level. "I know about the money."

Carol exhaled slowly. "I know." Her voice dropped. "I mean, I didn't know that *you* know. But I knew that's what he was after when he started asking about Otto's old cases."

"It was never Otto's case," Rita said. "This is *your* history."

Carol flinched. "You *know*-know?"

Rita nodded. "I never knew. But I figured it out." She offered a small smile. "But I'd still like to hear it from you."

Carol sighed. "I was the first one on scene. No one else was on the highway. I'd been driving, clearing my head."

"And you came upon the accident?" Rita prompted.

Carol nodded. "The armored truck had plowed into the tree. It was a disaster. Wood splintered all over the freeway. Foliage everywhere. When I walked up to it, still don't know why I did, I saw the branches had punctured the windshield. Stabbing the—" She broke off in a choke, then cleared her throat. "The driver was dead on impact."

"The paper said the bodies were burned in the explosion," Rita said. "You might've been the last person to see them."

Tears filled Carol's eyes. "Not quite," she said. "Theo Lake was there too."

"He arrived after you?" Rita clarified.

Carol nodded. "Yes, shortly after."

"He came when you called it in?" Rita asked.

Carol trembled harder. "I never called it in. It was too late. I saw they were dead."

That surprised Rita. "You didn't call it in?"

"When the tree came down, I knew Otto couldn't come, he was in Casper, at court that day. So I called Theo. At the office." She lifted her chin. "I'm not proud of it, but I pretended I was a nurse from the ward where his daughter was."

"But you knew him though Otto? Through the detachment?"

Carol flushed. "Of course. And … well, we'd been carrying on for a while." She paused, looking away. "If you know what I mean."

Rita went rigid.

Carol winced. "Theo was going through a hard time. Over his kid. And Otto and me, well, we were in a rough patch. And I was godawful scared, looking at those dead men. I remember feeling like a fawn, I was trembling so hard. I needed to feel safe, and men like your dad and Theo Lake always made me feel safe."

"Go on," Rita said, her voice flat.

"Theo was going through a terrible time too. His youngest, Brandi, was real sick, and he was having a hard time paying the medical expenses."

"I can't imagine how having an affair would make that situation better," Rita said.

"There was a lot of strain in his family," Carol said. "I was trying to offer some balm for the soul."

"So Theo Lake shows up," Rita said, "and you both take the money?"

"It was his idea. I'd only called him to help me, to comfort me. But when he saw what had happened, he suggested we take the money. Suggested that we split it.

Half for his daughter. Half for my silence. And then we'd never speak again." She shrugged. "I agreed and we loaded our cars. And did it just in the nick of time too, because the van caught fire. That's when Theo called the ambulance. But before it arrived, the armored truck exploded."

Rita let out a breath. "Help turned up, the crime scene was processed, and you and Theo Lake parted ways, and you never spoke again?"

Carol nodded. "Every now and then, I saw his name mentioned in the papers. He was a good cop with a fine reputation."

"I see," Rita said, her tone measured. "And your share of the money, what became of that?"

"At first, I didn't know how to explain it to your father," Carol said. "I knew it was right to support Theo in that way. But I wasn't sure it was right for me to take so much of it. So I hid it under the porch. Except Otto found it, by tripping over a loose board I hadn't fixed correctly. He made me tell him everything. Even about Theo. And he was mad as an old bee about it. Then Otto called him up. They argued for hours, it felt like, and eventually agreed to never speak about it again."

"And the event was never brought up again?" Rita asked.

Carol let out a bitter bark of laughter. "Technically, no, we never discussed it again. But it was the start of our dysfunctional cycle. Otto asked me what the hell I thought I was doing, not only sleeping with a lawman but grossly breaking the law. He kicked me out for the night. He even accused me of being drunk behind the wheel, because why else would I have exercised such poor judgment?" Carol smacked her lips. "Can you believe he did that?"

"Yes," Rita said.

Carol folded her arms. "Well, I wasn't going to let him call the shots, banishing me to a hotel for the night. Instead, I went to my cousin's in Cheyenne. I must have stayed a couple weeks. I didn't talk to Otto, which was fine with me, because my cousin thought I should take up with this fellow called Douglas. Not that there were any sparks flying with Doug. But at least he got my mind off things for a while."

"How nice for you," Rita said, her jaw tense.

"After a few weeks, I decided Otto had no right kicking me out of my own life. So I came back to Still and went to the house to fetch the money. But when I looked under the porch, the money had been moved. And in its place, well, there was a newspaper clipping about the accident."

"That's the fragment I found," Rita said.

"I confronted Otto," Carol said. "He said I could only have the money once the other witness was dead." She shook her head. "But he probably burned it."

Rita narrowed her eyes. "Why do you say that?"

Carol met her eye. "Because I can't find it."

Rita went still. "Is this why you really came back to Still? Not because of Otto, but because Theo Lake was dying?"

Carol shifted. "That's not the *only* reason. But naturally, while I've been here, I've had a look around."

"Like breaking into Jason's place."

"Rita!" Jason called, stepping out of the cement room. "Ambulance inbound. Forensics too. Mary Lou says Chester's got another vehicle, a rusted-out silver Chevy Malibu. It's been spotted heading up the road to the reservoir."

Rita stood and squeezed Carol's shoulder. "I gotta go, Carol. Get a ride with Jesse to the hospital. And if you so much as budge an inch from Admitting, I'm not doing that YouTube baby announcement with you."

Carol patted her hand. "Yes, yes, go do your job. Your dad would be proud."

Rita exhaled.

"Thanks, Mom."

Chapter Forty-Seven

RITA STARED out the passenger window, watching the trees blur past, their bare branches scratching across the sky.

"Jason…"

From behind the wheel, he glanced at her. "Uh-huh?"

"I've been thinking." She pulled her gaze from the window, watching his profile as he drove. "I know where the leak is."

He flicked his eyes toward her again. "Oh, yeah?"

"It's Candace."

His jaw tightened.

"She's in a relationship with my asshole assistant over at APEX."

Jason kept his eye on the gravel road. "Craig Dillard?"

Rita nodded. "I'm sure of it. And he's the type to make a name for himself, or at least pad his nest, with the least effort possible. Anything she's told him has probably been served straight up to Blaze, hot out of the oven."

Jason grit his teeth. "Shit."

"Craig said he was listening in on the scanner," Rita said. "And so did Blaze."

"Candace is gonna be bummed," Jason said. "She's a stickler for rules." His mouth turned down with disappointment. "Or so I thought."

"It's natural to want to debrief," Rita said. "I'm sure Craig offered a willing ear. Among other willing body parts." She grimaced. "Some say Craig's a charmer."

Jason grinned. "I take it he's not your style?"

Rita snorted. "My style? He's a child." Then she bugged her eyes at him. "Is he your style?"

Jason took his eyes of the road to bug his back at her. "I don't kiss and tell."

Rita laughed. "He's not your style. He's nothing like Blaze."

She returned her eyes to the view, scanning the bush. The clouds had thickened, pressing low and heavy, flattening the light and squeezing pale and elongated shadows over the landscape.

Something silver flashed among the foliage, and this time, it was not Carol's van. Chester's Malibu sat partially hidden behind the trees.

"There," Rita said, pointing.

Jason eased the SCSO truck to a stop. Together, they got out, boots crunching over the frozen ground, service weapons drawn. The cold wind whipped through the trees, shaking loose flurries of snow, which prickled Rita's face.

The driver's door creaked open. Chester stepped out, rifle held in a white-knuckled grip. His breath came fast, steaming in the freezing air.

"Stay back!" he shouted, his voice raw.

"Put down the gun," Rita called, picking her way through the frozen grass. It glinted silver in the fading light.

Chester raised the rifle. "Leave me be, Jonas!"

Rita stopped and lowered her weapon. Jason followed her lead.

"What happened, Chester?" Rita asked.

His grip on the rifle tightened. "It's a fucking mess."

Rita nodded. "We can help. We're going to work together to clean it up."

A shudder shook Chester's shoulders and he hung his head. "I made a mess of things."

Rita licked her lips, her heartbeat pounding in the back of her throat. "How?"

"Don," Chester said. His hands trembled. "And that shit, Teddy Lake. I wish he'd never come to town."

"Tell me how you met Teddy," Rita said.

Chester swallowed hard. "It was at The Shaft. Jesse pointed him out, said he'd come through the Gas-N-Go earlier that day, hitching a ride. Jesse figured the guy was skint and told him to swing by Ruby Joe's, 'cause she hands out free plates of leftovers to travelers like him."

"Ruby Joe's a friend of yours, isn't she?" Rita said. "She's made sure you've gotten home safe from time to time."

Blinking, Chester paused. Then he lowered the rifle.

"Suppose you're right," he said. "When my wife left me, she gave me three months of meals on the house 'cause she said I was gonna burn down the town learning to cook for myself. 'Course it only happened once that the fire squad came out, but rumors get around in a place this size."

"What happened with Teddy at The Shaft?" Rita asked, taking a slow and subtle step forward.

Jason matched her.

"Teddy had been on the sauce. Didn't even recognize Jesse when he said hi. And it turned out, he wasn't broke at all. He was buying pitchers of beer, running his debit card through Lacey's register faster than a pole dancer humps steel."

The wind howled through the trees, whipping snow across the ground in ghostly swirls. Rita and Jason stepped again, slow and steady, advancing across the rugged ground.

"Did you and Teddy talk about money?" she asked.

Chester nodded. "Teddy wouldn't shut up about how his old man knew about some money here in town. The more he talked, the more I realized I knew the accident he was talking about. I was only a teenager at the time. But I remember it 'cause we'd been coming back from my nana's upstate, and traffic was backed up for hours. Neighbors talked about it for weeks. Everyone figured the money had gone up in flames with the wreck." Chester exhaled sharply. "But Teddy was convinced otherwise. And the more I thought about it, the more I started thinking, what if he was right?"

Rita's gaze stayed locked on him, her feet lightly stepping. "And you believed Carol was involved?"

Chester gave a bitter chuckle. "The way Teddy talked, yeah. He kept bringing up the sheriff and his wife. Everyone knew Carol had been the first on the scene. It was funny, you know? The sheriff's wife, in distress. Her name was in the paper and everything. So I thought, what if she and Teddy's old man took the money?"

"And you wanted it for yourself," Rita said.

Chester let out a dry laugh. "Wouldn't anyone?"

Jason tensed beside her. They were close now, maybe twelve feet away.

He took another careful step forward. "Why?"

Chester sighed. "Gas-N-Go is goin' bankrupt. Ain't pulling numbers like it used to. All these computers in cars these days …well, half the time the guys can't make heads or tails of the manuals, and folk end up takin' their rides into the dealerships. And the store don't turn a profit like it used to, neither. No one buys cigarettes and porn no more, it's all energy drinks and damn long-lasting batteries. Ain't nearly as many repeat customers as back in the day."

"So you killed Teddy for the money?"

Chester nodded. "That was the plan." His shoulders shook again. "Like I said, I dropped Jesse home early for curfew. Then I swung back to The Shaft and picked up Teddy. Figured I'd drive him out, maybe up Beaumont way, and give him a scare. Make him think I'd leave him to freeze in the backwoods if he didn't tell me where the money was."

He let out a humorless chuckle. "But that jackass had other plans. Goddamned attacked me." His voice cracked. "Stabbed me in the leg with his damn penknife." Chester gestured at his thigh. "Said he was real sorry, but he needed a set of wheels and figured if he was gonna steal a truck, it oughta be one in good condition."

His breath hitched. "So I grabbed the wrench from under my seat and swung back at him. In self-defense, I swear. I hit him twice in the noggin before I realized what I'd done."

Chester hung his head for a moment, staring at the rifle in his hands. When he looked up again, his eyes were hollow.

"I should've left him out in Beaumont. Instead, I chucked him in the truck bed and drove back to the shop. Figured I'd chop him up, same as I do with game."

Rita's stomach twisted. "But?"

Chester's voice dropped. "After I took off the head, I tried to take off a hand. But I'd lost my stomach for it."

The wind howled around them and Rita shivered, concentrating to hold her weapon steady. "So you staged the body instead?"

He nodded. "Made some fancy marks on his chest.

Dressed him up for a distraction. Strung him up on display."

"Why the pentagram?" Rita asked.

"I'd seen plenty of posters around town. Then I heard it was Carly's thing. And Carly, well, she's a real hottie, but she's always given me a hard time. I supposed it was a bit of a jab back at her, for being so disrespectful. And figured some women getting together for some strange goings-on would be a good cover-up."

"So why dispose of the body at APEX?" Rita asked. Snow thickened in the air, swirling between them.

Chester shrugged. "It was the farthest spot in town, away from the Gas-N-Go."

Rita's expression hardened. "So you brought Carol back to your place to question her, since Teddy was dead and couldn't tell you the whereabouts of the money."

Chester nodded, his fingers twitching on the rifle.

"What about Jesse?"

Chester's breath came faster, misting in the freezing air. "I was trying to pin it on him."

"So you staged the fake robbery of the angle grinder?" Jason said.

Chester nodded. "Sure wish I'd never dropped it in the first place. Then you lot would never have come sniffing around the Gas-N-Go. And would've chased down that witch, Carly, instead. But then I made another mistake, I forgot to remove the padlock on the electrical panel. After your new girl deputy was out at the station, I planted it at Jesse's place."

"We found it in the shed," Rita said. "How'd you plant the bloody rag?"

"Sometimes when I'd driven Jesse home, his ma asked me to move something heavy for her. She had a lot of stuff, though none of it as heavy as the engine parts I got.

Anyway, I told her Jesse had asked me to check if one of the bookshelves was balanced. She didn't think twice about letting me in. While I was checking, I planted the rag in his room."

"So what led to you abducting Jesse?" Jason asked.

Chester exhaled sharply. "Damn kid wouldn't stop asking questions. He'd noticed me asking Don some questions about the accident and wondered if it was the same one Teddy had been talking about. He started asking me if I'd known all along about the hidden money. I didn't want to be sharing no money with him, most of his wage goes to his mom. But if I could bail out the Gas-N-Go, then Jesse would have better chances of making wages. So I told Jesse I was gonna promote him and gave him the day off to celebrate. But I told everyone else I fired him."

"And you put him in your cold room?" Jason said.

Chester nodded. "Used a different wrench and hit him a lot lighter than I hit Teddy. Only wanted to knock him out, so I could finish him off where I could clean up the mess." His voice wavered. "But I couldn't do it. He's just a kid."

"But you killed Don," Rita said, "your shop manager."

"And my friend," Chester said. His breath hitched. "I killed my damn best friend."

"Why?" Jason asked.

Chester swallowed hard. "Because when I drove back to The Shaft to pick up Teddy, Don noticed me." He shook his head. "At first, I didn't think much of it. I was just giving Teddy a ride, no big deal. But after Teddy turned up dead, I couldn't have Don telling you I'd been the last person to see him alive." He rubbed a hand over his face. "So I went to his place. He'd told me Lana was gonna be out. And he was just sittin' there, watching the race."

"And?" Rita said, her voice brittle.

"He offered me a beer."

"Did you take it?" Jason asked, staking a step closer.

Chester's gaze drifted again. "Sure. And I asked him to put up the volume on the TV. Then … I shot him." Chester gave a slow nod. "But I wish I'd used a wrench. Not nearly as messy as the gun."

Jason took another step. "Where are the wrenches you used on Teddy and Jesse?"

Chester's eyes flicked to the reservoir. "Chucked 'em into the water just now."

"And why did you dismember Don's head?" Rita asked.

"Because I thought I should make it look like the other murder." His voice cracked. "But Jesus—" He pressed a thumb to the center of his forehead. "That was a real mind fuck, taking off my friend's head."

Jason shifted his weight, inching closer. Chester's eyes flicked between them, frantic.

"Tell Lana I'm sorry," he said.

Then he raised the rifle to his chin and pulled the trigger.

Chapter Forty-Eight

"Come in, Martin," Rita said as he appeared in the doorway.

Martin hesitated, glancing at the district attorney seated on the black leather sofa. Hunter said nothing, his face as rigid as granite.

Martin cleared his throat and entered the office. His movements stiff, he closed the glass door behind him and took a seat in the chair in front of Rita's desk.

"I have some footage to show you," Rita said, rotating the monitor of her desktop computer. She hit play.

On the screen, the grainy security footage showed Martin handing Ginny a ten-dollar bill and receiving a five in return.

Rita clicked her mouse, opening another video file, in this one, her body cam showed Martin pulling into the park and handing off the goods to the driver of the Cadillac.

Then she opened the video file from Cash's phone that showed the vehicle admitted to the governor's grounds.

Martin opened his mouth, his breath catching. "I want a lawyer."

Rita shook her head. "You won't need one, Martin. Mr. Greene's here to give you a deal for full cooperation with the district attorney's office." She swapped a look with Hunter. "Not just a good deal, but a great deal."

Martin's gaze also darted between them. "I'm not sure what you mean."

"We're prepared to grant you and Ginny full immunity."

"We are?" Hunter said, swiveling his head towards Rita.

Rita nodded. "Yes."

"I don't know if I can do that," Hunter said.

"I've got evidence," Martin said, sitting straighter.

Rita's eyes sharpened. "What kind?"

Martin's voice dropped. "I kept tapes of all my interactions with the governor's aide." His fingers flexed against the armrest. "Including our first meeting when the governor himself was present."

"That was foresight," Rita said.

Martin gave a nervous laugh. "I knew I was a small fry. If anything went sideways, I'd be tossed to the wolves."

"So what was going on?" Rita asked.

"The governor was hoping to lure Maddox Corp. to Wyoming," Martin said. "And now he's due to make the announcement any day."

"What announcement?" Rita asked.

"Maddox is building a chemicals manufacturing plant outside of Cheyenne. It'll create thousands of jobs. And dislodge APEX from its seat of power here. "

"And the governor wooed them here by providing them APEX secrets?" Hunter asked.

Martin nodded.

Hunter was silent for a moment, thinking. Then: "It's not exactly how I thought we'd bring the man down, but it'll do." Then he got up from the sofa. He rapped his knuckles on the desk. "Thanks, Rita. Good work."

Then he left.

Martin glanced at Rita. "Is that it?"

Rita lifted her hands and smiled. "That's it. The DA's office will be in touch with you."

Martin swallowed and nodded. Then he strode out of the office without looking back.

Rita sighed and returned to her desktop, typing the final lines of a letter.

A knock sounded on the glass door.

She looked around the computer monitor to see Craig waiting at the glass door. She waved him inside.

"What's going on with Martin?" he asked, coming to occupy the chair his colleague had just vacated.

"Hang on a minute," Rita said, saving her document.

Then she clicked 'print' and the printer whirred into action. It spat out a letter-sized piece of paper and Rita signed it. Then she passed it to Craig.

"Would you like to accept my resignation, or should I send this to corporate?"

Craig froze, reading the document. Then he looked up at her. "You're resigning?"

"Yep," Rita said.

Craig took another glance at the letter, then met her eye again. "Do you think I'll get your job?"

Rita shrugged. "No idea, 'cause I'm not into guessing. But if I were you, I'd go for it."

Nodded, Craig exhaled. "Well, thanks, Jonas."

"One piece of advice before I go," Rita said.

Craig's eyes glinted. "Yeah?"

"Keep your mouth shut when it comes to shoptalk. Candace is learning this lesson too. Blaze isn't gonna help anyone get ahead anywhere. If anything, he might help *you* from time to time. But that's the extent of it."

Craig's complexion turned pink, then deepened to scarlet, and settled into a vivid shade of violet.

"Understood."

Rita gave him an encouraging smile. "We all make mistakes. I once accidentally leaked the identity of a mobster hitman by using his nickname, Mr. Snuggles, when I wasn't supposed to."

Craig laughed, his complexion gradually returning to its former hue. Getting up, he wished her well and left.

Rita sighed.

This was it. Her last day. The closest she'd ever be to APEX again, hopefully, for the rest of her life.

She pushed up from her desk and crossed to the electric kettle. Everything in here was branded. Every mug. Every mousepad. Every damn pen.

Nothing in this office was hers.

Except for the tea.

One by one, she shoved the boxes into her handbag. Then she slung her bag over her shoulder and left the office. She swiped her security card and stepped into the elevator. Was this the last time she'd ride the APEX elevator?

Unlikely, since she'd likely be working with Craig and L.E.O. again. But then, maybe Maddox *would* put APEX out of business.

She walked past the front desk, now devoid of Ginny's presence and the plants she had kept on her windowsill. Instead, a temp twice her age quietly typed.

Outside, a black limousine idled at the curb. As Rita approached the parking lot, the back door swung open.

Angela sat inside, the pleats in her royal blue business suit neatly pressed.

"Do you have a minute to chat, Rita?"

Rita tilted her head with a smile. "For you, Angela? Always."

Chapter Forty-Nine

RITA SLID into the plush interior of the limousine. Soft accent lights glowed along the mirrored ceiling, creating the illusion of extra space.

"No helicopter this time?" Rita said.

Angela smiled as she opened a sleek minibar stocked with glassware and bottles. "That was our first date. Chilled drink? I have several non-alcoholic options."

Rita leaned forward to peruse. "Tonic water, orange juice, or Clamato?" She wrinkled her nose. "I'll take the Clamato, unless you've got a protein bar?"

Angela handed her the red can.

"So where I can take you?" Angela asked.

Rita cracked open the can of Clamato. "As much as I wouldn't mind the Faculty Club's prime rib right about now, I'm meeting someone."

"I'll take you there," Angela said. She held out her palm. "Now that you've resigned, I have to take back the company car."

Rita laughed. "Craig didn't waste any time delivering my letter."

Then she stopped as Angela's hand continued to hover, expectant. "You're serious?"

Angela inclined her head and Rita dug into her pocket for the BMW fob. She tossed it to Angela.

She caught it and pocketed the fob. "Deputy Dillard is more motivated than you gave him credit for."

Rita scoffed. "Enjoy getting to know him." She took a sip of Clamato. "So this is our last date?"

"You're the one walking out on APEX," Angela said coolly.

"In uncomfortable shoes," Rita muttered, lifting a boot. "I'll be happy to return my uniform, too. These things still haven't softened. Always felt like a bit of a rat, strutting around in these squeaky things."

Angela crinkled her nose. "No one asked you to strut." Then: "Where would you like to be dropped off?"

"Casper Hospital, please." Rita pulled out her phone and sent a text to Cash, asking him to meet her at the front doors.

Angela relayed the request to the driver, then settled back in her seat. "In the meantime, we can have a chat."

"Good," Rita said. "'Cause I'd like to talk about how you've known along Jim was the snitch."

She tilted her chin. "Was it obvious?"

"Not really. But I'm good at sniffing out distractions."

The corner of Angela's mouth twitched. "Couldn't have you finding the real incriminating documents. Some pilfered trade secrets was as good a reason as any to satisfy Hunter Green's thirst for dirty water."

"You have a contact in Hunter's office," Rita asked, more a statement than a question.

Angela's smile broadened. "How else would I have known which documentation Hunter Greene was looking for regarding the governor's interests?" She lifted a manila envelope from the leather seat beside her and handed it over.

Rita opened the flap and flipped through a series of land titles, contracts, and confidential memos. Her gaze sharpened. "You're handing me the evidence?"

"APEX and the governor had an agreement," Angela said smoothly. "But then he went and used us, sold APEX's trade secrets to help him bring our competition to Wyoming." She adjusted her cuff, her smile turning razor-sharp. "So I'm closing the facility."

Rita found herself speechless for a moment, the freeway slipping past the window.

A moment later, she asked, "What's next for you?"

Angela relaxed against the seat. "Don't worry about me. I've made a hostile takeover bid for Maddox. Paperwork should be finalized before the weekend."

Rita blinked. "Today's Friday."

"Exactly," Angela said.

Rita shook her head. "Jesus. Remind me never to cross you, Angela."

Angela laughed.

The rest of the ride passed in comfortable silence as they watched the distant mountains shimmer under an opalescent sky, their jagged peaks cloaked in fresh powder. Pumpjacks nodded in the distance, tapping the frozen earth for treasure.

Then came the outskirts of Casper: truck stops, farm equipment dealerships, industrial yards interspersed with fast food joints and gas stations.

Finally, the limousine pulled into the hospital parking lot and rolled to a stop at the three-minute loading zone.

"Thanks," Rita said, unbuckling. "All the best to you, Angela."

"And you too, Rita." Angela's gaze softened. "Good luck with that baby."

"Good luck to you, too." Rita said, stepping out. She gave a wave. "Goodnight."

Then she shut the door behind her and the limousine pulled away.

Cash stood waiting under the covered entryway. As soon as he saw her, he approached and pulled her into a hug.

She leaned into him, breathing in his familiar scent.

"I've got something to tell you," she murmured.

"Don't tell me we're having twins," Cash said.

Rita laughed. "I resigned."

Cash pulled back, grinning. "You quit APEX?"

She nodded. "It's done."

His grin widened. "That's my girl. Otto would be proud."

Rita laughed. "Now all our problems are solved, huh?"

Cash snorted. "Sure. Except for that fifty grand."

"I was thinking of giving it to Carol."

Cash considered. "Or it could be a good education fund for the kid."

Rita nodded, her cheek brushing against his jacket. "That's true. Maybe we keep some of it for that."

"Sounds fair," Cash said. "We could still give Carol enough to get her out of town."

"Just enough," Rita agreed.

They shared a quiet chuckle before Cash took her hand and led her through the hospital's sliding doors.

Inside, a nurse greeted them at the front desk.

"Carol's ready for discharge," she said. "I'll bring her up."

"Thanks," Rita said.

She glanced at Cash as the nurse bustled away. "Jason's

cleaned out the guest room, now that Lucas Lake's gone home."

"That's good of him."

Rita nodded. "Jason's a good guy."

Her gaze flicked to the flat-screen TV mounted on the wall. A political ad was playing, Hunter Green, clad in a forest green sweater under a sport coat, beamed at the camera. The slogan beneath his name read: *'Take a chance on someone Green.'*

A chill ran down Rita's spine.

Cash noticed her stiffen. "What is it?"

Rita pulled out her phone and dialed Hunter.

He picked up immediately. "Hey, Jonas. Forget something?"

"No," she said. "But you sure as fuck did. You're running for governor?"

A brief silence. Then Hunter cleared his throat. "I was going to tell you, but—"

"Yeah. After I got rid of your competition for you."

"Hang on," he said quickly, "this is a good thing. Think of the relationship we'll have with me in this position."

"A smooth relationship, huh?" Rita said. "Then let's start with this, I want my sheriff's badge back. A raise for everyone at the station. And I'll need a new vehicle."

Another pause. Then a sigh. "You got it."

Rita put her phone away as the nurse rounded the corner, supporting Carol by the arm. She moved slowly, but color had returned to her cheeks. A bandage patched the wound on her head.

"Hi, Mom," Rita said, "You're looking well."

Carol smiled. "Thank you, Rita. I try."

"True enough," Rita said. "You've always been one to go after what you want."

Glancing at Cash, she squeezed his hand. Then she took her mother's hand.

Together, the three of them walked out of the hospital, headed home to Still.

The End

About the Author

Lauren Street has always loved a mystery. As a kid growing up in Bible Belt country she devoured every whodunit book she could get her sticky little hands on and secretly investigated all of her (seemingly) normal boring neighbors. Sometimes their pets and farm animals too. All grown up now and living in the UK with her thoroughly unsuspicious (and often unsuspecting) husband, she writes domestic psychological thrillers about families torn apart by secrets and lies. And she sometimes still peers over garden walls to check up on the neighbors.

Also By Lauren Street

The Nanny Problem

Rock-A-Bye-Bye

Nursery Crimes

Child's Prey

The Still County Thrillers

Still Here

Still Buried

Still Burning

Still Hidden

Still Missing

The Bishop Smoky Mountain Thrillers

Hide Me Away

Fuel To The Flame

Closer By The Hour

A Gamble Either Way

Calling My Children Home

Too Far Gone

Here You Come Again

A Friend Like You

The Company You Keep

One By One

Come Back To Me

The Only Way Out

Replaced with Nolon King

Replaced

In Her Place

Irreplaceable

The Salazar Redwood Forest Thrillers

The Girl Who Couldn't Stop Dying

The Girl Who Couldn't Get Out

The Girl Who Couldn't Be Found

Standalone Novels

Postpartum

9 781629 554662